TEEN   Meade, Lily
MEA
            The shadow sister

09/05/23

THE
SHADOW
SISTER

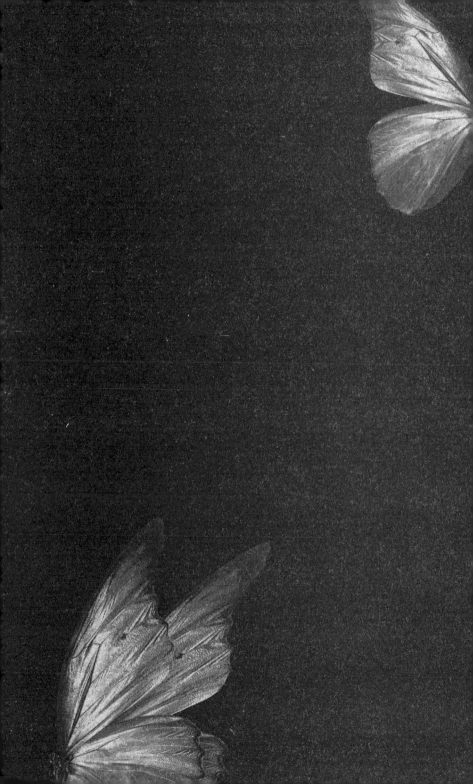

THE
SHADOW
SISTER

LILY MEADE

sourcebooks
fire

Copyright © 2023 by Lily Meade
Cover and internal design © 2023 by Sourcebooks
Cover design by Liz Dresner
Cover art © Shaylin Wallace
Images © CoffeeAndMilk/Getty, Missing35mm/Getty, Dole08/iStock, hsvrs/iStock,
vicuschka/iStock, Julia_Sudnitskaya/iStock, Al1974ex/iStock, Liudmila Chernetska/
iStock, RCKeller/iStock, Jean-François Botton/stock.adobe.com, boule1301/
stock.adobe.com, kolesnikovserg/stock.adobe.com, Kimo/stock.adobe.com
Internal design by Laura Boren/Sourcebooks
Internal images © boule1301/stock.adobe.com

Sourcebooks and the colophon are registered trademarks of Sourcebooks.

All rights reserved. No part of this book may be reproduced in any form or by
any electronic or mechanical means, including information storage and retrieval
systems—except in the case of brief quotations embodied in critical articles or
reviews—without permission in writing from its publisher, Sourcebooks.

The characters and events portrayed in this book are fictitious or
are used fictitiously. Any similarity to real persons, living or dead,
is purely coincidental and not intended by the author.

Published by Sourcebooks Fire, an imprint of Sourcebooks
P.O. Box 4410, Naperville, Illinois 60567–4410
(630) 961-3900
sourcebooks.com

Cataloging-in-Publication Data is on file with the Library of Congress.

Printed and bound in the United States of America.
LSC 10 9 8 7 6 5 4 3 2 1

To my mama, Laurie Meade, forever and always.

To my brothers Jeremy, Jordan, and Levi.
I am so blessed to be your sister.

To Taylor, for saving my mom during the pandemic
and saving me time and time again.

ONE

My sister is a bitch, but that doesn't mean I want her dead.

I can't say that, even though it's the truth. The truth doesn't matter when a person is missing. No one wants to hear that *the victim* was vindictive and cruel. It doesn't help the search—or the Home Again Narrative, as Mom calls it—to admit the girl we're all looking for is capable of terrible things.

And so here I stand next to the only person Sutton has ever truly cared about, a somber half smile on my face as I tell the reporter, "We all just want her home safe."

"More than anything," Andrew, her boyfriend, says. He actually means it too. Poor thing.

"It's so great that you're here to support Sutton," a young blond reporter says through a fake smile. She looks like a younger version of my mother. Considering the logo on her microphone matches the ones engraved on my mom's earliest journalism awards, that's probably intentional. "Are you affiliated with the church sponsoring the search effort?"

Andrew falters, looking sideways at me as his mouth opens and closes like he's a fish. Answering this question honestly will open a door he doesn't know how to close behind him. He's never been to Heights Above Church. It's a status symbol for wealthier Willow Bend residents. Dad doesn't even enjoy attending—he says it's nothing like the Black churches he grew up with in the South—but he goes for the same reason Mom does: networking. I guess God helps those who help themselves befriend the right people.

Andrew is not the *right* type of person. Not according to my parents. My mom, mainly.

He's not even that much less well-off than us. He simply works at the golf club to save up for his own car instead of getting one as a birthday gift like Sutton had. Yeah, he lives in Bend's End, which has never been the safest part of town, but he gets by. Sutton wouldn't associate with him otherwise. She's far too shallow.

Proof of that loiters beyond the too-bright lights balanced on the cameraman's shoulders that bathe Andrew and me in an unnatural glow. Waiting their turn like hyenas circling a lion's kill, Sutton's fellow cheerleaders pass around a single makeup compact like soldiers sharing a flask before combat. Their commander, the assistant coach, gestures instructions I can't interpret from this distance. They nod obediently, as if this is a pep rally performance instead of a search party for their cheer captain. Where's the head coach, Coach McCoy? A televised interview doesn't really seem like the best time to rely on the second-in-command.

No, Sutton—or her friends—wouldn't bother with Andrew if any part of him could embarrass her. I would know.

The biggest difference between us is that he's white, and we're not. It's pretty much the only thing keeping him out of jail right now. If the script were flipped, if Sutton were blond instead of simply light-skinned and Andrew were her less-fortunate Black boyfriend, he'd be facing interrogation under much less flattering lights and cameras.

"We're really grateful for the church's help," I say. I try to remember everything Mom has lectured me about as I choose my words. Everything I say and do must help bring Sutton home. "We know the police have a lot of responsibility, so we're glad we were able to come together to help the search."

"Do you think the police are doing enough for your sister? She's been missing for a week."

Dad's voice echoes in my mind with a resounding no, followed by thoughts of my mother's attempts at comfort, which grow thinner and thinner as each night passes without Sutton or any update on her case. Mom practically begged the police for their cooperation in this community-funded search effort. But I don't tell the truth. That's not going to make them love Sutton more.

"I, uh..." I start. "I am so grateful for everything that's being done."

"The way everyone has come together for Sutton shows how valued she is," Andrew says, easily beating my sentiment in a single line. His lower lip wobbles. "I miss her so much."

I don't know how he does it.

The reporter glances from the side of her eye at her camera man, her lip barely concealing a smirk. She moves in closer.

The media is so enchanted by the idea of Andrew as a monster, they don't even question my sincerity as they pick apart his. It's not his fault. He's a convenient suspect. The boyfriend from the other side of the nonexistent tracks. The perfect prime-time villain. There's no room for creativity in missing person cases; clichés are always welcome.

The weather matches their calculated tragedy. It's overcast, like it always is in Washington. The cheer team's matching pink FIND SUTTON shirts glow practically neon in the dewy parking lot, the rest of us cast in a dull gray. July is only a week away, but Andrew's white skin looks even paler than normal. His thin frame swims in a clearly borrowed button-down, practically skeletal as if *he* were the ghost we're chasing today. His blue eyes are icy and bloodshot at the same time.

I wonder when he last slept. I know the reporters are wondering the same thing, like I know how they'd like to ask: *What's keeping you awake at night, Andrew? Are you afraid for Sutton's safety? Or is it your guilt? Were you jealous of her money? Did you hurt her?*

There are questions I want him to answer too. I want him to explain how it's so easy for him to stand there and praise Sutton,

4

knowing her better than anyone. Maybe he's blinded by adoration of my sister, but he must know he's under suspicion. Is he truly innocent or just good at playing the part?

I don't let him answer any more questions, mine nor the reporters'. I thank the press and wave, pulling Andrew behind me as we head for the trees. I guess saving him from the ambush could count as a small mercy for Sutton, not that she deserves it. If she would even care. It's as much for me as it is for him.

The news crew eagerly welcomes the pink cavalry as our replacement, adjusting the lights and camera angles to take in the entire choreographed group. The reporter is so excited, even her practiced poker face can't hide it.

A missing girl must be like winning the lottery to local news anchors. A shot of one of us finding her dead body would be the highlight of their careers. Mom would certainly have been among them if it weren't her daughter we're searching for. A confession would be even more marketable than a body. I would let them claw one out of Andrew if I truly thought he were guilty of hurting Sutton. If I thought he were anything more than another pawn in whatever scheme she's truly up to.

But the cameras can't follow us into the woods.

Cameras aren't allowed in the search area. Cell phones are only tolerated to avoid losing track of anyone else in this recovery effort. There are so many rules to follow. Assigned grids. Appropriate engagement with evidence—aka don't touch anything you find on the ground. Or in the grass. Or in the mud.

The mud is everywhere. I feel like our dog after playtime in the rain. I wonder if my mother's boots are getting dirty this quickly too. She bought us matching pairs yesterday. They're these cute military-inspired canvas design with a ton of laces. I have no idea how to wash out the mud stains or if we should even bother. Does Dad know how to clean boots? He should. He goes fishing often enough.

"Casey," Andrew says in a tone that implies it's not the first time he's tried to get my attention. His hand is tight around my forearm, shaking it, but he lets go when I look at him. "Sorry," he says, though I'm not quite sure what he's apologizing for. He runs both hands through his copper hair. Sutton used to joke that he was the only white person allowed to touch her hair because she couldn't keep her hands off his either.

"I wanted to thank you," Andrew says. In the shade of the trees, all pretense of calm has escaped him. It's not even that warm yet, but the armpits of his oversize button-down are nearly see-through with sweat. Sutton would be mortified that this is how the world is seeing her favorite person. "You didn't have to help me with the vultures." He waves a hand toward the glitter of lights in the distance.

"It's fine."

"I've been assigned to Zone D, so I guess this is where we say goodbye."

"Bye, then," I reply.

Andrew lingers for a moment, staring at me as if I may say

more. I can't tell if it's awkward or creepy. Maybe this is just how he is. Maybe Sutton thought his intense gaze was sexy, but it makes me uncomfortable.

"We're gonna find her, Casey," he says. He repeats it, like I've noticed a lot of people do when they say empty words. It's clear he's trying to comfort himself more than me. But that's no surprise. I'm sure he misses her more than I do.

I nod in response. "I know we will," I say. "Thanks." Then, before he can say anything to worsen our collective misery, I walk away.

It's not my job to make Sutton's boyfriend feel better. It shouldn't be my job to comfort anybody, but that's all I've done since Sutton disappeared. I watch my step as I head off the marked path of the hiking trail. I'm supposed to search Zone B, near the lake. I could take the trail, but that could mean running into another well-meaning volunteer. I'd rather fall in a ravine than risk that. I know a shortcut that will be much faster.

I know this park. I've been coming here since I was in diapers, and so has Sutton. That's why this search is pointless. She only jogged this trail in the mornings, well before school. She rarely ever came here in the afternoon or evening. Sutton was a lot of things, but she wasn't naive. She knew the danger of being a woman alone on a trail in fading light. She was cruel, not careless. She wouldn't willingly endanger herself.

We'd have a lot more luck if we were all searching for the right girl. The Sutton they're looking for—an effortlessly loveable damsel, a heartbreaking accidental tragedy—doesn't exist. They won't find her by looking for mistakes she never would have made.

As far as I know—as far as anyone knows—she was last seen leaving the campus of Gwen Light's Upper School for Girls on our final day of classes last week. That's on the other side of Willow Bend. Maybe our oh-so-generous volunteers were less open to a search party in the middle of town, but I know she wouldn't have come here. I'm sure of it.

"Casey!" Ruth calls to me as I slide down a short hill to the small clearing—the starting point of Zone B. As she waves me over, the beads of the friendship bracelets we made in seventh grade dance on her deep-brown wrist. She doesn't show it—two summers of camp-counselor training keeping her calm—but I can tell she's glad to finally be joined by someone her own age.

Other volunteers, mostly adults, walk toward her from the main path. Ruth greets them in denim shorts, a light-green tee, and a reflective crossing guard vest. The only traffic to conduct here is that of the entitled middle-aged moms in white tennis shoes trying to convince Ruth to give them a search area away from the water and mud.

"If Sutton were on the main trail, we would have found her by now," Ruth says. "What if she slipped and fell somewhere? Isn't the safe recovery of one of our own more important than dirty laundry? God only made one Sutton."

I reach Ruth as the latest volunteer succumbs to her earnest church rearing. The woman swallows her response when she sees

the Heights Above Church emblem on Ruth's shirt. Sharpie sig-
natures from campers she counseled at last summer's Bible camp
peek out from under the yellow vest.

"I suppose you're right," the woman concedes.

Ruth smiles. "You'll be in the upper left corner of this grid,"
she tells the woman. "You're partnered with Nancy. Hi, Nancy!"
Another inappropriately dressed woman waves from the opposite
end of the clearing. "God bless you both!" Ruth says as they reluc-
tantly leave.

"That's the last of them!" she says as she turns to me, pocket-
ing her phone now that she's finished her shepherding duties. "It's
only you and me now. I gave us one of the more difficult areas.
Partly because I was tired of their complaining. It's one day! You'd
think people could suck up their discomfort with the general concept of nature to do a good deed." She blows a big breath through
her lips, her eyebrows raising with mostly exaggerated frustration.
She pulls a hair band from her wrist and starts to wrap her many
braids into a bun on top of her head. "I also know you probably
don't want to bump into many other people today."

I could hug Ruth for that, but I wait until she's done with her
hair before embracing her. "I really, really don't," I admit as she
wraps her arms around me. Her neck still smells like lavender soap
despite Ruth being outside all morning. I'm pretty sure I already
smell like deer crap, and I've only been here for an hour.

She pulls on one of my curls when we let each other go. "I'm
here for you," she says as I attempt to tuck the errant ringlet back

among the others trapped in my ponytail. I can tell by the itch at the base of my neck that I've already failed. I hope Ruth's braids mount a stronger defense against the humidity.

"We're here for Sutton," I correct.

"Yeah, speaking of, my dad wants to video call later. Are you going to be up for that?"

"I thought the cops said no photos or video?" Pastor Heights is a lot to take in during normal circumstances. Ruth tends to use her upbringing and status as a pastor's daughter when it benefits the situation, but her dad's commitment to bringing God into the equation is all-consuming.

"They did," Ruth admits. "But the church paid for most of this search. I doubt they're going to hassle the person bankrolling this."

I bend to tighten the laces on my new boots. "I guess it's fine."

"Thank you," she says as we head off through the brush and pines. "I really appreciate it."

I know it's true. Ruth is honest in everything she does. She's the kind of person to single-handedly coordinate the logistics of a community search to help her best friend, even while having to help care for her younger siblings with her only living parent out of town. Mom cried for hours when Ruth offered the church phone tree for Sutton's recovery effort.

She's the kind of daughter a parent would actually want. She'd miss her sibling if one of them disappeared. She wouldn't fake concern for cameras because her heart would be heavy with genuine worry.

Mine is seething with rage. I can't handle pretending Sutton was a sainted angel, taken down by unforeseeable tragedy. That she was the perfect sister—always thoughtful and never cruel nor vengeful, calculating, and manipulative. So, when Ruth asks me how I'm doing, I'm honest. Like she would be.

"I hate this." I don't say, *I hate her*, even though I do. "I'm so useless, Ruth. All Mom talks about is strategy and the Home Again Narrative. Everything has to be perfect for the press so they'll love Sutton and want to help find her. I'm supposed to pretend she's an angel. I can't do that."

I shove at a branch in front of me so hard, it snaps in half. My palm pulses, the branch's silhouette slowly fading.

"I'd talk to Dad about it, but he's worse than Mom. He's heartbroken. Anyone can see it, but he refuses to admit any vulnerability, so instead of being sad, he keeps getting mad over the smallest things. I'm either walking on eggshells or living in a dollhouse like some puppet. Sutton has managed to ruin everything without even being here. All anybody wants to talk about is how great she was."

Ruth stops where she's perched on a fallen tree log. What little sun there is breaks through the canopy and casts her in a spotlight. She's statuesque, which makes her next words all the worse. "How great she *is*," she corrects me. "You said 'was.'"

I don't respond. I simply stand there, watching her watch me as ice floods my veins. Ruth mistakes my silence as a need for reassurance. "Sutton isn't dead," she says. She jumps from the log and walks toward me, all that churchy compassion making her igno-rant of my sin. "You have to have faith that she'll return to you, even if you're mad. It won't always be this bad."

She reaches out to hug me again. Entwined with the bracelet we made is the promise bracelet her dad got her for her fourteenth birthday. It glitters in the light and looks expensive, like an heir-loom she may pass on to her own daughter in the future. I close my eyes, but Sutton's merciless grin chases me. In my mind is her wrist from that final night, wearing nothing but spite as she twisted it to flip me off.

I flood hot with rage like a dam has broken.

"You love her, right?" Ruth asks, like it's the easiest question in the world.

I smother myself in her shoulder, trying to squeeze out every-thing wrong inside me. Every terrible thought. *You love her, right?* I'm supposed to. I should. I would, if she hadn't—

I want to. I have to. It's not a real question.

I have no other choice but to say, "Of course I do."

TWO

Hours later, the only thing Ruth and I have found are allergies to plants we didn't know existed.

I rub one of my boot-clad ankles against the other, scratching at an itch that seems to have a mind of its own. I wish I'd worn summer clothes like Ruth, but I dressed like a clueless tourist. I should have known better. The sky is still gray—a darker and more foreboding sort as the day ages—but the sun is working overtime behind the cloud cover.

The heat is incessant and so humid. My boot-cut jeans trap every drop of sweat inside like stew broth. My socked feet squelch in my boots like the soles do in the mud. Even my simple band tee feels like too much. Ivy James's screen-printed silhouette is drowning in my perspiration. I'd take it off or tie it into a crop below my sports bra if we were anywhere else.

"We're done for the day, right?" I ask Ruth as we head back to the volunteer checkpoint at the trail's entrance. "I don't think I can take much more of this."

"I know," Ruth says. She pouts her full lips and gives my hand a reassuring squeeze. "Maybe someone else found something more useful."

Shame sends my sweating into overdrive. I swallow hard. "Yeah, hopefully."

Ruth's pocket starts vibrating. She lets go of my clammy hand to inspect it. "It's Daddy," she says. A selfie of her and Pastor Heights flashes on the screen. The contrast between them couldn't be more apparent. Sometimes people mistake my mom for a family friend, but most can spot the similarities between us despite our different skin tones. Sutton's always favored Mom more, not only in features but in how her skin is always lighter than mine even after a summer in the sun. Dad says I'm practically a clone of Grandma Remy, his mom, but I'm still clearly a product of both of my parents.

The same can't be said of the pastor and Ruth, regardless of her being adopted. He never looks more obviously white than when he's standing next to her. He smiles in the photo, his gaze still somehow judging me. Ruth's thumb hovers over the screen, but she doesn't swipe until I nod my acceptance.

"Hi, Daddy," she says as his face pops onto her phone. "Casey and I are almost done at the search today." She turns the phone toward me, and I try to wave hello to him and avoid tripping over a pile of rocks at the same time. I only succeed at one.

"Hello, Pastor Heights," I say, hopping on one foot as I try to catch up to Ruth.

"Casey," he says. "How many times have I told you to call me *David*?"

"Sorry, Pastor *David*," I say.

He laughs, but he looks tired.

"Daddy, when are you coming home?" Ruth asks. "You said you were going to try to get back for the search. It's been almost two weeks."

"I know I did, sweetheart, but it's complicated." The pastor rubs the stubble on his chin. I'm not used to seeing him with a five-o'clock shadow. "I'm very close to securing the finances to move forward with the new mission. You can last a little longer without me if it means we can bring more people to salvation, right?"

The saccharinity in his voice is too much for me, and I duck out of the frame again so he won't catch my grimace. Ruth sees it, but she's always had a better poker face than I do. "Absolutely," she tells her dad. "I miss you—*we* miss you. That's all."

"I miss you too," he says. "I wish I could be there for you and the Curetons right now. Is Casey still there?" Ruth flips the screen back to me. "Casey," he says. "I'd like to pray with you, if that's okay?"

I nod. This is another question that only has one answer. You can't say no when a pastor asks you to pray with him about your missing sister. Especially when his church and congregation con-tributed a large wad of cash to her recovery effort.

"Father God," he begins, closing his eyes. Ruth closes her eyes too. I don't. "We address this prayer from two different locations today. We know distance means nothing to the reach of your love, but the space between us and Sutton Cureton feels overwhelming in this moment, Lord. Sutton is a righteous daughter, a good girl on the proper path. Isaiah and Madison have raised her well, and we know that you see that. Her family needs her. Her sister needs her. We pray for her safety and swift return to us. We know you will bring her home. Amen."

"Amen," Ruth repeats.

"Amen," I say. "Um, thank you, Pastor Hei—*David*. I need to find my parents, but I'll tell them about your prayer. Thanks again for helping with the search today."

"It's the least I could do," he says.

I nod again, even though Ruth has angled the camera back to her. I wave goodbye to her and sprint ahead. I don't really want to check on my parents, but it's the lesser evil to another ten minutes of Pastor David's well-meaning microaggressions.

Sutton was the opposite of righteous and the last person I would call a good girl, but that shouldn't be the litmus test of her worthiness. No one should have something terrible like this happen to them, no matter the type of person they are.

None of these people truly knew her, yet everyone is claiming to be her best friend. Sutton didn't have a best friend, not as far as I know, but it's not like I know everything about her life. I know she liked something only when it meant she'd taken it from me. I know who she spent time with when she'd leave me stranded after promising to drive me somewhere. I know she hated me. I know she wished—every day—that I had never been born.

It's the last thing she said to me.

I hate her too, but I want her back anyway. I want this all to stop.

When I return to the park entrance, I can still see the line of media vans at the edge of the parking lot. The cheerleaders are gone. The reporters don't notice me from this distance, but I recognize the bright blond hair and silhouette of my mother's figure addressing them. Sutton's face stares at me from the back of her T-shirt. Mom and I fought this morning when I said I couldn't find the matching shirt she got for me. She delayed our departure for half an hour to let me search for it, but it's still hidden deep under my bed.

I have no desire to be on camera again, so I seek out the other person wearing Mom's exact outfit. Sutton's face is even bigger across my father's broad shoulders. Her flat-ironed hair frames her open-mouthed smile, like she's laughing at us for trusting her. Laughing at these people for worrying about her, fearing for her, wasting their time trying to find her. Laughing at me—mocking me like always—for not buying a second of it.

Dad is working under a big tent with refreshments and supplies. He doesn't hear me sneak up on him, so I watch his big hands carefully position small flashlights on a pop-up table like they're favors at a child's birthday party.

His brows are furrowed as he lays out his little rows, his

bottom lip under his teeth. This changes when he spots me. A big fake smile takes up his whole face, and his brows relax, but there's no joy in his eyes. No relief or pleasure at the sight of me, even as he claims the opposite.

"Baby girl," he says. "You're back."

I decide to answer the question before he can ask. "We didn't find anything. I'm sorry, Dad."

"No, honey," he says, reaching out an arm to pull me in. He tucks me against him, and somehow he smells woodsier than the actual forest. He's overly warm like everything else today, but I don't want to pull away. "Don't apologize. It'll be okay."

He gestures to his army of flashlights. "These are for the people who've offered to search into the evening. So many people care about your sister, Casey. We're gonna—" He lets out a big breath. "She's coming home."

His hand tightens on my shoulder. From my vantage point, I can see more of the beard on his chin than his face, but even through the coarse midnight hairs, I can tell his jaw has tightened.

"Are you okay?" It's a useless question, because of course he isn't, but it's all I have. This is my door. My invitation for him to open up to me. I hope and dread he takes it. *I'm here, Dad. You still have me.*

He lets go of me instead. I step back as he returns to his flashlights, realigning a row that was never off-center. He's not looking at me when he speaks again. "I heard some volunteers talking earlier," he says. "They didn't see me, but they were talking about her."

"What did they say?"

"They said she probably ran away." The words escape him in a rush, so fast that I almost don't catch it. He doesn't say anything else, but I can tell he's been carrying that weight all day. He turns to pull more flashlights from a box.

Sutton's face smiles at me once again from across his broad shoulders, and I fight the urge to punch my father in the back.

Instead, I take one of his hands and pull him into a hug. Even though he's twice my size, he falls into my arms. I've always loved my father's hugs. Nothing has ever felt safer than the sound of his heartbeat beneath my ear. But today his pulse is racing, not mine.

"She wouldn't do that," I lie. "She would never leave without telling you," I say, even though she regularly snuck out past curfew. "She would never hurt us like that." She absolutely would. "There's no reason she'd run away. It makes no sense. She has everything she could ever want." The only truth. "And she definitely wouldn't have left Andrew behind."

He laughs at that, shaking us both with the mirth of it. I tighten my arms around him, but my hands still don't meet on the other side. I lift my head from his chest, meeting that low-angle view of his beard again. He looks down at me. In his eyes, I see a familiar sight.

We're all devastated by Sutton. I've seen the same sorrow reflected in the mirror hundreds of times. But there's no anger in his gaze. He doesn't blame her for this.

"She loves us," I say, before correcting myself. "She loves *you*.

She loves Mama. And Romeo." He laughs lightly again. "She wouldn't hurt us like this. Not on purpose."

I bury my face in his shirt again. I want to believe what I'm saying, but I can't hide my doubt. It doesn't matter what I think as long as he's comforted. If Dad trusts Sutton—if he believes in her—maybe that's enough to bring her back, no matter why she disappeared.

She has to come back.

"I found you," comes a voice from outside our cocoon. Dad eases his grip on me to greet Mom. "My favorite people," she says as she approaches. She tucks wayward strands of her long blond waves behind her ears; they escaped the updo she'd put them in so they wouldn't obscure Sutton's screen-printed face on her back. "Well..." she amends. "Most of them."

She takes the hand Dad has freed from holding me, and it's like a switch flips in him. Flips in them both. His arm loosens around me from an anchor to a buoy floating at sea. "Hey, Maddie," he says. "Our girl was helping me finish up here."

Mom takes my hand, looping the three of us in a small circle, and I let her, even though I can't look her in the eye. I stare at our shoes. My boots almost look as caked with mud as Dad's. Mom's look exactly like they did in the store, save for some new grass stains. I keep my eyes low as I confess my failure. "We didn't find anything," I tell her.

She tugs on my hand to pull me closer, and before I know it, I'm inside a three-way hug with my parents for the first time since middle school.

"Baby, it's all right," she says. "I'm proud of you for coming today. We're gonna find her."

"We will," Dad echoes, as if I hadn't just reassured him of that.

I'm the first one to break the chain of love, shrugging out of their embrace. "Are we done for tonight? Can we go home?"

Mom looks to Dad. He doesn't say anything, but they seem to communicate through glances, because she nods. "Yeah," she says. "We can head out. Let me check in with the volunteer liaison first, and then we can go."

She walks away from the tent. Dad follows, still holding her hand. I hurry to catch up. My shoes squelch again in the wet grass. "What's a volunteer liaison?" I ask.

"The police officer responsible for civilian reports," Mom answers without stopping, using that practiced reporter voice of hers. "He'll have heard from all the zone heads and should have an update if anyone found anything. It's the police's job to keep us informed on the investigation's progress."

Dad's fingers flex between hers at her last comment, but his face betrays no further discomfort.

I don't know exactly where we're going, but I lag a few feet behind them. The tree line is another two hundred yards or so ahead. I hope we don't have to go back into the park. The sky is getting more restless by the minute, clouds churning through shades of agitated gray. It's definitely going to rain, and I'm not dressed for it at all.

"That's him," Mom says, gesturing at a white man emerging

from the evergreens. He clearly recognizes us, even at a distance, because he stops dead in his tracks and makes an aborted move to turn back.

But he's too late.

We've already noticed the other police officers flanking him. I can see the bag one of them is carrying, even from behind my parents. Mom lets go of Dad's hand and starts to run toward the cops. We race after her.

The cop tries to shift the evidence bag behind him, but we all see it. Mom halts like she's hit a brick wall, falling to her knees as her momentum catches up to her. Dad skids to a stop beside her. I'm frozen behind them, the distance between us growing greater and greater despite the fact we're no longer moving.

No one makes a sound, but the sight before us screams like a siren. I know it will be burned into my retinas, haunting me behind every blink.

A single running shoe. Something you'd see abandoned on a sidewalk in the city and never think twice about. A piece of garbage.

Except this is Sutton's running shoe.

And it's covered in blood.

SUTTON

MORNING OF

I don't care what Casey thinks about me.

I don't care if she's mad at me. Don't care if she thinks I'm the worst sister ever. Don't care if she wants me dead. It really doesn't matter to me at all.

I wait in the car for Andrew to come outside. As I drum my fingers on the steering wheel, my thumb kisses the pendant of Grandma's bracelet, and I decide then and there that I'm never going to give it back to Casey, even if I have to hide it in a new location every day.

Ma Remy was *my* grandmother first. Mom and Dad began our family with *me*. Casey wouldn't even exist if it weren't for me. They had a second child so I could have a sibling. Without me, she would have never been born, and honestly, most days I wish she weren't. My life would be so much simpler without her. I know she feels the same way.

Casey doesn't understand that everything she has was mine first. Everything that comes so effortlessly to her, I had to work for. She has Daddy wrapped around her finger. He'd do anything for her. He dedicated his last book to her, simply because she hung out in his office while he wrote. I spent weeks researching genealogy to have something to talk about with him, and he waved me off, saying I didn't understand the perspective he was using to approach the material. I could have if he'd given me a chance.

She didn't even do anything to help. She never has to do anything. She gets everything she asks for, and more she doesn't even need. I work so hard to make Mom and Dad proud. I'm so close to being scouted for cheer, and it's like it doesn't matter. She just sits in her room chatting about music or dropping in on Dad when he's busy. She doesn't have extracurriculars or hobbies or go anywhere, and she's still their baby girl. The spitting image of Ma Remy, with those perfect curls that she flaunts at me.

Newsflash, Casey: it's a lot easier to keep your hair natural when you don't have to wake up early for practice and shower away sweat every day. You're not a better Black girl because your scalp is as much of a virgin as you are.

It's so easy for her. Always.

Andrew knocks at the driver's side window. He steps back as I open the door, then looks around his street like he always does when I come to pick him up, like he's ashamed.

I hop down, smiling as he watches the hem of my school uniform bounce up with the movement. His eyes are almost the same color blue as my mom's, but his are deeper, like water under moonlight. They shine for me and me alone. He's the one thing I never have to share.

I want to drag his lips to mine, then bury my face in his neck and stay there, wrapped up in him. We've waited so long for today. I know he didn't think I could do it, but I did. I'd do anything for him. This is only the beginning.

"You didn't tell your parents, right?" I ask as I hand him the keys.

"No," he says as I circle my baby, the bright red Jeep I got for my sweet sixteen. He waits until I climb in on the passenger side before he slides into the driver's seat and continues, "You told me not to."

"I don't want to tell anyone until we know for sure. If it doesn't work out, I don't want—"

"I know," he says, patting my nervous hands.

He pulls out of his driveway slowly, as if the patchy gravel is a hidden minefield. He's still not used to the backup camera in my car, checking the mirrors before I remind him of it. His cheeks flush a brighter red than the graffiti spray-painted on his neighbor's fence, but the embarrassment fades as we drive. By the time we merge from the cul-de-sac to the main road, his skin is as porcelain fair as usual.

"Sutton, I want you to know," he begins as we start to work our way out of Bend's End, the cheaper area of Willow Bend. "This isn't why I'm here. I'm not gonna leave you. I—"

"I know," I say this time, cutting him off. I twist toward him as much as the seat belt will allow. "I know," I repeat.

"I don't want you to think I was only in this for your money or what you could offer me—"

"I've never thought that," I interrupt. "Not once."

"Your parents already don't like me, and I want to show them I'm worthy of their daughter. I don't want to be a mooch, okay? I don't want them to think I'm some deadbeat that's latched on to you."

"They definitely don't think that," I say. "I promise."

Andrew rolls his eyes, and I can't help but laugh, which gets him laughing, which only makes me laugh harder. "Okay," I concede through giggles. "My mom *totally* thinks that. But that's gonna change."

"When hell freezes over," Andrew scoffs.

"With climate change, that could happen this fall," I say. "You never know."

He laughs again, but this time I don't join him. I take it in, memorizing the sound. He doesn't laugh enough. His laugh was how I met him. I heard it at the golf club, while I sat through yet another garden party hosted by Coach McCoy's wife. Andrew was on the periphery of the outdoor café, lifting the hem of his uniform to shield himself from the ice his coworker was tossing at him. He didn't see me then, and it was even longer before he laughed because of something I said, but I'll never forget that first day.

We're finally back in the thick of Willow Bend, so I know we don't have much longer together. Quiet overtakes the car. I want to turn on the radio to fill the silence. More than that, I want to talk, but I don't want to make him any more nervous. He's already so anxious.

At the next stoplight, he glances over at me. His fingers drum against the steering wheel. "I like your bracelet," he says. I'm pretty sure he couldn't care less about jewelry, but he's always been good at noticing details and complimenting me.

"This?" I lift my wrist as if I'm wearing anything else to show off. He nods.

"It was my grandma's."

"The one who died?" He immediately scoffs at his own tactlessness. "Babe, I'm sorry. I—"

"You're fine," I say gently. Ma Remy's absence still hurts, but even the most careful wording wouldn't help that. She's only been gone three months. Every reminder of her cuts like a rock in my shoe, yet I have no choice but to keep going.

I rub the silver of the bracelet again, tracing the grooves of the intersecting chain, avoiding the pendant this time. It hangs toward my palm like a teardrop, a dark green bulb except for where the plants inside it meet the surface. My favorite part is the tiny white flower kissing the center, opening its few petals to the world. That's the part I claimed as mine when Ma Remy promised it to me.

There's only one other car in the school's parking lot when he pulls into the school parking lot, but I know he can't stay much longer if he wants to make his appointment on time. And if he notices whose car it is, he won't leave. He'll insist on staying until the lot fills and the bell rings. He may even cancel his trip entirely.

I don't know if anyone is in the van waiting for me. But I can't let Andrew suspect anything. He has to leave now.

I unbuckle my seat belt and reach down for my backpack. Andrew catches my arm. "I love you," he says. It comes out watery the first time he says it. He tries again. It's no better.

If he cries, I'll start crying. I didn't wear waterproof mascara today.

I silence him with my lips. It can't be a deep kiss, not with the center console separating us, but I put everything I have into it. I want him to understand that we're tied together forever, that I'll never leave him. I want him to know that I trust him. That I believe in him, in us. No matter what happens today.

"I love you too," I say when we break apart, my face still so close to his, he practically inhales my words. "It's gonna be okay."

He lets out a sigh as he leans back in his seat, nodding.

"Remember though, you can't tell anyone that I loaned you the car."

"Of course," he promises. "But are you sure you're going to be okay walking back? It's a long walk."

I shake my backpack. "I brought my running shoes. I'll be fine."

He still looks uncertain, but another car pulls in across the parking lot. I open the door and slip out before bouncing on my toes. I twirl to face the rolled-down window and blow him a kiss. He has to go. He needs to leave before he starts to worry about anything else.

"The Garden at four, okay? You'll be there?"

I give him a bright smile. "Rain or shine, baby."

"Rain or shine," he repeats.

I watch him drive away, waiting until he's out of sight. Then I walk to the forest-green van parked in the reserved section of the parking lot. He's replaced the left taillight since I broke it, but the paint is still scratched around it. I guess insurance didn't want to shell out for detailing.

My hand tightens around my phone in my pocket. I remind myself there's nothing he can do to hurt me now. I have the upper hand. It's too late.

It doesn't matter anyway. The van is empty.

I'm safe.

THREE

No one looks at one another on the drive back home. My parents aren't touching, not to hold hands across the center console or squeeze the other's thigh. They *always* touch. They always find a way to connect that's gross, awkward, and embarrasses me but also reminds me—*promises* me—that they are solid. Unbreakable.

What if this destroys them?

I've always had my family. When my classmates talked about split holidays and custody arrangements, I was smug. *That's never gonna be me*, I told myself. Even on our worst days, I knew I'd never be separated from Sutton in some *Parent Trap* arrangement (even if I wished otherwise). Dad would never move back south without us. I'd never have to help one of my parents figure out online dating. I've prided myself on the fact they both first thought Tinder was a camping app.

I don't know how to be the child of a shattered relationship. I want life to go back to normal. I want Sutton to come home and fix this.

Why would Sutton go jogging after the last day of school? It doesn't make any sense. She should have been celebrating. She should have been happy junior year was over, with all the college prep pressures. The only time she ever went for a run in the afternoon was when she was angry or stressed. I should know. Many of our fights ended with her grabbing her keys and running shoes.

I know she was mad at me that day, but...

I lean back against my seat and watch the storm outside. Rain pelts the windows like a thousand anxious knocks. Is Sutton out in this weather? Is she cold? Is she feeling anything at all? The windshield wipers only amplify the silence within the car.

Dad turns onto the private road that leads to our gated community. Mom doesn't react until we pull into the driveway, and then it's as if nothing has happened at all. "Casey, don't forget to take your shoes off when you get inside," she reminds me as she steps out of the car. "I don't want you tracking mud through the house."

I don't have time to respond before she's walking away, her own boots slapping against the rain-soaked stone path cutting through her garden. Dad waits for me to climb out the back and shuts the door after I hop out of the black SUV. He doesn't say anything.

Mom is still unlacing her boots when we get inside. "The

police said we can't be sure it was Sutton's shoe until the blood tests come back," she says without looking up. "We'll have to wait."

Dad clears his throat, looking at me. We know this already. We were with her when the police tried to talk us down from panicking over the obvious truth. "Then we'll wait," Dad agrees. "We can do that, right, Casey?"

Mom looks up at me, so I have no choice but to nod. I'm saved from any further response by Romeo, our corgi, who slides into the tiled entryway on his stubby orange legs. He jumps up, his little paws sliding down my jeans, falling seriously close to my muddy boots.

"Cas—" Mom starts, the beginning of a scolding on her lips. It's almost normal, her getting upset about the house getting messy. I bite back a smile.

"I've got him," I promise. I bend to pick him up. "Hey, buddy, how are you?" He kisses my neck and chin in response, squirming like a furry worm in my arms. He presses his front paws against my chest, angling himself for a better view of the front door. He's focused, searching for something. Someone.

I stroke his back. "I'm sorry," I say. "Sutton's not with us." Romeo deflates in my arms, burrowing his head against my breast like a pillow. He doesn't whine—he's too proud for that—but I feel a disappointed exhale tickle my clammy skin. I set him back down on the floor, and he treads over to the door anyway and sits there expectantly.

"I—um," Mom starts too loudly. "I have some work emails to address. I'll be in my office if you need me, Isaiah."

Dad nods, "Yeah, sweetheart. That's fine. I was about to let Romeo outside anyway. He probably wants to go out." He scoops him up again and heads the opposite direction, toward the back of the house. Mom turns for the stairs. Neither of them acknowledges me.

I take my time unlacing my boots. Mom left hers on the tile, so I don't feel any obligation to find somewhere else to put mine. I leave my wet socks on top of them for her to launder or Romeo to chew. I don't really care either way.

The hardwood is cold under my bare feet.

As I pad down the hallway, my fingers ghost over the framed newspaper clipping of the first time Dad hit a bestseller list, a memento older than I am. There are so many items in this house that have existed long before I came along. Even more that will outlast me, like they outlasted those who first created them.

I pause before one of the many framed pictures that hang alongside our parents' professional achievements. A younger Sutton smiles from behind a distracted toddler me on Halloween. In another we're wearing matching flamingo floats by the pool. I'm older than in the last photo and almost as tall as Sutton, as she hadn't yet hit her first growth spurt. The camera immortalized the comical horror on my face as I slipped on the edge of the pool, falling backward into the water. Sutton is halfway to the water herself, the float falling to her feet as she reaches for me.

She's not laughing at me like she would if this happened today, like my parents or anyone seeing this on the wall would now. Her face, still soft with baby fat, is focused on me. I barely remember hitting the water because she dove in and pulled me to the surface before Dad could even set down the camera.

I rub at my bare wrist as I enter the living room.

Dad is back inside, sitting on the couch. I glance at the glass doors to our deck, but Romeo is nowhere in sight. He must be looking for Sutton somewhere in the house. Dad wouldn't have left him alone in the backyard, not with the pool uncovered for summer.

"Hey, Daddy." I announce myself. He seems deep in a serious bout of brooding. "Are you hungry? I could make us something." Admittedly, I don't know what I would make. Sutton has always been his kitchen protégé. I inherited Mom's ability to burn water. I can't remember the last time someone went grocery shopping.

"I'm fine," he says. He pats the empty spot next to him.

I join him on the couch, sliding into the dip in the leather that his weight creates. He smells like rainwater, even though none of us were outside long enough to get soaked.

He doesn't speak for a while, so I join him in a silent study of the coffee table. It's relatively new. Sutton and I are old enough now that Mom and Dad don't worry about us shattering something so fragile. Not accidentally, at least.

Below the glass is a recessed display area, with several family heirlooms artfully laid out. It's a showcase of what Dad has dedicated his career to: proof of the ties that bind us, artifacts of the people who met and loved and persevered to bring our family to today. He's been curating the display in his downtime between grading papers and consulting with the Familiar Roots ancestry app.

I've seen most of his efforts already, but a trip down memory lane seems like a far better alternative to our present. I lean forward to get a better look.

In the far corner is the first deed of property ownership our ancestors claimed after slavery, circled by photos of that same land changing through the decades. Closer to the center is a faded dollar and some rusted nails that sit next to a black-and-white photo of my great-grandfather balancing Grandma Remy on his shoulders. They're in front of the first iteration of Cureton Construction, which is still a prosperous company back in the Carolinas.

Right in front of us rests a new addition: a small cloth bag with pressed flowers and plants peeking from the rim. It sits carefully atop a sketch of a middle-aged woman in a simple work dress. Her head is shaved, and she has a scar on the left side of her forehead. She's not looking at us or whoever drew her portrait. She is stone-faced, her attention directed toward some unknown horizon. But the artist loved her. You can see it in every line.

"That's your great-great-great-great grandmother," Dad says, pointing at the sketch. He makes a joke of the mouthful of *great*s, taking an exaggerated breath after finishing the sentence.

"Grandma Remy's great-great-grandma," I confirm.

Dad smiles at me with pride. "Yes, exactly. Her daughter had a son, that son had Ma Remy's father, who then had her." He scoots forward to the edge of the couch for a better view of the bag, and

I follow him, eager for a history lesson instead of whatever awkward conversation could follow. "The plantation records named her Hanna, but family records say she went by Henny in private."

"Then that's what we'll call her," I say. Dad has taught me that it wasn't uncommon for a person to have multiple names in the slavery era. If a plantation owner bothered to call the people they enslaved by names, they weren't usually the ones they were born with. Slaves were considered nameless until they were purchased from the auction block. Their new given names could be mocking or condescending or simply meant to prevent the owner from having to remember unique or difficult-to-pronounce names when barking orders.

"Her daughter, Mima, drew this picture of her," he says. "She drew it two weeks before her mother ran away from their plantation. It was Mima's most prized possession. It was all she had left of her mother after Henny disappeared."

"Oh," I say. My heart sinks. This isn't the direction I wanted our conversation to go tonight. "I thought..." I can't really claim to have imagined a happy ending for my enslaved ancestors, but I didn't want this. I know my purpose right now is to be a rock for my parents to lean on, to keep steady through this storm until something finally gives way. But I don't know how to push past my own doubts and fears to assure him everything will be okay when generations of proof otherwise is right in front of us. I fight the urge to stand, to leave Dad to revisit this alone.

"It's all right, Casey," he says. He takes my hand in his. "Henny came back."

"She did?"

"She did." He squeezes my hand. "It's a good story. Do you want to hear it?"

I squeeze back in response.

He points to another document, an old map, under the glass. "They lived here, on the Cureton plantation. That's where we got our name. Henny, Mima, and Mima's husband all came from the same plantation, though only Mima and her mama were related. Many freedmen chose to change their names after emancipation or escape, but your grandma always taught me that—"

"Too much has been taken from us not to reclaim ourselves," I finish. Ma Remy was so proud of our family history. Her passion became Dad's, which fed and nourished his career ambitions. She would have loved this heirloom display. She would have lectured Dad on leaving himself out, reminding him that we are living history and as important to our legacy as our ancestors. I almost wish she were here to tell this story with him, but maybe it's better that she's been spared everything that's happened since Sutton disappeared.

Dad is quiet for a long moment but then continues, "Our family lineage nearly stopped here. After she was emancipated, Mima was almost executed for murdering her former master."

"She killed him?" I ask. This is by far the most scandalous family story he's ever told me.

"Let me finish, Case," Dad admonishes me, but there's a chuckle in his voice. It's a familiar lightness that's been missing with Sutton gone. I make a show of sealing my lips.

"As the story goes, Mima never believed her mama ran away. She was certain their master had murdered Henny, and the whole town believed Mima killed him in revenge. Mima was arrested and put to trial, which should have been a death sentence in her time. But it was ultimately proven—to an all-white jury—that Mima hadn't even been in town when the crime occurred. She was still punished, stripped of the few resources she and her husband had managed to piece together after being freed, but she escaped with her life."

"And she found her mom again?"

"Henny came back for her, just like she'd always said she would," Dad confirms. He points to the pouch of dried flowers, careful not to touch the glass. "This was all Henny took with her. That's why I put this in here. It's in an important part of our family story. We always come back home."

A silence spreads over us like dust as Dad stares down at the glass, avoiding my gaze. I have questions I want to ask, like why Henny left alone when it seemed her daughter was so important to her. If she left of her own choice at all, or if there are more unsavory things he's kept from this retelling—like he's kept this entire story from me until now.

But digging at the roots of an old family tragedy doesn't seem like the best idea given our current circumstances.

"I'm grateful you shared this with me," I say, for lack of a better response. I'm not sure what the proper etiquette is when your father gives you a lesson in family trauma after you come home from searching for your missing sister. "I didn't know any of this."

He sniffs loudly and clears his throat. "No, and that's on me." He shakes his head as if to pull himself from a trance. "You were too young to hear some of this before. I planned on telling you though. It's my duty to connect you to your heritage, but with your grandma's illness this past year and then losing her—" He cuts off abruptly, and I'm reminded how emotional it is to talk about anyone's death right now. "I've been distracted. But you can learn more when you help me this summer. You're still gonna do that, right?"

I nod. The low thrum of family togetherness slips out from under me. There are cracks in our happy family facade that pre-date Sutton's disappearance. And this is one of them. Working to help Dad with his research this summer is how I'm earning my Ivy James concert money back after what Sutton did. I'm lucky he even offered me the opportunity to recoup my savings this way. He and Mom were so angry with me when it happened, no matter how many times I told them it wasn't my fault. I like learning from Dad, but I hate that I now *need* to. Ivy could announce a new tour at any time; there's no way I could save up enough with a part-time job to afford a ticket as soon as they're online. I swallow my rage and plaster on a fake smile. "I'd love to learn more about Henny and Mima."

He slings an arm around my shoulder and squeezes. "Good, good," he says. "You can help me finish the table. There's lots more we can add to the display. Won't that be fun?"

It doesn't seem like a question that needs answering, but the look he gives me is so pleading, I can't help but nod. He lets go of my shoulder and focuses on the dried flowers again, as if they have unspoken answers. As if they hold some key to understanding why this is happening to us.

"Mima sewed this bag. She picked these flowers," he says. "Her mama carried it with her always. She *always* planned on coming back."

"You see," he says when he finally looks back at me, black eyes glassy. "We've been through worse than this, baby girl. We will overcome. Justice was done in our favor then, and it will be done again. No matter—" He inhales sharply and swallows. "No matter what happens."

I nod again.

"She's gonna come back," Dad says. "She has to come home."

And then he does something I've never seen in my living history: he cries.

FOUR

omeo follows me back upstairs after Dad fakes an excuse to lock himself in his office like Mom, but it's not out of any sense of canine loyalty. When we pass Sutton's bedroom, he stops to paw at her door. He's starting to scratch grooves in it. He's never damaged any of our doors before, because Sutton never once locked him out. She always had endless patience for him, even when he'd wake us all in the middle of the night during puppy potty training.

He presses hard against the door as if he thinks being more stubborn will solve his problem, though it hasn't helped him so far. He is Sutton's dog after all.

His ears perk up when he looks at me.

"We aren't supposed to go in her room," I tell him, but he doesn't falter. He presses his little nose in the crook of the door as if to show me how to open it.

I keep walking to my room, which is across the landing. "Come on, you can hang with me," I try. "If I leave my door open, you can still see her room. How about that? What do you think, buddy?"

He is *definitely* Sutton's dog because the headstrong little mutt doesn't even entertain the idea. He sits on the hardwood and whines while pointing his manipulative eyes directly at me.

"Fine!" I walk back and open the door for him. He runs straight for the tiny set of stairs Sutton placed at the foot of her bed. He walks a circle around her unmade bed, creating a nest from the blanket and sheets, untouched for the past week, before plopping down. "You better back me up when they chew me out for this."

He only yawns in response.

As I close my own door behind me, I wonder if my parents will say anything about my letting Romeo into Sutton's room. Mom probably will. Scolding or lecturing me is the only way she communicates these days. I'd say she's overcompensating since she has only one daughter to discipline, but she's never been as nitpicky with Sutton as she is with me. I sometimes wonder why they even bothered to have me when Sutton was clearly a golden child from birth. But unlike Dad (who was an only child), Mom came from a bigger family. She's the youngest of four. She always says, *Siblings are good for the soul*, but if that's true, you'd think my aunts and uncles would be calling more to comfort her.

As I shuck off my sweaty jeans, one pant leg catches on my

ankle, and a rush of pain hits me so unexpectedly, I nearly fall headfirst into my dresser. When I finally shake them off, I see my new boots gave me something from the search after all.

The back of my right ankle is as red as the sunburn Mom got last Fourth of July, when she forgot sunscreen on the first day of our beach vacay. My skin looks like a strawberry tart on the verge of burning, golden brown with a bubbled red center.

I hop to the edge of my bed, wondering if I should take off my bra or crawl under the sheets as is. The blister throbs with my pulse. Either way, I should probably wrap it so it doesn't pop on my bedsheets.

My pants vibrate on the floor. I poke at them with my good foot until my phone reveals itself. Then I attempt to pick it up with my toes, but that ends disastrously. My nightstand wobbles with the effort, toppling the picture frame resting on it. My empty savings jar—still decorated with the music notes I painted during Ivy's last album announcement live stream—wobbles too, but it can crash to the floor for all I care. It's pretty much useless now.

I fix my toppled picture frame. The glass is fine, and so is the print inside. Grandma Remy smiles, her frail arms wrapped around eight-year-old me. I'm staring up at her from below, not looking at the camera but clearly happy. My hand is closed around her wrist. You can barely see her bracelet peeking through my fingers, but I know the feel of those grooves by heart. If I close my eyes, I can almost feel the pendant in my palm, but it's only a fantasy.

It's gone. Just like Sutton.

I collapse on my bed. My phone vibrates again in my hand. I unlock it to reveal two new text threads. Only one is a true surprise.

Casey, this is Andrew. Can you text me back?

I didn't know Andrew had my number. Sutton must have given it to him at some point. He texted me an hour ago.

And then, a few minutes later, barely enough time for me to respond even if I had read it on time: Did they really find her shoe at the trail?

I swipe them both aside in favor of Ruth's texts that just came in: Are you okay? then I can talk for a bit if you need.

I take a picture of my angry foot and send it to her. She responds immediately.

Ruth: I TOLD YOU TO DOUBLE SOCK WHEN WEAR-
    ING NEW SHOES!
Me: I'm not an Active Person. I exist to consume mu-
    sic and hot chips.
Ruth: That's why you trust the summer camp coun-
    selor.
Me: I'm sorry. I repent. Ask God to make it go away.
Ruth: That's not how He works, lol
Me: Yeah, probably has more important things to do
    anyway.
Ruth: Like find your sister.

Her typing bubbles flash for a few moments, building a crescendo of dread in my stomach. When she finally replies, her message isn't nearly as long as the wait implied, but it hits hard: Was it true? Did they find Sutton's shoe?

I wonder if any of the emails Mom needed to answer ask this same question. The police were obviously trying to keep the find secret, but news seems to have spread through the search party like cottonwood pollen in the thick of spring.

> **Me:** Yeah. It was covered in blood.
>
> **Ruth:** No no no
>
> **Me:** My parents are trading off between denial and
> devastation.
> My dad cried downstairs.
>
> **Ruth:** Isaiah cried?!
>
> **Me:** I don't know what to do for them. It feels like me
> being here makes it worse that she's not. Even
> Romeo doesn't want to be around me. Maybe
> he can tell that I'm not entirely certain this isn't
> Sutton's fault. I know that sounds bad.
>
> **Ruth:** I'm sorry, Casey. I don't know what to say.

So we don't say anything for a long while. My foot still throbs, but the longer I sit with that pain, the less overwhelming everything else seems. There's nothing Ruth could say. There's no way to ease my parents' anguish or this anger I can't seem to suppress.

I'm stuck in this purgatory of gated grief and uncertainty, which coats everything in a poisonous haze. I don't know what to do—I'm afraid to do anything for fear that one wrong move will crumble everything that's left. What if she comes back and we're already ruined beyond repair?

What if she never comes back at all?

I slip under my covers, counting my breaths by how many times my foot throbs between each inhale and exhale. When that stops quieting the scenarios running through my mind, I open the thread and admit in text what I haven't been able to say out loud: I hadn't really considered that something bad could have happened to her.

Ruth's typing bubbles stay on the screen longer this time, and the final message is her shortest: a single heart emoji.

A couple of minutes later, she texts again: I wish I could call you, but the nanny left early, so I'm responsible for the bedtime rush. Do you want to talk tomorrow?

It's fine, I reply. Good night.

Ruth's dad makes her do a lot of the caretaking for her youngest siblings, even when he is in town. They hired a nanny after Ruth's adoptive mom died from complications after her fifth pregnancy, but Pastor Heights doesn't like other people being involved in child-rearing. He would have homeschooled all seven kids if his wife hadn't set her foot down on that from the beginning.

Even if Ruth didn't need to care for her siblings, I wouldn't blame her for wanting to disengage from our conversation. How do you respond to someone telling you they don't trust their missing sister? I'm supposed to be the one crying for her on TV, not her teammates. I'm supposed to be the one spearheading a search effort. I'm supposed to comfort my parents through this tragedy.

That's what this is. A tragedy.

If that shoe is Sutton's—and it probably is—then this isn't a prank. Something happened to her. Something bad. Outside of her control, of anything deliberate she could do to hurt us.

My mother raps against my door: three knocks in rapid succession and then a solitary fourth. And like always, she ends it by opening the door, making the taps more of an announcement than a request.

She takes a half step inside, leaning against the frame. She's pulled her hair into a high ponytail. Her layers of screen makeup are gone, showing how sleep-deprived she truly is. Even her eyes look more gray than blue, as if their color is draining with her energy.

"Did you let Romeo into Sutton's room?"

I drag myself to the edge of the bed, carefully swinging my legs to the floor. "He was begging."

"I would appreciate it if you asked me first. I want to keep Sutton's room as neat as possible in case the police want to take another look."

"Dad said they barely looked at it the first time," I protest. "It's not considered a crime scene because she didn't go missing here."

"There could still be evidence to help them find her. They

may change their mind." Mom clears her throat and stops leaning, as if standing straight will broadcast her lecture clearer. "I don't want you messing with her things."

"I didn't touch anything!" I stomp a foot without thinking, sending a new wave of agony through my leg to match my anger. The accusation awakens the worst in me. For a moment, I can see nothing but Sutton in Mom's condemning stance, despite all that sets them apart. If I had torn her room apart, I would have been justified.

But I'm innocent. This time, at least.

"I just let in the dog."

"Still," Mom says, proving pettiness is hereditary.

"Is that it?" I ask her even though I already know the answer. Mom gets a look in her eye when she's latched on to a good story. Dad used to point it out with pride when we watched her interview someone on TV. *Look*, he'd say. *She's turned on her ice eyes. They're in for it now.*

She turns her ice eyes on me.

She wants to interrogate me.

"I know you hung out with Andrew at the search today," she says. It's not framed like a question, but she clearly expects an explanation. I won't give in. I'm sixteen, not six. I learned long ago that the first one to break a silence never wins the argument. Mom knows that too, but she's too upset with me to care. "I told you not to associate with him."

"I didn't *hang out* with him," I argue. "I stood with him

while we talked to the press. Remember, like you told me to this morning?"

"I told you to talk to my colleague, not to endorse Andrew as if his innocence is supported by the family."

I roll my eyes. "I didn't endorse anyone." I barely said anything kind about Sutton. Without Andrew there, it probably would have been a boring clip. I didn't offer the reporter anything that would help the story stand out. Andrew did.

"Cassandra," Mom says, my full name like a warning. "I saw the footage. You pulled him away before they could ask any hard questions."

"The coach and Sutton's friends were waiting," I say pointedly. "I didn't want to take up all the time. Besides, they would have eviscerated him if I left him alone."

"You should have let them!" she yells, surprising us both with the volume of it.

"I'm confused," I say, letting acid creep into my voice as I stand and walk toward her. "I thought this was about Sutton."

"Of course it is," she snaps.

"How does letting her boyfriend be torn apart by the press help us bring her back? If she's out there, if she's alive—"

"She's alive," Mom says. The fight almost leaves her voice as she forces it out, her jaw tight. Defiant. "She's alive."

"You said we have to make them love her if we want people to help us. They have to care. Why would anyone bother if the media demonizes Andrew like they've already figured out what happened?"

"You don't know him."

I laugh. "Andrew would never hurt anyone. I don't know what he even sees in Sutton."

"He's not who you think he is."

"Neither was Sutton," I remind her. "You've asked me to pretend she was perfect for the cameras, but you know better. You know she was awful. And you didn't care. It never bothered you how Sutton treated me. All you cared about was how she made *you* look. It's still all you care about. This isn't about Andrew. You're mad I didn't follow the Perfect Family script like Sutton would have. At least Andrew knows how to play his part."

Mom steps back from my doorframe as if she's been slapped. She takes in a quick breath and then delivers her final response like the snap of a whip. "He had her car the day she disappeared. Did you know that? The police didn't find it until two days later. Tell me how that's my fault. Try it."

I can't. *Two days.* That's way too long.

My mind goes blank for the first time all day, but it's not a relief. It floods with new thoughts. Suspicions I never once entertained since Sutton went missing. From the first evening she didn't come home and even into the next morning, when my parents transitioned from angry to panicked, I was sure Andrew was harmless. He is, right? He couldn't have hurt Sutton. He would never.

She *loved* him. More than me. More than anyone. He had to love her back.

His panicked texts about the shoe float to the surface of my mind. One message after the other, with no breathing room for a response. Was it concern for his girlfriend or fear for himself? Possibilities circle around me, every thought worse than the last. Did he want reassurance or intel from me?

Did he hurt my sister?

I don't know. Now I can't be sure. I have nothing.

Mom's ice eyes have melted, but there's still righteousness in them. She's proud of herself for one-upping me, for weaponizing knowledge she'd kept from me. She knows she's won this argument.

I close my fist around the cool metal of my doorknob. "Well," I say. "If Sutton's dead, I guess you should start being nicer to your other daughter. You have only one left."

And then I slam the door in her face.

FIVE

can't sleep. It has nothing to do with the early summer heat, though that doesn't help my night sweats. I try listening to Ivy James's earliest album, before the trials of fame tainted her lyricism with deeper heartbreak. Her first songs have an optimism she doesn't seem to carry with her anymore. That's normally not an issue for me—I've always been a cynic—but my reserves of hope are becoming dangerously low.

I curl deeper into my blankets as Ivy's vocals whisper from my phone's speaker, muffled in this nest of cotton sheets. "*The world comes up to cushion us,*" she sings. "*A towering cocoon. I get wary as the light fades, but you say we'll be there soon.*"

I try to let her serenade me, but I'm distracted by the ever-climbing notification number on my group chat app. All my online friends are messaging back and forth about other artists' music drops and theories on when Ivy will finally announce her next tour.

I've been silent in those conversations since Sutton disappeared. I don't know how to explain what's going on. I never minced words about my sister, so my fellow Jamies know there are times when I wished I were an only child. But not like this. They would get how conflicted I feel over what's happened. But they didn't know Sutton. Not truly.

All I can think about is the last thing I said to Sutton.

It was the night before she disappeared. I discovered she stole the bracelet Grandma Remy gave me, and I confronted her, attempted to tear her room apart searching for it. She laughed at me, sitting on her bed like some kind of movie villain with Romeo curled in her lap. Her hair was already wrapped in her satin head wrap for the night. She watched me pull open drawer after drawer in her dresser with perfect calm.

I dropped to my knees and crouched to look under her bed. Sutton simply lifted her legs and rested them on my back while I searched. "Find anything?" she asked from above me. "I lost one of my cheer tops a few weeks back. Maybe you can locate it for me."

I sat up, shoving her feet off me. "It's not even in here, is it?"

She shrugged. "Who says I have it? Maybe Grandma's ghost took it back since you're a lying, selfish little brat."

It was my turn to laugh. "Look in a mirror, Sully."

"Don't call me that, *Cassandra*," she snapped, her smug facade cracked by the childhood nickname. Romeo shifted in her lap, glancing between us like he could feel the tension rising. He hopped down from the bed to avoid any potential carnage. Sutton frowned. "I'm not giving it back," she said as she squatted to reassure him. She gently scratched behind his ear. "You will never find it."

"I'll tell Mom and Dad," I tried.

"Do you think that's gonna work after what happened last time?"

Phantom tears haunted my eyes at the memory. I tried hard not to cry in front of her, doubling down on rage instead. "I hope you get hit by a truck," I told her, meaning every word of it. "I wish you were dead."

She didn't even flinch. "I wish you were never born," she replied. "We can't always get what we want."

But I might have.

I hated her. I hate her. Even now, thinking of her fills me with fury. She's been gone for a week, but I never thought she was in actual danger. Before today, I would have agreed with the volunteers who theorized she ran away. It didn't totally make sense, but none of her decisions ever do. I was so sure she was behind it all. Her disappearance, the chaos, the pain. It was all her. It had to be.

I never once thought Andrew could hurt her, but he didn't tell me about the car. No one did. Apparently, I'm important enough to stick in front of a camera but not worthy of knowing what's really going on.

Sutton loved her Jeep. I assumed the reason it hadn't been returned to the house was because the cops were holding it for evidence. That's probably true, but if Andrew had her car, the police didn't retrieve it from the campus parking lot. He lives in Bend's End, the poorer side of Willow Bend. He doesn't go to our private school—or, more accurately, the all-male counterpart to it.

Two days.

What could he have done with the car for two days? What could he have done with Sutton? Why? I try to close my eyes and rest, but I keep seeing Sutton screaming. I see her dark pupils transfixed on some unseen horror, filled not with her tears of rage that I'm used to but with fear.

I wanted her to suffer, but this... It's finally hitting me that Sutton may never come home. Her room may stay empty forever, a time capsule of who she was when she disappeared because she'll never get a chance to outgrow her current obsessions. Never have a priority higher than college application essays and cheering at away games. Never hug Romeo again. Never anger me so much, I want to shove her down the stairs.

I don't know what to do without a sister.

I need her back. I need to yell at her. I need to scream. I need her to cut me open the way she always did. I need the fight. I can't stay locked in this battle position, braced for a strike that'll never come. If she never comes back, I'll never be whole again either. A part of me will always be lost with her, unable to heal or fully face everything we never got to say. I can't—I can't—I can't stop now. I can't forgive a dead person. I'm not ready.

In that moment, I have an overwhelming ache for my older

sister. I want nothing more than for her to hold me. To reassure me that everything is going to be okay like she used to when I was little and got scared. I can't remember the last time Sutton touched me more than with an accidental finger brush while passing food at the table. We haven't embraced under anything but parental force in years, but she is the only one who can fix this void. I hate her and I need her and I miss her, and I may never ever get her back.

I'm breaking. My body can't sustain me. It's too small to contain my grief. My rage. My fear. I sob for the first time since she disappeared. I drown out Ivy's muffled vocals. I toss my phone, and Ivy's heartache stops, but mine continues. It hurts worse and worse, emotion squeezing my ribs tighter with each jagged breath.

Finally, the tears stop. I lie there in my sorrow and sweat, waiting for something to claim me. Exhaustion or absolution. Anything.

Numbness arrives. My breathing slows simply because I don't have enough strength to feel any more than I already have. When I close my eyes, I still see Sutton's terror playing behind my eyelids, but I can't keep them open any longer.

As my mind starts slipping into sleep, I'm brought back to full consciousness by a scream.

"Isaiah!"

It's my mother. Her voice sounds far away and right beside me all at once. My heart pounding in my ears, I've barely scooted to the edge of my bed when she screams again. "Casey!"

By the time I reach the hallway, my dad is at the railing with one of his golf clubs, taking the stairs three at a time. I race after him.

"Isaiah!" Mom yells again. We find her at the dining table, surrounded by a fresh pile of missing person posters. She's shaking, half in and half out of her seat like she doesn't know where to go. She's crying hysterically. Her phone is in her hand.

"Maddie," Dad says as he approaches her. He sets the golf club aside. "What's happened, baby?"

Mom drops the phone and wraps her arms around him, still shuddering despite his support. "They found her," she says through sobs. "They found her. They found her."

The strength leaves Dad. He struggles to sit without letting go of Mom. She won't stop crying. The unanswered question chokes us all. My throat goes dry. I can't find my voice to ask it. Dad looks too afraid to ask himself.

Mom slowly removes himself from the crook of his neck. She takes each of his shoulders in her hands so they're looking directly at each other. It's like I'm not even here, but I still feel her words like a shot to the heart.

"She's alive."

SUTTON

THREE MONTHS BEFORE

'm gonna kill Casey.

She lied. She lied to me about a will reading. Who does that? What kind of twisted, evil person deliberately misleads their sister about the timing of the will reading of their final living grandparent? She told me it was Thursday—also known as *tomorrow*—so I went to cheer practice *today* like I always do. I put my phone on silent like I always do. I didn't check it for three hours.

Like. I. Always. Do.

And now I'm home in my room with Romeo and a jewelry box of old diamonds and gold necklaces but not the only thing I wanted from Grandma Remy. Not the only thing I needed from Grandma Remy. The only thing that has brought me any comfort to think about since she died two weeks ago.

I've been crying for the past hour. I didn't even bother washing off my makeup first, so I look like a clown's wife on a rainy day. Mom and Dad don't care about what Casey did. They don't blame her at all. She told them it was an accident, playing innocent like she does every time she screws me over.

I know better.

They're more disappointed at me than anything else. "You need to get better with time management, Sutton," Dad said. "We've talked about this."

I know we did. I knew the timing of the will reading was important because we had to coordinate time zones with my great-uncles back in Carolina. The business details of what Ma Remy chose to do with her shares of Cureton Construction there were as important as her possessions here in Washington. I'm not a complete brat, okay? I know this wasn't just about me.

Maybe I'm not great at showing up on time. Sometimes I get distracted, but I cared about this. I canceled a date with Andrew to go. I put it in my freaking planner outlined in red next to my homework assignments. I was going to show up. I was going to be there. I loved her.

They think I should be happy with what I did inherit. Grandma willed all her jewelry to Casey and me, but Casey—*sweet angel Casey*—gave up everything else in exchange for Ma Remy's favorite bracelet. Her silver chain bracelet with the teardrop pendant, its white flower kissing the surface. Her proudest possession. The one piece of jewelry she wore every single day. The bracelet Ma Remy promised me.

Romeo sniffs around the abandoned jewelry box I shoved in the corner of my bed. His little brows furrow, like he can tell something is missing too. It's not that the rest of the jewelry is bad. In fact, the pieces are gorgeous, and any girl would be lucky to have them. But they aren't her bracelet. It's all I wanted. Casey had to know that.

We were supposed to share. Maybe, if I talk to her, we still can.

"Come on, Romeo," I say, heading for the door. He toddles down the padded stairs attached to my bed.

I knock on Casey's door five times before she answers. She's smiling, texting on her phone as she stands in the doorway. She's already wearing it. The silver sparkles against the terracotta of her skin. The green pendant swings below, mocking me.

She looks up from her phone and rolls her eyes at the sight of me. "I already apologized," she says.

"This isn't about that."

She sighs, looking behind her to where her laptop rests on her bedspread. Her screen is rapidly updating, probably with messages from her online friends. She's obsessed with this singer called Ivy James, and it's all she ever talks about. She has three posters of her on her wall, but that isn't enough, so she wastes most of the time she doesn't spend with Ruth talking to strangers online who also like Ivy's music. They call themselves *Jamies*.

"What's it about, then?" she asks. "I'm busy."

I take a deep breath, then let it out slowly before I start my pitch. "Grandma left her jewelry for us to share. While I appreciate you giving me so much of it with no strings attached, I'm still willing to share. That's what Grandma Remy wanted. She wanted us to share *all* of it."

"I'm not giving you the bracelet. I gave you everything else."

"That's what I'm talking about, Casey!" I try. "I don't want all of it, okay? I want to share it, particularly the bracelet. I want us to take turns. It's what Grandma would want too."

"You wouldn't know what Grandma wants," Casey says. "You weren't at the reading."

And whose fault is that, you absolute demon? I squeeze her doorframe so hard, I almost give myself a splinter. "I just want some time with the bracelet, please."

"No, Sutton," she says. "I know you think I kept you away intentionally, screwed you over like you always do to me, but this isn't my fault. Even if I hadn't given you the wrong time, you probably still wouldn't have shown up. You never do."

"That's a lie. I—"

She cuts me off. "You were never there! You don't get to rewrite history because you regret it now. Maybe if you spent more time visiting Ma Remy when she was getting her treatments instead of going to your practices, you wouldn't have had to rely on me to know what's going on with our family."

"That's not fair." I look up at the ceiling to stop myself from crying, then turn back to her with a hardened gaze so she can't call me out on it. I spent as much time with Ma Remy as I could. I even offered to drop cheer to be with her more this past year, but she made me promise to stick with it. She was the person who convinced Mom and Dad to let me start competitive cheer in the first place. She was proud of me. She believed in me.

"You got literally everything else," Casey says, moving the wrist with the bracelet behind her door as if to protect it from me. "Why do you want the one thing I asked for?"

"Because..." I start, but I can see she doesn't care. It will never matter to her how much that bracelet means to me. The significance is lost on her. No amount of explaining or begging is going to change her mind.

"Because?" she repeats sarcastically, a smirk twisting her full lips. She knows she's won. There's nothing I can do to get her to give it back.

On her nightstand next to her bed, a picture of Ma Remy sits in a place of pride. From here, I can see she's wearing the bracelet as she holds Casey, blissfully unaware of the monster in her arms.

Behind the frame is a nearly full mason jar painted with dozens of little music notes. Casey's been saving up to go to an out-of-state Ivy James concert with her fellow Jamies. Mom and Dad weren't exactly jazzed about her meeting random strangers from the internet, despite proof they are real teenagers and not creepy men, but they OK'd it as long as she pays for the trip herself.

She's been saving for over a year. Ivy hasn't even announced her next tour yet, though less than five minutes of talking to Casey and she'll tell you it will happen "any day now," so she has to be ready the moment the tickets drop. She missed out on the last tour because tickets sold out before Mom could buy them for her. If she doesn't have the money ready the day this mythical sale starts, she'll lose her chance for who knows how long. Casey says Ivy's already taken a much longer break between albums than usual.

"I'm giving you one last chance," I tell her. "Share it with me."

Her smile doesn't falter. "No."

"Okay," I say. I twirl on my heel before heading back to my room. I hear her ask what I'm doing as I grab my own laptop from my desk, but she has barely stepped into the hallway when I return.

"What are you gonna do? Show me statistics?"

"No." I open my laptop so the screen is visible and vulnerable and hold it over the staircase railing.

"You wouldn't," she says.

"Share the bracelet with me," I warn her.

"Or you'll break your own laptop?" She laughs. "How does that hurt me?"

I drop my laptop from the landing, and it hits the hardwood of the first floor with a sickening crunch. Casey rushes to the railing. We can both see the damage from here. The screen has shattered, and several keys have popped off.

I pinch my wrist until tears well in my eyes again, blinking them forth until my anger can supply the rest. "Now you'll never go to your concert," I tell her. "Not when I tell Mom and Dad how you broke my laptop when all I did was ask you to share what Grandma gave *both* of us. They'll make you use your savings to buy me a new one."

Casey looks at me, the horror slowly dawning on her. "No," she says, but her voice is already cracking. "I'll tell them you did it yourself. I'll tell them the truth."

"Why would I break my own laptop, Casey?"

"No," she repeats. Her bottom lip starts to tremble. "I'll tell them."

"They'll never believe you."

Casey leans over the railing to survey the damage again. It must finally sink in, because she starts sobbing. "I hate you," she cries. "I hate you so much."

My own tears taste victorious. "The feeling is mutual," I tell her.

SIX

The sun has risen, and we still haven't seen Sutton.

The sleep that escaped me earlier is trying to take me now. The night was black when we first arrived at the hospital, but morning light has crept in through the tall windows to assist the fluorescents in fighting my fatigue. It isn't helping much, especially with yet another hour without updates on Sutton's condition. I pick at the empty Styrofoam cup in my hand, reducing it to slivers of rings.

The detectives have already come and gone, but they were no help. They didn't even find her themselves. She wasn't anywhere near the trail we searched yesterday or the shoe they found. She was spotted miles away by a random driver who called in the sighting. The driver hadn't recognized her from the news coverage or any of the flyers stapled across town. They were just concerned about the state she was in. Sutton was found wandering a street leading to the highway, past the limits of both Willow and Bend's End.

She was naked. Naked and dirty, like she was in such a rush to escape wherever she had been that she had no care for modesty. When they told us that, my parents looked as if they were going to vomit, but my brain immediately flashed to countless memories of Sutton screaming at me if I even cracked the bathroom door to grab my toothbrush while she took forever in the shower.

The cops barely asked us any questions. They were already here when we arrived at three in the morning. They led us to the seats we're sitting in now, hard plastic things that feel like a last-minute addition to the otherwise bright and modern glass and white scheme of the hospital waiting area.

They showed us some screenshots from a mapping software of the intersection where she was found, asking if Sutton had any reason to go there. "No," Dad bit out harshly, though he's the only one of us who got any sleep last night. "There is no reason my daughter would be there or anywhere *naked* at midnight."

"I understand this is a difficult situation, Mr. Cureton," the lead detective—a white man who'd introduced himself by his first name, Brendan—said. "But sometimes these things don't have logic to them. If your daughter was under the influence, if she had taken something, she might return to an area familiar to her."

"There's no reason that area would be familiar to her," Dad said.

"She wasn't high or drunk," Mom added. "The doctors said so. They said she's clean." Then, quietly, as if to reassure herself, Mom continued, "They said she's going to be fine."

"They're still running tests," Brendan's partner said. He never introduced himself or said anything except to correct a detail or name a location on one of their printouts. The whole thing was clinical, almost boring. It felt like we were the latest cogs in a practiced machine. No one wanted to be here. After my parents refused to incriminate Sutton, the cops left with promises to get to the bottom of what happened.

We're not holding our breath.

I know Dad is still thinking about the detectives. He looks angrier than Mom, though Mom hasn't shown much emotion since the doctors' last update. When we first arrived, all they would tell us was that she was alive and being evaluated. An hour ago, however, the doctors claimed Sutton doesn't remember what happened to her. This almost relieved my parents, until the doctors clarified that Sutton doesn't remember *anything*. She claims she has no idea who she is.

"We've done scans, and they don't show any physical reason for Sutton's memory loss. This is most likely trauma related," one nurse who sat with us said. "It is highly likely that she'll regain her memories over time."

I'm sure this so-called amnesia will clear up before cheer camp later this summer. It has to. I can't imagine a whole summer of this after everything else we've dealt with in the past week.

"Can you tell us if she was—" Mom started, looking to Dad before continuing. Dad closed his eyes and leaned his head against the wall behind our plastic seats. "The detectives were only here for a few minutes. They didn't tell us much. Was she...did someone..."

The nurse didn't need Mom to complete her sentence. "The rape kit came back negative. She has no internal sexual trauma and only minimal bruising. She's in really good condition, considering. Her only wounds are superficial and less than a day old, probably from wandering outside without clothing."

"She's okay?" Mom asked.

"She will be," the nurse confirmed. "With time. Like I said, this may be a long recovery. Her physical wounds will likely heal long before the emotional ones."

Mom reached for Dad's hand, jolting him back to attention. He squeezed her palm, nodding at the nurse. And that was the end of my parents' questions. Outside her immediate health, they seemingly had no lingering curiosity. Sutton had been gone for over a week and showed up in a part of town none of us have ever visited. Even if she refused to talk about what happened, there had to be some clues the doctors or detectives could go on.

Sutton has always had endless excuses. She's never met a trouble she couldn't talk her way out of. But she's not defending herself. If she's unable to explain what happened, there must be something that hints at what she went through this past week. Something that doesn't line up.

"What about the blood?" I asked. "Where did it come from?

If Sutton doesn't have any big wounds, why did they find her shoe covered in blood? Was it not her shoe? Whose is it?"

"Casey," Mom said in a warning tone.

"Uh," the nurse hedged, clearly out of the loop. "Any evidence found separate from your daughter will have to wait for the crime labs. That's not connected to the hospital. I can't help you with that, I'm sorry."

"Maybe it wasn't her shoe after all," Dad offered.

That was the last thing anyone said for the past hour and a half. We're due for another update, but all I want is to sleep. My body is ready for this all to be over.

My parents don't look tired, though I know Mom has gotten less rest than I have. She bounces one of her legs, her feet still in her house slippers. Dad pulled an old Seahawks jersey over his sweat-pants, but that's the only additional effort he made. I remembered the rain and slipped my messy jeans over my sleep shorts before we left.

This is the most disorganized and unpresentable my family has ever looked in public. I'd point it out to Mom if I thought she'd laugh instead of snap at me.

I rest my head on one hand, watching the giant hallway for anyone with a new update. Fifteen minutes or fifteen years later, a brunette guy in blue scrubs strides toward us. Mom straightens from where she'd leaned on Dad's shoulder.

"Are you the Cureton family?" he asks.

Mom nods.

"Are you ready to see your daughter?"

My parents stand, and I follow them, a half step behind as we head down the hall. He keeps talking as we walk. "As you've already heard, your daughter is suffering from traumatic amnesia, and as much as you want her to, she may not recognize you when you see her. I know it will be hard, but try not to overwhelm her."

"I promise," Mom breathes out in a rush. "I just want to see my baby."

The man leads us down a narrower hallway. The rooms in this corridor have windows for observation, but most are obscured by soft blue-and-white curtains. He stops at the last door, scanning a laminated badge against a machine near it. The action doesn't seem to unlock anything. The door has a normal latch, but he waits for the machine to blink green anyway.

"We are working with the police to protect your daughter, Mr. and Mrs. Cureton," he says. "All hospital staff must check in before interacting with Sutton, and she'll be allowed no visitors but the three of you."

"Thank you," Dad says.

The nurse opens the door but steps aside to let us enter alone. Mom hesitates, then pulls Dad in after her. I hover in the doorway.

Sutton reclines in her hospital bed, her face tilted toward the outside window. She blinks slowly at the early morning sunlight, letting it wash over her skin. I can't see any physical injuries from what her oversize gown leaves visible, but she's changed. Her hair falls in curly waves against her shoulders. It's the same color as always, a deep brown so dark, it passes for black unless it's under direct light, but it seems shorter. It takes me a moment to realize Sutton has flat-ironed her hair for so long, I forgot what her natural hair looks like.

I thought her hair would look more damaged if ever freed from her weekly heat routine. I guess I thought she'd look more damaged in general. If—*when* she came back to us.

She doesn't look like she's in pain. Her face betrays no emotion at all. Not fear. Not relief. Not exhaustion. Her first sign of connection comes when our parents circle her like predators isolating prey. Mom can't help but hug Sutton. Sutton allows it, but her arms don't move to reciprocate. They rest at her sides like a doll's until Dad takes one hand in his and kisses it.

She doesn't push them away, like how I'd imagine a trauma victim would react when people invaded her personal space. She actually smiles at Dad. It's small and quick, the kind of smile you'd give a stranger you pass on the street when you accidentally make eye contact.

Mom, still squeezing her with every ounce of strength she has, can't see how Sutton looks at her. I don't know how to describe her eyes. They aren't quizzical. But it's nothing like how she looked at Dad. There's no warmth or recognition in them at all.

When Mom finally lets go and steps back from her bed, she sees it too and tries to school her own expression to hide her hurt. "I'm sorry," she says. "They told us not to overwhelm you, but we've missed you so much. I love you, Sutton. I'll love you through anything."

Sutton doesn't respond. She leans back against her pillow and goes still again, her eyes the only part of her that's moving. She looks back and forth between them, but her face betrays no further hint of recognition.

Mom looks to Dad with panic in her own gaze. His back is to me, so I can't see his reaction. "Sutton," he says. "We're your parents. I know you must be scared, but I promise we won't hurt you. I'll never let anyone hurt you again. Okay?"

Sutton's lips part as she studies them, but eventually she replies, "Okay."

I'm not used to hearing her speak without sarcasm or frustration.

"Your sister," Mom says, attempting to transition the conversation to include me. "Your sister is excited to see you too."

She gestures for me to come inside, her eyes pleading.

I take my time moving past the hospital equipment, not ready to pretend I'm hurt when Sutton acts like I'm a stranger too. When she looks at me with emptiness in her heart, it won't be any different from before she disappeared. She can't hurt me any worse than she already has.

Sutton's still looking at Mom with that weird expression when I step into view. She slowly shifts her focus, but when her gaze hits me, something lights up within her. Her eyes lose the glassy sheen I assume medication has given her. Her eyebrows rise, her mouth opening wide. I stand firm, resisting the urge to retreat, though I'm unable to suppress a sudden fear that she's going to lunge at me like a wild animal.

And she does—move toward me, that is. She pushes herself forward, leaning as close to me as she can manage without dislodging her IV. She takes a fast, excited breath like Romeo at the sight of the treat jar.

"Casey!" she says, though no one has mentioned my name.

Her face breaks into a wide smile. There's no malice in it, but it chills me like no horror movie ever has.

"I remember you."

SEVEN

They hold her at the hospital for two more days.

As I try to keep Romeo from pulling his ancient leash into a neighbor's rosebush, I work to smother the part of me that thinks that isn't long enough, the part that smokes like a forgotten stove at the idea of our family reunion. There is nothing good or nourishing left in me. I'm spent from all that happened while she was gone. *This is what we all wanted*, I try to remind myself. *You wanted her back.*

I did. I do. I'm glad that she's okay—well, that she's alive. "I'm so excited for your Sutton to get home," I tell Romeo as he balances along the sidewalk's curb like a furry tightrope walker. He perks up at the sound of her name.

"She's on her way home," I tell him. He pulls on the leash again, ready to head back to the house and meet her there. I slow on the incline of the hill, forcing him to pause.

Mom told me to tire him out before they got back. She's afraid he'll scare Sutton if he's too hyper. I'm doing my best to walk him to exhaustion. It's usually not a difficult task with his stubby little legs, but I can't see him responding to the return of his favorite human with anything but intense joy no matter how tired he might be.

I thought Sutton's return would mean the end of the Home Again Narrative and all the posturing that entailed, but the situation only morphed from missing person case to regimented care plan for supporting a *traumatized* recovery. I suppose that makes sense. I guess, in a way, it should feel like progress. A relief.

I never expected life to snap back without consequences. I understand that Sutton went through something horrific, supposedly. It would probably be worse if we were expected to act like nothing happened, so this is fine in comparison.

I can give her space. I can respect boundaries. Even if Sutton can't.

"She asked if you're going to be there tomorrow when we pick her up," Mom told me last night when she stopped by my room. She gave me a cold burger and fries they'd picked up on their way home from visiting hours at the hospital.

"I can't," I reminded her. The fries were mushy on my tongue, flavorless. "You told me to watch Romeo."

"He can be alone for a little while," she tried. "If you want to come, we can make it work."

It was clear from her tone what she actually wanted. She was following the rule book like always, scripting the words of a good mom through her mental teleprompter so she could give the performance of prioritizing me, but I knew the truth. She didn't want me at the hospital any more than I wanted to be there. The salt on my stale fries was less bitter than Mom was. She wished Sutton had asked for her instead.

I did too. I didn't say that though. I told her I was fine with dog duty and would see them when they all got back home, and she dropped the issue without any further pushing. Just like I knew she would.

It finally stopped raining after three days of unseasonable downpour, but I'm still cold this morning. It has nothing to do with the sheen still glistening on the perfectly paved streets of our cul-de-sac, nor with my thin layers. Romeo stops in a patch of grass to give a full-body shake that almost lifts his tiny feet from the ground. I bend to scratch behind his ears. It's an apology of sorts. I haven't been the best adventure buddy this morning.

"Romeo," I say, voice serious. He sits on the wet grass, his big eyes giving me his full attention. "Your mama Sutton is coming home today." His tail starts to flicker, but he doesn't move. "But she's been through something. She's going to need us to be patient with her. She may not react the way you expect her to, but that doesn't mean she doesn't love you anymore, okay?"

He stays still as if considering the weight of my words in a way I know he's not truly capable of. Then he shuffles forward and bumps my chin with his wet snout, then chases it with his tongue when I stumble back with a chuckle. This is the best I'll get from him, but I know he'll be fine. He's the type of pup who tries to cuddle up to total strangers. He probably won't even notice if she acts weird around him.

If she doesn't remember him.

I don't know why the idea bothers me so much. Sutton hasn't had any miraculous memory recovery since claiming to know me. She seems to know I'm her sister in a primal way that she still hasn't found with our parents.

She smiles more when I'm around. As long as I was in the room, she was more agreeable to the needle pokes and other tests the doctors needed from her.

"It's a good sign," the doctors claimed, but it feels like a lie.

Because that's all it is. There's nothing to her recognition beyond my name and a focus that seems almost antagonistic, like a staring contest where she's waiting for me to crack first. She clings to me when I'm around and asks our parents about me when I'm gone, but all it does is remind everyone of everything that's wrong with this situation. This isn't Sutton. She would never act like this.

That's how I know she's faking it. I don't know why she's pretending to have amnesia or how it could possibly help her. I don't know what happened while she was gone or what she's trying to hide from our parents, from the cops. But I know my sister. I know she's lying. And she knows the best way to shift attention from her bad behavior has always been to make me look worse instead.

This is her best plan yet.

Mom is so busy resenting me that she's lost all investigative drive. All she wants is her firstborn to fall into her arms again. It will be so easy for Sutton to manipulate her in exchange for affection. I bet she's already started.

Dad doesn't even need manipulating. He just wants to feel needed. Helpless, confused Sutton will feed right into his patriarchal drive. He hasn't looked me in the eyes since he cried in front of me on the couch.

I'm the outlier. I'm the one who could expose her lie. I don't get to complain about being the only person she remembers. It would make me a monster to question her. She's weaponized my doubt.

My phone vibrates in my pocket.

Mom: We're at the gate. Have him ready.

I pick up Romeo and climb the hill to our house. Romeo doesn't have to worry about playing games of respectability. He can be as obnoxious as he wants. "You're gonna prove me right," I tell him as he bounces in my arms with each step. "Sutton may have everyone else fooled, but there's no way she'll be able to hide how much she missed you."

He wriggles in agreement. I set him down in the yard as the car pokes into view, creeping slowly toward the driveway like a new parent driving a newborn home. Romeo begins running around in circles on our manicured grass. His dropped leash swirls behind him like a lasso seeking a hold.

The car stops in front of the garage, and Dad steps out of the driver's side with a pained smile and two armfuls of plastic hospital-branded bags and paperwork. He looks back inside the car before shutting the door behind him, but he doesn't linger. He heads into the house with his cargo while Mom exits the passenger side.

They left before I woke up this morning, so this is the first I've seen my mother today. She looks more put together than she has since Sutton was found two days ago. Her blond tresses are slicked back into a high ponytail like some sorority freshman, but her outfit is typical posh-mom chic. She's wearing stonewashed jeans and a loose blouse. She's dressed for a picnic. Expertly photogenic.

"Thank you for handling the dog, Casey," she says as she comes around the back of the SUV. Her hand rests possessively on the handle of the back driver's side door. I can't see Sutton through the tinted windows, but I know she's watching me all the same. "Can you record them reuniting?"

"Of course," I say, pulling out my phone with one hand while I pick up Romeo's leash with the other. "No problem."

"Ready?"

I hit the record button. "It's filming."

Mom opens the door and steps around it to offer Sutton her assistance. Sutton doesn't seem to struggle with the concept of exiting a car, but she lets Mom take her arm and help her step down. Mom shuts the door behind her before Sutton turns her attention to me. She smiles at me again, just like that first night.

Wide, with teeth.

Her eyes lock on mine, but I don't hold her gaze. I tighten my grip on Romeo's leash and gently tug him forward. Anything to take the attention off me. I double-check that I have Sutton in the frame of my camera. I can tell she's still looking at me through my phone's viewfinder.

"Honey, look!" Mom encourages her. "It's your dog, sweetheart. Romeo missed you so much. Do you want to say hi?"

Sutton looks away from me and watches Romeo cautiously approach. He inches toward her. His head dips low to the ground like when he's broken into the treat jar. He looks up at her, his eyes as determined as her own incessant stare. His mouth parts, but his tongue doesn't come out in a welcoming lick.

He growls. His whole body vibrates with it. And then—before I can react—he leaps at her, jaws snapping. Noises escape him that I've never heard before, vicious barks and guttural throat sounds. He pulls so hard on his leash that the weave snaps.

Mom screams. She grabs Sutton by the shoulders and pulls her back. Mom shields her with her body, shifting her stance as if to defend them both from Romeo. But he stops. He growls, then tries to move around Mom's feet to get at Sutton. Dad rushes back outside as I catch Romeo by the collar.

"Keep it away from her!" Mom yells at me.

It doesn't take much for Dad to understand what happened.

"Madison," he says, resting a hand on Mom's shoulder. She flinches away. She steps toward the house, Sutton behind her.

"Maddie, he's a dog. He's confused. She probably smells different. It's gonna be okay. It'll be fine."

Romeo does not seem to agree. He lets out a frustrated huff as he shifts in my arms, eyes still narrowed in Sutton's direction.

"I don't want—" Mom starts.

"We'll keep them apart for now, okay?" Dad says. "You can keep him with you, Casey, right?"

I nod.

"Come on," he says to Mom. He offers a hand, and she takes it, following him inside with Sutton. I wait a few minutes before going inside myself, but they're all long gone by the time I step in the entryway. I set Romeo on the tile and detach what's left of his leash from his collar. His dog tag tangles in the threads. I work to remove it while trying to ignore the inscription:

ROMEO CURETON

SUTTON'S DOG

He follows as I head upstairs. I worry for a second when he stops at Sutton's door. I can hear Mom and Dad speaking to Sutton on the other side, but he doesn't linger. He hasn't let his guard down though. He paces the length of my room when I close my door behind us.

"You don't buy her act either, huh?"

He huffs again.

I flop on the floor next to him. He toddles over to my armpit before nuzzling at my neck as his anger fades to a whimper. I reassure him with some belly rubs, wishing it were this easy to fix my own problems. We lie there for a while. Romeo's asleep when someone knocks on my door.

"Come in," I say from the floor.

Dad cracks open the door, but not enough to let Romeo escape. "Hey, baby girl. Your sister is fine. I've talked with your mom, and we think it's best that you take the lead on Romeo for now. I'm sure he'll warm up to her in time, but if you could keep him in here and take him on walks, that would be a big help to us. Can you do that?"

It's not really a request. "He'll need a new leash. He broke his."

"I'll take you to the pet store in the morning. We can go for ice cream after?"

"Just us?" I ask.

"Just us," he promises.

I nod. He locks the knob from my side of the door before shutting it, as if Romeo could figure out how to open it himself. It's almost funny. Sutton is the one who is supposed to be kept under a close watch, and yet I'm being banished to my room like a prisoner too. A convicted coconspirator when I had nothing to do with the crime.

Romeo breathes hot air on my chest from where he's cushioned in the crook of my arm. I move slowly, freeing my phone from my pants without waking him. When I unlock it, it's still in the camera app. Sutton's silhouette is in the little square in the corner.

I click it.

The video opens at full volume. I press quickly at the side of my phone to quiet it. The last thing I need is to broadcast my mom's screaming across the house again. I watch silently, Romeo's small snores my only soundtrack.

Sutton climbs out of the car in an Oscar-winning display of fragility. Her hospital bracelet is still on her wrist, a glowing white beacon of invincibility. Her smile upon noticing me replays. I fight the urge to fast-forward. I want to see her response to Romeo. I want to see if her charade cracks when he doesn't react how she expected him to.

But she doesn't look surprised when he lunges at her. She doesn't show any emotion at all. Not an ounce of fear or an instinct for self-preservation, no flinch or jump to protect her ankles from the tiny aggressor. She doesn't even react when Mom screams and manhandles her toward the house, something that surely should have rattled an actual abduction victim.

The only emotion on her face in the entire video comes from that single smile directed at me in the beginning, her empty black eyes staring directly into the lens.

EIGHT

I can't find Romeo's car carrier.

I've been searching for almost forty minutes, and I'm beginning to truly doubt we ever had one. My phone vibrates in my back pocket again as I push aside old raincoats and rummage on the floor of the supply closet. I ignore it. It could only be one of two people, and Ruth won't mind if I'm delayed getting back to her. Andrew, on the other hand...

Andrew contacted me again this morning.

You didn't reply to my last message, my phone accused as soon as I turned off my alarm. I saw on the news that they found her.

He didn't send anything else, but I don't know how he expects me to respond. Am I supposed to feel bad for him? I'm struggling to sustain the level of pity I'm obligated to give Sutton as her sister.

Her boyfriend is pretty much a stranger to me. Sutton always did her best to avoid having our circles overlap, even if it meant breaking promises and ignoring things our parents asked her to do, like pick me up from school or youth group.

She never wanted him to know me. He was hers. Now I guess he belongs to no one. She hasn't mentioned him, and I know Mom and Dad are not going to bring him up.

Two days. That's how long he had her car after she disappeared. She's barely even been back that long, and he thinks it's okay to ask me about her?

My pocket vibrates again. I lean back from where I'm crouched in the closet, sitting on the balls of my feet. I pull my phone out.

Andrew: I'm not too poor for a phone with read
   receipts.
Message clearly received.

I groan. Romeo whines in response from where I've locked him in my bedroom. "I'm coming," I tell him. "I'm done with this."

When I open the door, he races out as if he's been trapped for years, but he slows enough to let me pick him up. I press him to my chest as I take the stairs two at a time.

Following Mom's overly soft voice to the living room, I see photo albums scattered all over the coffee table. Snapshots of young Sutton and me in matching bathing suits at the beach cover the heirloom display Dad worked so hard on, smothering the sepia snapshots of ancestors with bright prints of our first Disney trip and last winter's Christmas card.

Mom is next to Sutton on the couch without an inch of space between them, yet another album spread across their laps. Dad is on the other side of the room, barely in the living area at all. He's surrounded by books too.

"What are you doing?" I ask. I'm not sure who I mean to direct the question to, but Dad is the only one who answers.

"I'm working," he says. He punctuates it with a pointed look at his laptop on the dining table in front of him, like I hadn't clearly seen him studying Mom and Sutton instead.

At least his books make sense. The ones piled next to his computer aren't family memorabilia, though they seem pretty old. They're likely research. Still... "You never work out here," I remind him. Especially with books this old and fragile. Protecting items like that is pretty much half the reason he set up his own office.

Dad sighs. "It's part of the normalcy routine."

Isn't normalcy supposed to mean acting normal? I hope he doesn't expect me to earn back my money helping him out here instead of in his office. Seeing Ivy in concert isn't worth the exposure to Sutton's carefully choreographed performance.

Romeo shifts in my arms, vibrating a little but not yet growling.

"What is he doing out here?" Mom snaps at me. She turns at a protective angle in front of Sutton. Mom's hair is in a messy bun this morning, and some loose strands tickle Sutton's face as she moves. Sutton grimaces, shaking her head free.

She sees me. "Good morning, Casey."

For the first time, she doesn't pair her attention with that gross grin, but I still feel more likely to growl than Romeo.

"I thought you told her to keep the dog away from Sutton," Mom scolds Dad. "We talked about this. I don't want him upsetting her."

"I did," he promises. His shoulders tense, but when his mouth opens, nothing comes out. He looks from me to Sutton. "She doesn't seem upset to me."

She doesn't look like anything. Sutton stares at us as we all watch her, a blank slate. There's no fear in her eyes. No apprehension. She doesn't even seem to care about all the attention. It's a really good act.

"Look, Dad," I say. "I'm fine watching him. But he's going to pee in my room if I don't take him outside, and you promised to drive me to the pet store to get a new leash."

"Can't he do his business in the yard?" Mom asks. "Just let him out. Then you can come join us." She pats the spot next to her. "Wouldn't you like that, Sutton? For Casey to join us?" She speaks like she's talking to a toddler, but Sutton perks up anyway.

"The front yard has no fence, and the back has the pool. You remember last summer. His legs are too short to swim properly. He could fall in and drown, Mom."

She lets out a frustrated huff, like there's no solution to the issue at hand. But there is. The only problem is that it breaks up the little family charade.

"I can get him a mini fence to keep him safe in the yard if *someone* takes me to the pet store," I try.

"Can I come?" Sutton asks.

"What?" Mom's babying voice drops in shock. I don't blame her. Sutton hasn't asked for anything since she got home yesterday. She's been saving this tactic, I guess. They'll give her whatever she asks for, and she knows that, but I don't know why she'd want to go to a pet store of all places.

"Can I come?" she repeats. She looks at Dad while she asks it this time, like she thinks he might give a more useful response.

"What about Romeo?" Mom asks. Romeo barks once at being acknowledged.

"He doesn't have to come," Dad says. "You could stay home with him while I drive the girls—" He backtracks. "Or I could. I'll stay here." He pushes his chair back and stands, opening his arms for Romeo.

I squeeze him tighter instead. "You don't need to come," I say to both Mom and Sutton. "I'm fine going alone with Dad. It's probably easier that way."

"Nonsense," Mom says. She's already getting up. She sets the album from her lap with the others on the coffee table and offers Sutton a hand, which she ignores. Mom tries to shake off the rejection as if she had been looking for her bag instead. "It'll be good to get out. Don't you think so, honey?" She's not talking to me, but Sutton doesn't respond. She doesn't move from the couch.

"I can go?" she confirms one last time, looking at me.

She's going to make me the villain again. There's no way for me to say no. This is what she really wants. To remind them that she's broken and fragile and should be given every ounce of attention. That I'm the true screwup. I'm the one who can destroy everything our parents are trying to repair. By refusing her. By not playing this game. She smiles at me again, a small one, almost a smirk.

"You can come," I say.

I hand Romeo off to Dad while Mom sets about getting herself and Sutton ready. I don't wait for them. I grab Mom's car keys from the hook in the entry as I slip out the door, pressing twice on the button to unlock all the doors. I want to sit in the passenger seat, but that's always been Sutton's favorite spot. I'm not up for another fight I'm not allowed to win, so I get in the back seat.

I pull out my phone while I wait for them. Andrew contacted me again, but Ruth wants to know if we'll be coming to church this Sunday. Everyone will understand if she's not ready, she promises. We're just happy for you.

It's up to Sutton, I reply. Everything is now. But Sutton has always hated Heights Above Church. She's normally on board with the socializing and networking Mom needs for work and Dad tolerates—she loves the golf club—but even before, she'd find excuses to avoid going to church. She'll surely use her newfound power to get out of it. Probably not this week.

Ruth: Totally fine. I'll tell them.

Me: Thanks. Is your Dad back yet?

Ruth's typing bubble pops in and out on the screen, but Mom and Sutton approach the car. Sutton's curls are pulled back in a low-effort ponytail that looks like Mom's handiwork. Sutton picks at it as she trails behind her.

"Do you have the keys?" Mom asks as she gets in the driver's seat. I hand them to her. We both wait for Sutton to get in across from her, but when a door opens, it's the one across from me instead.

Mom twists to get a better look at her. "Honey, you don't have to sit back there like yesterday. You can sit up front with me if you'd like."

"I'm fine back here," she says.

Mom parts her lips again, clearly trying to figure out another tactic. Before she can find a convincing argument, I open the front passenger door.

"If she doesn't want the front seat, I'll take it." I'm already buckling in before I finish my sentence. "You know," I say as Mom pulls out of the driveway, "if I had my own car, I could've done this by myself. I could be driving."

"You have your learner's permit," Mom says. "That doesn't mean you're allowed to drive alone. It means the exact opposite, actually."

I look back at Sutton, instinct bracing my ears for a snarky comment, but she's not paying attention to me. She rests her head on the window, watching the evergreens blur by. She's humming under her breath, but it's too faint to recognize, and I don't plan on asking.

"You got Sutton a car when she had her permit," I remind Mom. A car that is still absent from our driveway, the police still searching it for information Sutton can't—or won't—share.

Her thin lips twist into a frown. I scrunch my own full lips (thanks, Dad) in response. She lets my point hang in the air for several blocks, scored by Sutton's continued humming from the back seat. Mom sneaks a peek at her in the rearview mirror before addressing me again. "Sutton had cheer practice and extracurricular activities to go to," she says. "All your friends are online—" I start to argue, but she catches herself. "Except Ruth. You don't need a car right now."

"Well, neither does Sutton," I snap, unable to stop myself. Mom brakes at the red light a little too harshly, jolting all three of us. She glares at me. Sutton's back to watching me too. I'm already in trouble, so I continue, "It's not like she's going anywhere now, is she?"

"We're going to the store," Sutton says.

Mom chuckles. "We are," she agrees. Her eyes sparkle with joy at Sutton involving herself, uninvited, into the conversation. Mom tries to make eye contact with her in the mirror again. "Is there anywhere else you want to go?"

But Sutton has checked out again. She's back to staring out the window and humming that unknown song.

"What are you singing?" I ask her. If she can interrupt for no reason, I can too.

"What?" she asks, all faux innocence.

"What are you singing?" I repeat. "Or humming or whatever."

"I wasn't," she says. Even Mom wrinkles her brows because it's a lie. She's been humming the entire drive. She was clearly repeating a melody.

Silence overtakes the rest of the journey to the Willow Town Center. I'm out of the car before Mom has fully parked. She calls out a plea for me to slow down that I pretend not to hear, but it doesn't take either of them long to catch up with me inside.

The pet shop has a distinct odor I can almost taste, an aroma that is somehow wet and tartly earthy. I head for a display of live mealworms and crickets that's by the pet feed aisle. Sutton makes a move to join me, but when she catches sight of the squirming bugs, she stops.

I bite back a smirk.

I guess even *serious* trauma can't override an irrational fear of bugs. Some things never change.

Mom loops her arm through Sutton's and forces her toward me anyway. Sutton's complexion goes ashy and gray with each step.

"All right," Mom says as they approach. "What do we need?" She lets go of Sutton's arm to flag down an employee, beckoning some poor teenager toward us. Relief washes over Sutton's face as she takes in her small freedom.

"Casey?" Mom prompts me. It takes me a moment to remember she asked about the shopping list.

"A new leash and an outdoor enclosure," I recite.

"I can absolutely help you with that," a white boy with acne says with the bare minimum of fake enthusiasm. "Leashes are in aisle A4 over there"—he points to somewhere behind me—"and outdoor accessories are toward the back. You'll need someone to pull down your choice from the upper shelves, but that's what I'm here for. Where would you like to begin?"

"I—" Mom starts. "Sutton?"

Sutton ignores her, glaring at the bug display behind us like it can't be trusted.

"Casey," Mom tries instead. "Why don't you and your sister get the leash together? You can pick out some new toys or treats too if you'd like. I'll look at the fences, okay?"

I nod.

I grab Sutton's arm and pull her behind me. I'm not as soft with her as Mom was. Sutton's arm is so thin, I can almost close my hand around it, but she's not a child. She not as fragile as she's making everyone else think. She doesn't fight me as I drag her along. She doesn't flinch when I let her go.

"You don't need to do this," I tell her. "She'll do what you want if you're nice to her."

Sutton picks at her ponytailed curls again. A ringlet of dark auburn, not unlike my own, comes free. She lets go of it, like it burns her. Her hands flex at her sides. "I can be nice," she says.

I scoff.

"I can do it," she insists.

"Yeah, whatever." I spin her to face the wall of leashes. "Pick out a leash for your dog."

I keep one eye on her as I browse the opposite shelf of treats and toys, and Sutton takes on her new task with utmost sincerity. I've decided on both a bag of chicken treats and a chew toy before she's selected a leash. Then she presents it to me like my opinion matters to her.

"It's fine," I tell her. There's nothing special about the green camo print. It's not really her style, but it doesn't matter. "It's your choice," I remind her.

She scrunches her nose, pursing her lips. "No," she says. She puts the leash back and starts all over again.

God, I hope Mom finishes soon. I'm sick of this routine already. I'm not a babysitter.

I squeeze the rubber squirrel in my hands. Does Romeo even like squirrels? If she's going to pretend his leash is a monumental decision, I may as well put in some effort into picking out his new toy. He's my only true ally in the household at the moment.

I crouch to examine a carton of plush and squeaker toys. No squirrels. He deserves better. I could probably get away with buying him two new toys. I don't think Mom would push back too hard.

"Sutton," I ask as I dig in the bin. "Do you want to pick out a toy too?"

She doesn't respond. Again. I suppress a deep sigh. This is getting old. "Sutton," I repeat. "Please answer me."

Nothing.

I'm gonna kill her. I spin around. "Sutton!" I snap, but she doesn't say anything. She can't. She's not there to hear me. I twirl again, taking in the empty aisle. She isn't here.

She's gone.

NINE

"Sutton?"

No. Where did she go?

"Sutton!" I call again. "Sutton, please." *I didn't mean it.* I stride down the aisle. "Sutton."

The aisle opens into an expanse of bins filled with various sale items. I spin again, but the maze of it all seems endless. Where is she? Is she still in the store?

A hand touches my shoulder. "Sutton," I say, turning, but it's not her. It's another employee. A plump Black woman, far older than the kid who helped Mom. She looks older than Mom. *Oh no...* How am I going to tell Mom? We just got Sutton back.

"Are you looking for someone, sweetheart?"

"My sister," I breathe out. "She was right behind me. I lost her." It's my fault this time. She was my responsibility. They'll never forgive me.

"Calm down," the woman says. "Breathe." I'm reminded of Ma Remy, especially when she asks, "Does she look like you?"

"Yeah," I say. "We have the same curly hair and eyes. But she's taller than me and thinner, and her skin is lighter—"

"I saw her," she says. She points toward the side of the store with a wall of aquariums. Sutton is standing before them. She's pressing her right hand against the glass of a goldfish tank. Her left holds a sparkling pink leash that trails on the linoleum floor.

She's alive.

She's fine.

She *left* me for no reason.

I barely remember to thank the employee as rage blurs my vision. It takes all the self-restraint I have not to stomp over and lash out at my sister. My anger is so all-consuming, I feel like I could scream and shatter the glass, drowning us both in fish water. "What the hell is wrong with you?"

Sutton turns those soulless eyes on me again. The side of her mouth flickers, like she's considering smiling. She better not.

"You left me."

"I'm sorry." Her hand trails down the glass, startling the school of fish. They scatter in all directions. She drops her hand, stepping back. "I didn't mean to scare you," she says, but I can't tell if she's talking to me or the fish.

"It's fine," I lie. "Don't do it again."

"I won't," she says. She attempts to take my hand with her wet, clammy one.

I pull out of her grasp, mumbling an apology, but she doesn't even pretend to look hurt.

When is Mom coming back? I don't know how much more of this I can take.

I haven't figured out the rules of this new game. Mom and Dad's roles are clearly assigned, but my purpose is murky. Sutton and I are not on the same team, yet she seems determined to position us that way. I feel like a weak pawn in The Hunger Games, lured into a false alliance with a more powerful player until I'm strangled in my sleep.

The light filtering through the tanks shimmers as Sutton slowly moves back to the goldfish she was watching. I watch her watch them. She's enchanted in a way she hasn't been since she returned. The fish's rhythmic swimming seems to bring her genuine contentment.

My stomach clenches as what I'm seeing clicks into clarity. She's calm. The apprehension, the calculating look in her eyes is gone. I'll do whatever I can to extend this peace.

"Do you want a fish?" I ask her. "I'm sure Mom will buy you one."

She doesn't respond how I expect. She starts to shake her head, then frowns. "Do you think they remember?"

"What?"

"If I take one home with me, will it remember being here?

Will it miss its family?" She tilts her head up, taking in the wall of pacing Pisces. "The other fish. Will it remember them?"

I sigh. There goes my hope. We're back to her mind tests already. That must be what this is, right? Sutton must know what she's saying.

"I read somewhere that a goldfish only has a ten-minute memory," I tell her, "so it can't really remember anything."

Just like you. How convenient.

Sutton hands me the leash she picked out for Romeo so she can return to the tank. I pace behind her in an invisible cage, trapped until Mom returns. I pull out my phone twice as time drags on, but the service inside this giant fluorescent box is either nonexistent, or Ruth still hasn't responded to my last text. I'm almost tempted to reply to Andrew's passive-aggressive messages when Mom rounds the corner.

"Finally," I groan, dropping the leash in Mom's cart. It slides down the outdoor enclosure box but doesn't slip through the gaps at the bottom.

"Did you get him a toy or treat?"

Shit. I completely forgot about Romeo's present when Sutton disappeared. "I was gonna ask her," I say in defense. "We got distracted."

Mom sighs with a nod, like the idea of Sutton flaking is already a relatable occurrence.

"Honey," she says. "Did you want to pick out a treat for your dog?"

"No," Sutton responds, without looking away from the tank.

"Okay—" Mom starts, but before she can placate her, Sutton is talking again.

"I want a fish," she says. "Casey said you would buy me one."

"That's not what I said!" I argue. "I told her you would probably get her one if she asked you, Mom. That's all."

"I'm asking," Sutton confirms. "Can I have one?" Her eyes flick between Mom and me like she's trying to figure something out. "Please?" And then—looking directly at me as if for permission—she adds, "Mom?"

It's the first time Sutton has acknowledged Mom as her parent and not some random person of authority since she's come home. This is it. Sutton could ask Mom to buy out the whole store, and she'd take out a new mortgage without a second thought.

"Yes, of course," Mom surrenders easily. "You'll need a tank and supplies."

"Yes," Sutton says. "I want this one, *Mom*," she repeats, putting emphasis on the word now that using it once was successful. She points at a big goldfish in the corner of the tank. Unlike the others, this one doesn't swim away from her finger.

"Absolutely," Mom agrees. "I'll go get someone to pull him out for you, all right? Casey, watch the cart and your sister while I'm gone."

Like I have a choice.

She isn't gone nearly as long as before, but I'm equally as relieved when Mom comes back. I slip into the background as

Sutton and Mom direct the employee's net toward her chosen victim.

I ache for a return to our life before, despite how I despised it. Days ago, I was sobbing over the possibility that I'd never get the chance to yell at my sister again. I didn't realize how different the agony of survival could be. Death would have immortalized Sutton, but her return forces me to confront her faults alone because there's no room to acknowledge, let alone examine, them in this recovery.

I'm grateful for the olive branch she's given Mom. A momentary relief from being the only soul she acknowledges in this new journey she's forced on us. I'm happy to be the shadow sister, invisible until necessary, forgotten by choice.

But Sutton doesn't let me hide for long.

Her new trophy is bagged and tagged. She cradles it in both hands as Mom lets the employee lead us to the aquarium accessories aisle.

"What do you want to call it?" Mom asks.

"He's hungry," Sutton replies.

"We'll get him some food, but he needs a name."

"Hungry," Sutton repeats. Her fish doesn't seem concerned with any possible outcome, circling in its small bag of water. It occasionally stops by Sutton's fingers, nipping lightly through the bag like it's truly famished.

Mom doesn't seem to want to grab any other supplies until this critical issue is solved.

"What about naming it Juliet?" I offer. "To go with Romeo."

"You can't call a boy fish *Juliet*," Mom argues.

I roll my eyes. "Don't be transphobic to Sutton's fish, Mom. How do we even know if it's a boy, anyway?"

"I like that," Sutton says, still staring at her fish. "Juliet."

"It's settled, then," Mom says. That lonely look I'm becoming familiar with flashes across her face again, but she doesn't let it linger. "Thank you, Casey." She addresses with me with intention. "I appreciate your help with Sutton."

I wave it off, hoping she won't press it. I don't know how to explain that I understand, that I wish Sutton were clinging to her instead too.

Romeo takes to becoming a big brother just fine. He doesn't care that Sutton has replaced him with a fish, especially when it means he gets more outdoor time. Dad offered to help me set up the enclosure, but it wasn't that complicated. We were halfway done when Mom called him in to help set up Sutton's new lighted aquarium—the Rolls-Royce of fish prisons. I managed fine on my own. I always have.

> **Ruth:** I hate our nanny. I don't even know why we
>   hired her.
> **Me:** Would you rather watch all your siblings yourself?
> **Ruth:** I pretty much am. She barely does anything. I
>   wish you were here.

I glance up at Sutton's bedroom window from where I'm lying on the grass by Romeo's pen. I see Mom's silhouette conducting an orchestra of instructions inside.

Me too, I text back. I'd prefer real babies over this forced coddling.

> **Ruth:** It will get better.
> **Me:** Uh huh. Yep. Totally. Sure. Thanks.
> **Ruth:** LMAO okay okay, but it can't get worse?
> **Me:** I can't believe you said that. You've jinxed me.
>   She's gonna ask for a pony next.
> **Ruth:** What are you gonna name it? Mercutio?
> **Me:** Othello.
> **Ruth:** Uh... someone's screaming and someone else is
>   crying. I gotta go BUT we are definitely unpacking
>   that reference later. Don't kill your sister.

What if she kills me first? I send off, knowing I won't get a reply. Other apps have red notification badges on my home screen, but I have no energy to respond to anyone else. I press my head hard against the ground even though it's going to ruin my curls. I want to believe Ruth. I want my relationship with Sutton to improve, but I don't know what that would look like anymore.

Romeo hops around inside his little playpen, chasing butterflies that seem to know how close to fly to taunt him but not risk being eaten.

I don't need to be out here with him. I could go inside. He's safe. But what's the point? All that waits inside is my own room and the awareness that everyone else is with Sutton in hers. I get that no matter what my opinion is, she has a right to that undivided attention. And I'd rather she monopolize our parents than cling to me.

I don't want to be the focus. Not really. Still, where does that leave me? What am I supposed to do in this purgatory where we don't have to bury a body but it's not socially appropriate for me to ditch the family that's ignoring me to hang out at my friend's house?

"I'm fine, Isaiah!" Mom shouts from Sutton's room, loud enough to startle Romeo and his butterfly clique. He pauses his pursuit, looking at me with a head tilt.

"Maybe time to head back in, buddy," I whisper as we wait for an aftershock.

It arrives less than a minute later.

"I'm fine," Mom repeats from upstairs, less angry but still too loud. She says something else, but her volume lowers enough to make it impossible for me to understand with the distance. I can't see her shadow in the window anymore.

"Sounds like family fun time is over," I say as I stand. I lift Romeo out of his pen. "You wanna see Daddy? Wanna help him study in his office? Or the living room, I guess."

Dad's already downstairs by the time I shut the sliding glass door behind me. He's doing busywork in the kitchen. His back is to me, and he doesn't face me despite hearing me enter. "Are you hungry, baby?" he asks, head buried in the refrigerator. "Think it's about time we had something other than takeout."

I set Romeo on the floor. He waddles over to help Dad in case anything falls out of the fridge.

"I'm good for now," I say, "but I'll eat whatever. Let me know when it's ready."

Dad's not so invested in the dinner menu as to ignore Romeo. He bends and lowers a hand from the fridge frame to scratch behind Romeo's ears. I wait as Dad starts pulling meats and veggies onto the counter, but he won't look at me, not even to question why I'm still there.

"I'll be upstairs," I announce to no one. There's not really anywhere else to go.

Mom almost runs into me as she races down the stairs. The mascara she put on for our errand earlier runs down her face, but she forces a watery smile anyway.

"You should probably let your sister be for a while," she suggests like I intended to play hide-and-seek with her. "I think today was a lot for her. She needs some space." She doesn't wait for me to reply, sidestepping past. I hear Dad's voice overlapping with hers as I reach the top of the stairs.

I linger outside Sutton's closed door despite Mom's warning. I don't really want to see her, but this has gone on long enough.

I open the door.

Sutton sits cross-legged on the floor in front of the new aquarium on top of her dresser. The makeup and cheer camp pictures that sat there before are in a haphazard pile in the corner of her room. Her focus is on the single fish swimming in the giant tank. The LED lighting paints her in waves, but the glow makes her appear gray.

When she notices me, standing at the precipice of this figurative and literal mess she's made of our home and family, she has the audacity to ask, "Do you want to feed him?"

"I want the truth, Sutton." I shut the door behind me so our parents can't overhear. "I know you're faking it. I'm not buying this for a second."

She tilts her head in confusion like Romeo, but it's a lot less cute. She lifts the box of fish food sitting between her folded legs. "He's still hungry."

"I don't care about your fish!" I snap. My eyes flash to her open window, waiting to see if my voice carried, but the only visitor is another butterfly inching along the windowsill.

"Tell me the truth. Tell me what really went on while you were gone."

"I don't remember," Sutton says.

"Then how do you remember me? I looked it up. This isn't how amnesia works. You don't selectively remember people. You can't pick and choose. It's manipulative, Sutton. Why are you focusing on me and not Mom and Dad?"

Sutton's face is serious. "I love you, Casey," she says simply and leaves it at that. Like that justifies her behavior. Like that explains everything. Like that makes any sense at all.

"No, you don't." The words come out in a rush that breaks open my heart and my tear ducts before I can stop them. I blink rapidly, but some tears still escape. Sutton watches as I wipe them away. "You don't love me," I remind her. "You don't love me like you love Mom and Dad. You don't love me like you love Romeo. Even he can tell something is wrong with you!"

Sutton opens her mouth, closing it just as fast, like she's mimicking her fish. She starts to get up from the floor, but I step back, and she drops back down to sitting.

"You definitely don't love me like you love Andrew. You've proven that time and time again. What does he know, Sutton?"

Her brows furrow. "Who?"

I could strangle her.

I unlock my phone before scrolling for her Instagram. Hundreds of selfies dance across my screen, most featuring her blond, blue-eyed boyfriend: at the golf club, diner dates, trail runs, and even at games where she cheered, though he doesn't go to our school. She takes my phone from me and taps on a picture of her kissing his cheek. In the photo, her eyes are closed, but he isn't looking at the camera either. He's drinking her in.

"He's not with the others." She points to the frames on her shelves. They're carefully curated to only contain pictures of our parents, Grandma Remy, and other school friends and extended family. There's only one with me, and it's from when we were both in elementary school. No, of course, there aren't any photos of him in her room. Mom broke her Leave It the Same rule to take them all out.

"Why did he have your car, Sutton? What did you do? Why are you lying?" I surge forward, voice breaking, "What happened?"

"I don't know," she says. She pretends to look sad for me, frowning at my lack of emotional control, but she's empty of true empathy. I know she doesn't care. I knew it before any of this happened. I shouldn't keep letting her get to me like this.

"Fine, then," I give in. "Don't tell me. But what about my bracelet? Where's the bracelet Grandma gave me?"

Sutton snaps to attention, locking her gaze on my own like she's looking through the scope of a sniper rifle. All pretense evaporates from her expression. I wish I had confronted her in front of our parents, because the look on Sutton's face—the ice in her glare—is the most *her* she's been since she came home. It would take less than a second for them to see through her like I have.

"It's not yours," she replies sharply. Of this, she is sure.

"How do you know that?" I ask her. "If you don't remember anything."

"I..." She falters, caught. She breaks eye contact, returning her gaze to Juliet. But her contentment is gone, her mouth set in a hard line. "I don't know," she says. "I just feel it."

And *I* feel alive again. I've got her.

"It doesn't matter if you have everyone else fooled, Sutton. I'm going to find out exactly what you're hiding, and then everyone will know who you truly are."

SUTTON

ONE YEAR BEFORE

I feel like everyone at the diner can see right through me.

I changed out of my school-branded gear after practice and before driving here, so it's not like I'm wearing a blinking neon sign that says, *Look at the private school girl!*

Still, the middle-aged white guy in the booth opposite mine is definitely watching me in a way that implies I'm not blending in as well as I'd like. I hope Andrew doesn't notice. I picked this place so he would worry less about money. I've noticed how carefully he selects treats at the movies and always picks the value items off a dinner menu.

I'm not sure how to approach the topic without offending him. I'd be fine with more dates where we don't spend any money at all. I only want to spend time with him.

I run my thumb over the edge of my car key yet again. It's

a calming ritual, and my finger is developing a groove from the pressure.

I click the power button on the side of my phone, waking the screen. Romeo smiles at me on my lock screen, his tongue chasing the camera lens to kiss me. 7:13 PM, the time crowning his head reads.

A new text notification covers his furry face.

Casey: Remember, you promised to get me at 8.

I groan, leaning back against the cold vinyl of the booth. I start to type out an honest response, but I think better of it and start over. I've only had my car for three months, and part of the deal is picking up Casey from school and her other activities. She suddenly has lots of errands for someone who spends most of her time in her room.

But she didn't *have* to go anywhere today.

She should have known better than to make plans when she knew I had a date with Andrew. I've been very clear with her about my schedule, but she still had the audacity to okay youth group at Heights Above tonight with our parents before we left for school this morning. I didn't even get the chance to argue about the conflict.

She definitely isn't going to youth group to learn about the Bible or whatever. I know she only agreed so she could hang out with Ruth at her dad's church. They do that all the time since Mrs. Heights passed. Grace used to let them hang out at the house, but now most of Ruth's time at home is spent being a sur-rogate parent.

I don't blame Ruth for making the most of the time she has available. But Casey knew I'd be busy tonight.

Me: I know. I'll be there.

I'll be there even though it cuts my date short. Andrew was supposed to be here a half hour ago. We're barely going to have any time together if he doesn't show up soon. If he shows up at all.

I tap into our text thread. I check our last messages for any clue to his absence.

Me: Meet me at The Garden? It's a diner near your place.

Andrew: Are you sure you want to go there?

Me: Do you not like it? The reviews said the food was good and affordable.

Andrew: It's great. I'll be there.

His last text was two hours ago. I check my missed calls, but there's nothing there either. I flip my phone down on the table and pick up the menu to busy myself. That signals the waitress, a girl with warm-ivory skin and equally warm eyes, to check on me.

"Are you ready to order?" she asks. Her name tag introduces her as Elizabeth.

"I'm going to wait a little longer for my boyfriend to arrive," I tell her. "But thank you."

Elizabeth's kind eyes look down on me in pity. She doesn't voice her suspicions, but she refills my empty water glass without touching the full one that mocks me from across the table.

Andrew will be here. He promised.

He's not like the boys at the male academy match to Gwen Light's Upper School for Girls. He never leaves me on read. He doesn't make fun of me when I know the answer to an obscure trivia question, or when I get excited over small things, or even when I complain about Casey.

He's so good to me, so kind.

If there's a problem, it must be me.

Is this blouse too dressy for a diner date? Is he embarrassed to be seen with me in his own neighborhood? A lot of our dates have been during his breaks at the golf club or picnics at my favorite trail. I wanted to show him I can compromise. It doesn't always have to be about what's easiest for me. If we find some spots more local to his side of town, we won't have to wait as long between dates. I know commuting is an issue since he's still saving for his own car.

The door chimes. I look up like I have the last six times, hoping it's him.

It is.

He's rain dusted and breathing heavily, but when he sees me, his smile is like the sun coming out from the clouds. I feel brighter, and I can tell he's happier with each step that brings him closer to me.

"I'm so sorry, Sutton," he says as he slides into the seat across from me. He takes a grateful sip from the water glass Elizabeth left for him. "The buses were running late, and my phone died."

"I thought this was closer to your house," I say. "That's why I picked it."

"It is, but I had work today. The club is on your side of town, you know that." His finger marks a line in the condensation on his glass.

My cheeks burn. "Of course, right. I'm sorry."

He shakes his head. "You don't need to apologize for me being late."

Elizabeth returns to the table. "He arrived!" she says with a pointed look at Andrew. Maybe I was wrong about her politeness. "Would you like to order now?"

"Yes," I say. "Give us a few more minutes to decide, but we'll be ready soon." I lift my menu again, but Andrew reaches across the table and presses it back down.

"No," he says. "I'll have water. I already made you wait. I don't want to put you out anymore."

My aborted laugh comes out as an awkward grunt as I try to suppress how ridiculous I think that is. "It's not a problem, babe." I dismiss Elizabeth once more. "I've got it covered. Don't worry about it. Order what you want. I read the twice-baked potatoes are really good."

"*Sutton.*" I've never heard Andrew say my name in such a harsh tone, and it must show on my face because he backtracks. "I can't expect you to foot the bill every time we go out."

"I'm sorry," I say. "I know you don't have a lot of disposable income. I swear I'm trying to be mindful of that. I really—I want to pay tonight, but we can do something different next time. We don't have to spend any money at all. I don't mind."

"*I* mind," he says. "I'm not some sugar baby. I don't want to be a gross little gold digger hanging off your tennis bracelet like a leech."

"That's not how I see you at all."

This time he's the one trying to stop a laugh. "You're the only one. I think you need to face it, Sutton. We've had a great few months, but we were never going to work. I don't hold anything against you. Thanks for slumming it with me for a while, but you can go back to your friends and Willow parties. You don't need to drag me around like an obligation."

"You're not an obligation."

Andrew takes my hand in his, his thumb stroking my wrist softly. Deliberately. Final. "I shouldn't be anything to you anymore."

"W—what did I do?" I ask. "I can fix it. I can do better."

His hand tightens around mine. His other hand covers his face. He leans an elbow on the table. "No," he whispers, defeated. "Don't. Please don't blame yourself."

"I know I've made some mistakes because of my privilege," I say. "But you can call me out. I'm sorry about the money thing. I didn't mean to make you feel embarrassed or like you can't provide for me."

"It's not that," Andrew says. He drops both hands. "I know you don't care about flashy dates, but my problems are deeper than splitting the bill. It's not fair of me to drag you down into them."

"Andrew, you're my boyfriend, my friend. Let me in."

He pauses, then speaks quietly. "I'm going to lose my home, Sutton. Even with everyone in our household working, we can barely cover the rising rent, and our landlord told my parents that he plans to sell our house at the end of our lease because the current housing market makes it more profitable to sell than to keep renting to us. I don't expect you to date a homeless guy."

"You won't be homeless," I promise. "We won't let it happen. We'll work together to find a solution. We'll find a way to fix this, find someone to help."

He scoffs. I can feel him retreating into himself. I won't let his shame take him away from me.

"But even if it all fails," I say, scooting around the booth to slide in next to him, "I'm here for you. I don't care what anyone thinks. I love you. I'd stay with you even if we both had to live in the woods like Bigfoot. Even if we lose everything, I'll stay."

"Are you sure?" He won't look at me, like he's afraid to see the truth on my face. I tilt his chin up with a finger. A drop of rain falls from his hairline to my palm.

"I'm in it to the end. Rain or shine, baby."

He sighs, breath tickling my skin. "I love you too," he admits and closes the distance between us.

My phone vibrates on the table. I slide it to me.

Casey: Almost time. You still coming?

"Do you need to respond to that?" Andrew asks.

I put my phone on silent and set it back down, moving closer to him again.

"No," I tell him. "I can stay as long as you need. Let's get something to eat and talk. It sounds like you've been going through a lot. Let me listen."

TEN

It turns out there is such a thing as too many choices.

Ruth seems entirely at home with the dozens of yogurt flavors and toppings in front of us, but I don't know where to begin. I guess I shouldn't be that surprised by the extraness of a place called Fro-Yo-Yo.

"It's not that bad," Ruth says. She pulls me toward a stack of paper bowls beneath an ancient-Egyptian-style art print of people playing with yo-yos. DID YOU KNOW YO-YOS HAVE BEEN AROUND SINCE 500 BC? a plaque below the print reads. FROZEN YOGURT IS A BIT YOUNGER, BUT AS MUCH FUN.

"I didn't say anything."

"Your face did."

"Where did you find this place?" I accept the bowl she hands me and follow her toward the soft-serve machines.

"I spend a lot of time in the Town Center waiting on the

nanny," Ruth says. That makes sense. That's why we're here today after all. Four of Ruth's siblings have doctors' appointments, so her nanny agreed to drop us off at the shopping center to minimize the number of heads she needed to keep track of.

I'm not sure my parents would have agreed to let me hang out with Ruth had they known we were leaving the safety of her house, but I guess ancient Froyo is a decent price to pay for a bit of freedom.

Instructional posters teaching yo-yo tricks decorate the area around the soft-serve dispensers, but the actual flavors seem mercifully normal. There are simply *a lot* of them.

"You can try samples!" Ruth says, pointing out mini cups next to the machines. "I've been here before, but you should experiment. You can mix and match."

"I'm not an experimenter," I say. "I like things to stay the same. Do they have vanilla?"

Ruth groans so loud, the mom of the family ahead of us does a double take. "Sweet baby Jesus in heaven, Casey," Ruth says. "What is the point? Like, seriously—why do I bother trying to expand your worldview when this is how you treat me?"

"Expand my—" I laugh. "Ruth, you're acting like frozen yogurt is the eighth wonder of the world."

"I take what I can get." The family ahead moves toward toppings, and Ruth takes their place, pulling the levers of three flavors, one after the other. It takes her less than a minute to fill her bowl. She wasn't lying about coming here before.

"Try something out of the norm for once," she says. "For me?"

"Fine," I say, dragging out the word like her request is a huge chore when it's the opposite. I'm grateful for an afternoon free of Sutton. For the first time, I'm beginning to understand what Ruth must deal with having so many younger siblings. Sutton isn't a child, but she may as well be for how our parents treat her. How *I'm* expected to treat her. I've missed interacting with a peer.

Ruth is acting totally normal. I honestly couldn't ask for a better best friend. She hasn't brought up my sister once since Dad dropped me off at her place, though I know she must be curious. Everyone is.

She even agreed for me and Andrew to meet at her place sometime next week so I can talk to him without my parents knowing. She's not fully on board with my suspicion of Sutton, too kind-hearted for her own good, but she trusts me. She listens to me, even when no one else will.

"Tell you what," I say, "I'm gonna make your day."

"Oh yeah?"

"You can pick what flavor I have."

She gasps. "Praise be," she says, setting her concoction on a nearby counter. "It's a miracle." She grabs my bowl from my hands and spins to take in all the options, *hmm*ing dramatically. "Well... you do like pineapple on your pizza—like a heathen—so maybe you'll like it in a dessert." She lowers a lever and fills my bowl with pale yellow Froyo.

She hands it to me and folds her arms like a contestant

waiting on results in a cooking show. I make a show of inspecting the scoop on my spoon before taking my first bite.

"Not bad," I say, but my smile gives me away.

"I knew it!" She picks up her bowl and leads me to the toppings bar. I'm much more at home here. There's little that peanut butter cups, graham cracker crumbs, or gummy worms could do to offend me. I pair brownie bites with fresh strawberries and step back while Ruth builds a much more elaborate palette.

The music playing in the store transitions from a recent radio hit into the opening notes of "Broken Heart-Shaped Glasses," one of my favorite Ivy James songs. I don't bother hiding my smile when Ruth catches my gaze with an "I told you so" grin.

"Okay," I admit. "Maybe this place is growing on me."

"My taste is impeccable, I know."

Ruth joins me at the register. I attempt to pay for us both, but Ruth claims she's close to a free reward on her loyalty card. I argue that her meal would also be free if I paid for it. It gets me nowhere.

Ruth pays the cashier and sticks two extra dollars in the tip cup as he punches two holes on her well-worn loyalty card.

He hands me a card too, even though I didn't pay for anything. "Come back soon," he says.

We choose a table near the front window. The chairs are taller there. Once I'm seated, my feet no longer touch the floor. I swing them back and forth, feeling like a kid again.

"How's your sister?" Ruth finally asks, making the sweet tart of the pineapple turn sour in my mouth.

"She wanted to come with me today," I say, "even though she doesn't like you."

"Of course she likes me!" Ruth protests. "What's not to like about me?"

I bite my tongue about Sutton's endless complaints about youth group, Ruth's conservative wardrobe, her many siblings. There was also Sutton's two-hour tirade when Pastor Heights invited us to a church-sponsored "purity" ball. Now that I think about it, none of Sutton's comments have ever been directed at Ruth herself. She's never actually said Ruth was annoying.

"She doesn't hate you," I concede. "She probably likes you better than me, honestly. She just doesn't like the church."

Ruth nods with her lips closed around her spoon. "*Oh*," she says, drawing out the word. "Sounds like her. Makes sense. I bet we'd even agree on some of her complaints."

I nod. Ruth is definitely more devout than either Sutton or me, but she's less of a stereotypical pastor's daughter in private. She has faith, but several of her social beliefs would not be met well by her father if she voiced them to his face. It's not like Ruth and I spend most of our time hanging out at Heights Above out of choice. It's usually a choice between the church or her house. Her dad has a parental control app on her phone that tracks her location, so she doesn't exactly have the freedom to leave whenever she wants. At least at church, other people can keep an eye on her siblings so we don't have to babysit.

"She could have come," Ruth says. "You said she did okay at the pet shop."

"My mom was there too," I remind her. "They're not going to let her go anywhere unchaperoned for who knows how long."

Besides, I'm having more fun without her. After the past few days, it's nice to have some space from all the family drama.

"You can have my loyalty card," I tell Ruth. I slide it across the table. "Mom and Dad aren't likely to let me out of the house much this summer either."

"I'll keep it safe for you," Ruth says, picking it up and twirling it between her fingers. "Oh, he punched the whole thing!"

"That's strange," I say. "You should use it."

Ruth doesn't say anything. I look up from my Froyo, and her lips are pursed like she's trying to hold in a laugh. "I think he wants *you* to use it."

She pushes the card back toward me. There's a number written on the back.

"What?" I look to the register. The boy winks at me. His blue eyes match his teal uniform.

I stumble over every syllable trying to exit my mouth. "I don't—I, um... You can keep it."

"I will take the free yogurt," Ruth agrees, "but I won't be calling him."

"Why not?"

"Casey," Ruth says, looking like she's about to laugh at me again. "He likes *you*. And I'm a lesbian."

"Right," I say. "I'm sorry. I'm not my best today." I stick another spoonful of yogurt in my mouth, but my cheeks still burn at the attention.

"No apology necessary. I'm very happy to file this in my Casey collection of embarrassing memories."

"Come on," I groan. "I have a legitimate reason to be distracted."

Ruth nods. "This time," she concedes and doesn't press it any further. We eat in a pop-soundtracked silence. I try to commit this moment to memory, the contentment of escaping responsibility and being in the company of the sister I chose instead of the one forced upon me.

"See?" A voice breaks in, ringing as melodically as the door chime announcing a new customer. And another new customer, and another, and another.

Six girls of varying shades but identical moods file in. It disrupts the ecosystem of the place, distracting kids at other tables. An employee steps out of the way, the white cleaning cloth in his hand fluttering like a flag of surrender.

"I told you I wasn't making shit up," the first girl says. A father nearby frowns at her language, looking at his toddler. "I couldn't make this place up if I tried."

Four of the girls head straight to the soft-serve machines, but the leader—a white brunette with expensive highlights—stays behind with the final member of the group. The straggler watches her friends with the same wariness I had for Fro-Yo-Yo, but she has a more justifiable reason to avoid the chaotic group arguing over flavors.

Her arm is in a sling. Her manicured fingertips tap the cast encasing her wrist, colored the same hot pink as her nails. She uses her free hand to tighten her strawberry-blond ponytail, which complements the blush tones of her coloring. "It's a lot," she says. I feel a kinship with Cast Girl.

At least I do until the leader speaks again.

"You can wait with Coach if that's easier," she says. "Tell me what you want, and I'll get it for you." They both turn their heads toward the front window, and I follow their gaze. My appetite leaves the building.

I recognize the man sitting in the front seat of the forest-green van in the parking lot. He's clearly browsing his phone from his bent head and slight glow on his face. I can hardly see his face, but I don't need to.

Even if I couldn't place him by appearance alone, the logo emblazoned on the van would make it a dead giveaway. Gwen Light Academy's crest shines in the summer sun. WILD WILLOW CHEER SQUAD reads the custom paint job.

"We should go." I'm already halfway out of my seat. I can't deal with this today.

Ruth frowns, brows furrowing. "What?"

They're Sutton's teammates.

I should have recognized them from the search party or the halls at school, but they look less like clones when they aren't color coordinating every part of their outfits. I didn't even notice one of them had an injury when I saw them at the park. The pink of her cast must have blended in with the neon of their FIND SUTTON T-shirts.

"We have plenty of time before the nanny comes back," Ruth argues, oblivious.

I consider rushing out the door to avoid them, but that's more likely to cause a scene than staying put. Then Ruth utters the killing blow to my attempt to stay unnoticed.

"Casey," she asks, as the music lulls between songs. "What's wrong?"

The whole shop hears.

"Casey?" repeats Cast Girl.

"Oh my God," echoes the leader, likely the captain. "It's Sutton's sister." The rest of the pack turns from the soft-serve machines.

And just like that, our paradise is gone.

The girls at the machines start hurrying through their orders to come over, but one shouts across the shop, "How's Sutton?"

"I'm so glad she's home and okay," the captain chimes in. She moves forward as she speaks, and I instinctively step back, my abandoned seat pressing against my spine. I catch Ruth's eyes and see the apology forming in them, but nothing can be done now.

Cast Girl doesn't crowd me like her friend, but she asks, "She *is* okay, right?"

The entire shop is listening to the conversation now. The

cheer girls, the families—they all wait for my response. Sutton was on prime-time news for a whole week. They know her name. They know her face. They practically know more about what happened to her than she does.

And now they can see her in me.

"She's—" I swallow the bile rising in my throat. "She's good." I can tell by their faces that it's not enough of a response, but I don't know what else to say. "She doesn't remember anything."

"Is she going to get better?" Cast Girl asks.

"Yeah," comes a voice from the toppings bar. "Cheer camp is in August. Will she be better by then?"

I open my mouth to respond, but I don't get the chance.

"Screw cheer camp, Amelia," the captain says with an eye roll. "I'm pretty sure Sutton and her family have more important things to worry about."

"She's one of our best tumblers, that's all."

"Amelia!"

"I'm not saying she needs to be on her A game. It would be nice—"

"Is she even gonna do cheer in the fall?"

"She may not come back to school at all."

"You shouldn't say that, she—"

Their voices and questions overlap. I try to answer what I can, but there aren't really answers to give. I have no idea what happened—or what's going to happen. I have no idea when or if Sutton will return to normal. I don't know why we're going through this. That's why Ruth and I came here. This was supposed to be an escape.

Ruth gathers our half-eaten bowls and walks toward the trash. The team takes the hint to lay off the questions, though they're still focused on me.

"Can we come see her?" Cast Girl asks.

The others fall silent to hear my answer. I feel like an awards-show announcer presenting a deeply competitive prize. No matter what I say, someone will end up disappointed. But their affection for my sister is evident, even if she won't remember them.

"That's not really up to me," I say honestly. "You'd have to ask my mom. She's in charge of who's allowed to see Sutton."

"I have her number from carpool!" Amelia says. "I can text her!"

"No!" chorus all the other girls.

"Until you learn how to pull your foot out of your mouth," the leader says, "there's no way in hell you're gonna be the one to talk to Sutton's mom."

I can't help but agree.

"Could you be our go-between?" Cast Girl asks. She's already pulling out her phone before I have a chance to respond. "Your number?" I rattle it off, and a few seconds later, my phone pings.

Unknown Number: This is Natalie. Sutton's friend.
Let us know what we can do to help.

I save the contact as Ruth makes her way toward the door.

She opens it for me. I don't waste a second following her out, but I pause and look back. They're still watching me.

"Thanks," I tell Natalie, though I'm not sure what for.

As we pass the green cheer van on our way through the parking lot, the man in the van looks up from his phone and does a double take at the sight of me. It's the assistant coach, once again filling in for Coach McCoy. I hold his gaze long enough to see the exact moment he realizes I'm not my sister.

If I didn't know better, I'd say he looked relieved.

ELEVEN

Ma Remy was kinda hot, once upon a time.

I'm beginning to seriously doubt Dad's claim that I resemble a younger version of my grandma because I'm looking at several photos of her. I've never had such effortless elegance, and there is no way I could pull off bell-bottom jeans, even if they managed to somehow come back in style.

Her hair is wild and sun-kissed like the rest of her, glowing through the time-faded print. Her smile is immortal. I can see it in this snapshot of youth the same as through the memories of my childhood. The same as the last time she smiled at me, tired and sedated but still mine.

"I miss her," I say.

Dad smiles softly at me and nods, but I only hear laughter. The sliding door is closed, but the sound of Sutton's teammates in the pool is inescapable. Romeo sits anxiously on our side of the glass, his tiny huffs fogging up the foot of the door with his disapproval.

"You can go hang out with them if you want," Dad says. He lifts the lid off another box of Grandma's photo albums and memorabilia. He's still working at the dining table instead of his office, though Sutton isn't even in the house. She's in the backyard with Mom.

I can see her from where I'm standing. She's perched at the far edge of the pool, her legs dangling in the water while the rest of her is completely dry. Her bikini shows off her athletic figure. She looks perfect. Entirely normal. Exactly like her frolicking friends. Except she's not interacting with them at all. She simply watches them.

"I'm supposed to help you," I say. "I'm fine here."

"You can skip one afternoon," Dad offers. "I'm not tallying your hours for payroll, Casey. One day off isn't going to make you miss your concert. You go have fun."

I tear my gaze from the yard, returning to the family history laid out before me. "I'm having more fun here," I say honestly.

I don't even know the girls on the cheer team. I should recognize my sister's friends. I've seen them all dozens of times when my parents dragged me to support Sutton at competitions.

I won't pretend I always paid attention. Those bleachers were where my Ivy James fandom took root as I browsed and befriended other fan blogs on my phone as the hours dragged on and on. I'd listen to music while the rival teams performed, only taking out my headphones when Sutton's group finally took the stage. But while Sutton showcased her assimilation and teamwork, my community thrived in her shadow.

We both preferred it that way. She never formally introduced me to her friends, and she never asked about mine. It shouldn't be so unsettling that I can barely name a fraction of the girls in our yard today, but it is.

Mainly because the person who feels like the biggest stranger is Sutton herself.

"Well, I'm happy to have you with me," Dad says. He ducks his head to hide his smile, like this acknowledgment of affection could hurt him somehow. I return my focus to our task too.

I haven't seen many of these pictures before. Ma Remy liked to display photos of family at her house, but it was mostly pictures of us as children with her. She also displayed some very old frames of her and her two brothers, along with snapshots of their children and grandchildren back in the Carolinas.

I've seen pictures of younger Ma Remy before, of course. Mom always loved pointing out the prints of Dad as a little kid. Those are the ones Mom is most excited to redisplay now that we've inherited my grandma's scrapbooks. But Dad is more interested in Ma Remy's memorabilia from before he was born.

"Who is this?" I ask him, pointing to a picture of a tall man with his hands wrapped around young Ma Remy's waist at a park. She's laughing. Her hair is pressed slick from the top of her head down to just below her ears, where big roller curls hem her head, like a petticoat peeking out from the bottom of a skirt. They're both wearing warm-weather clothes, but with them being from the South, that doesn't mean it was summertime when the photo was taken.

"That's my father," Dad says. "Spring of 1975, about a year before I was born." He doesn't linger on the photo. He returns to unsealing two boxes of journals and prints. I know better than to ask him to elaborate, though he usually loves waxing poetic about family history.

I know he won't talk about Grandpa Booker. This is the first picture I've seen of him. He died before Dad was born. Before Ma Remy even knew she was pregnant, a month before their wedding. He'd survived the Vietnam War only to die on American soil right before his life was set to begin. No one has ever told me how or why.

Everything I know about Grandpa Booker is what he never knew himself, what he was never able to experience. He never got to marry the love of his life. He never knew he was going to be a father. He never met Dad, let alone Mom or me or Sutton.

He never knew us, and we don't know a lot about him. He was estranged from his family and didn't talk about them much to Ma Remy before he passed. For someone as obsessed with heritage and legacy as Dad, the lack of knowledge we have about Grandpa Booker has always been a sore spot. It's not that Dad is ashamed of his father; I think he has a hard time with all that he will never know about him or his family.

Daddy looks just like him. I start to sift through the pictures on my half of the table for ones featuring Booker. Dad pages through one of his mother's old diaries. His eyes are misty behind his glasses. He's too distracted to really pay attention to me.

Booker is always smiling. In almost every photograph, he's grinning wide at the lens. I have to assume Ma Remy is behind the camera because the only ones where he's not facing the camera are where his smile is directed at her instead. He always looks so happy. It's like a flashback to Dad before Sutton's disappearance.

The only print he's not grinning in is the single one of him in uniform. Though Dad was never in the military, Grandpa's serious—almost pained—expression reminds me of my father now, so I set that one aside.

I run out of photos that aren't in scrapbooks, so I start to skim through one of the journals Dad isn't reading. A navy-blue patterned one with an illustrated iris on the cover has several Polaroids tucked inside, so I slow my flipping to give a closer inspection to the content.

I'm distracted by the word *ivy* repeated several times on a single page. Ma Remy wasn't writing about Ivy James twenty years before she was born. It looks like a list of ingredients.

Ivy—woven into marriage wreaths, for protecting homes and blessing luck on a person.

Cleavers—for binding?

Bay Leaf—purification? Needs more research.

Grandma listed several combinations of herbs and flowers, crossing out certain matches with various levels of frustrated scribbling. It seems like she was testing something.

She reasoned her experiment was failing because of the absence of a plant she couldn't identify. She sketched out various small flowers and weeds around the potential lists.

"What's this?" I ask.

Dad looks up at me from the journal he's reading, then reaches out a hand for me to pass it over. He pushes his glasses up his nose, but he doesn't spend more than a few seconds reading before he snaps the blue cover closed and puts it back in one of the boxes. "This is one your grandma's diaries," he says.

"It didn't seem like a diary," I say. "Or a field guide. But it had information and sketches about plants. It looked like she was trying to solve a puzzle."

He glances down at the box. He doesn't look like his father anymore. "It's probably from when she was trying to remake the pendant on her bracelet."

"Remake it? She told me it'd been in the family for generations," I say. "Did it get lost?"

"For a time, yes." Dad puts the journal he was reading on top of the one he took from me and then puts the lid back on the box. "She found it eventually, so it doesn't matter. You don't need to be reading about Ma Remy swooning over your grandfather. Trust me, she does not mince words in these journals."

I giggle. "I think can handle it."

"They don't have anything we'd want to put in the display," he insists. "Maybe when you're older."

I want to argue, but I know better. "Well, I want to put this in the display." I hand him the picture of Ma Remy and Booker embracing at the park. "He looks like you. He belongs in our heirloom collection."

Dad's face moves in an imitation of a smile, but it doesn't reach his eyes. "Okay, baby girl."

Romeo barks. He paces the length of the patio door, vocalizing like a canine doorbell. I look up in time to see Natalie open the door and step inside. She quickly shuts it behind her before Romeo can escape, then squats to scratch the top of his head in greeting. He stops barking immediately. He must recognize her from sleepovers, but he sniffs her cast with the same wariness he gives Sutton.

"Hi, Mr. Cureton," Natalie says. "Casey. Thanks for having us over."

"Of course," Dad says. "It's good for Sutton to see you. I hope you're enjoying the pool. We haven't touched it much this season."

Natalie waves her injured hand with a half-hearted chuckle. "Everyone else is having a great time in the water, but I thought I'd come in and get something for me and Sutton to do instead. I can't get my cast wet, and she doesn't seem in the mood for swimming either."

"What do you think she wants to do?" I ask. She's rarely in the mood for anything but watching people (or her fish) nowadays.

Dad gives me a look for being rude, but Natalie doesn't react.

"I thought she'd like to peek at some pictures or videos of practice on her laptop," Natalie says. "Your mom suggested it. She thought it could help her remember."

I highly doubt selfies from school will awaken memories in Sutton if having her teammates circling our pool like sharks isn't enough to break her apathy.

"That's a great idea," Dad says. "Her computer should be in her room. Casey can show you."

"That would be great." Natalie smiles.

She looks to me with an easy kind of camaraderie she hasn't earned. She doesn't need me to show her where Sutton's room is. She's been here many times before. This false deference, waiting for me—it's as annoying as Sutton's newfound interest in me. Sutton always scheduled her hangouts and group sleepovers so I was as unavailable to interrupt as possible. I've never been cool enough to join their little in-group. There's no point in pretending different now.

I don't say anything as I head for the stairs. When we reach Sutton's room, I let her enter first. She pauses to look at Juliet's tank. "Cute fish," she says. I don't respond.

I shift some things around on Sutton's neglected desk. "You really think some pictures will help Sutton remember?"

"More the videos than pictures, to be honest," Natalie says from her perch by the tank. She's not really helping me look at all. "She started recording practices a few months ago, so she should have hours of footage to pick through."

"Why?"

Natalie finally ditches Juliet to help me search. She pulls open a drawer with her good arm. "She said it was to review her moves, but she asked me not to tell Coach about it. I think she was embarrassed. I'm not sure why. She's one of the best on the squad."

I suppress an eye roll. Sutton's always the best at everything. You'd think people would feel freer to critique her since she doesn't know them anymore. It's not like she's going to get pissed at Natalie. If she can't remember why she should care.

Natalie keeps talking even though I didn't ask a follow-up question.

"I think she's scared about having an accident too," she says. "She got really upset when I messed up my wrist, like she could have prevented it. I told her it'll be fine by the time cheer camp comes around in August. In time for someone else to break something." She laughs lightly, as if injuries are such a regular occurrence on the cheer team that it's become a joke.

Natalie breaks eye contact awkwardly when I don't laugh. "It's not a big deal," she says, her attention focused solely on the messy drawer she's opened that's too small to hide the laptop. "Coach McCoy is really well respected. He does personal training for important people outside his work with the school. Like bank officers and Fortune 500s. Real big shots. He knows what he's doing. We're safe."

"Maybe we should look in the closet," I say to stop her rambling. "When we brought Juliet—the fish," I add at Natalie's confused expression, "home, my parents had to clear space to fit the tank. They might have stuffed it in there."

It's not immediately visible, but after some shuffling, I see a rectangular flash of silver pressed against the wall of Sutton's closet. I pull it out and flip it open.

Natalie gasps. "What happened to it?"

This isn't the laptop she's looking for. It's the one Sutton destroyed. The screen is shattered, and a few keys are missing. Why did she keep this? Does it even work anymore?

I press the power button. After a moment, the screen flashes to life, fluttering slightly under the cracks but still capable.

The cursor blinks expectantly on the password screen, but even if the power bar in the corner signaled more than 7 percent battery life, I wouldn't have the first clue how to unlock it.

"This is her old laptop," I tell Natalie. "The police must have taken her new one when she went missing. That's probably why we can't find it."

"Oh," she says. "It looks like this works. Maybe we could still use it? Do you know the password?"

I shake my head.

She starts to stand. "Thanks for helping me look anyway, Casey."

"No problem." I poke at the keys. They still work too, even the ones with missing tops. What did Sutton have saved on here? She wouldn't have kept it if it weren't important. And was Natalie right? Is there something on the computer that would help restore Sutton's memory? I guess the laptop is as much of a mystery as my sister.

TWELVE

I don't know how Ruth handles so many siblings.

Her youngest sister, Esther, pulls on my pant leg as I finish making her almond butter and jelly sandwich. "No cross," she says in her serious three-year-old voice. "No cross."

I look around the kitchen, which has at least three different cross or crucifix decorations. "Um, Ruth?"

"No crusts," Ruth clarifies from the other room.

"Can do. Do you want it in squares or triangles, Essy?"

"Angles," Esther decides. I finish preparing her snack and lead her back to the playroom, where Ruth is brokering a custody dispute between the twins and a stuffed elephant. It's only the three youngest with us today. The other three are grocery shopping with the nanny, but it's still a lot to handle even with both of us here.

I don't know how Ruth does it on her own. She's so calm in the face of all this toddler chaos, but even that feels wrong. Ruth isn't a calm person. She's not serene and quiet, like she almost always is when we hang out her house nowadays. It wasn't always like this.

I remember a sleepover back in grade school, when the sprayer at the sink got loose and chased us like a snake while we attempted to make Kool-Aid. Ruth slipped on the water and accidentally spurted the flavor packet all over her face. I laughed and laughed, and she retaliated by blowing the rest of the powder at me, painting us both neon blue. Her mom came in to check on us, and we both froze as she grabbed the flopping hose. But instead of turning the water off, Grace spun and sprayed us in the face, laughing even louder than we had.

I miss her mom, but I don't vocalize it.

"When is your dad coming back?"

"Next week," she says. The twins separate, one with the elephant and the other with a baby doll cradled in the skirt of her dress. Ruth heads back to Esther and me at the little table. Esther fits perfectly in her tiny chair, but Ruth and I have to sit on our knees to be the appropriate height.

Ruth rips the plastic wrap off a new set of brochures and splits the pile, giving half to me. I begin to fold them again. I avoided a paper cut through the dozens I folded before Esther got hungry, but I don't think I'll end today unscathed.

"He says he's got everything pretty much secured now," Ruth continues. She's so much quicker at this than I am, but she was doing it for hours before I arrived. Her dad and second-oldest brother smile at me in vibrant ink as I crease the cover. RISE ABOVE reads the new camp name in a font that looks like wooden planks on a dark green background.

"I don't really see why we need two summer camps," I admit.

"This one isn't for us," Ruth says.

I know. That's why we're folding these pamphlets. The new camp is for lower-class kids who can't afford the fees of the church's current New Heights Youth Retreat. The land is already purchased, but Pastor David is fundraising to help offset the costs to keep it free so it can be a safe place for "at-risk" kids. At least, that's what the brochure claims.

Nothing sounds worse to me than being trapped in the wilderness with Pastor Heights and his condescending prosperity gospel. He'd probably preach that you can overcome poverty simply by believing in God hard enough, but I'm not going to say that in this Noah's ark–themed playroom.

"Where's this going to be?" New Heights is more than an hour drive out of town, near a secular lakeside resort.

"Bend's End," Ruth says as she polishes off another stack of ten brochures. She moves them from the table to an empty box. I've folded three in the same amount of time.

A photo with a gas station bordering the forest says the same, not that I bothered to read it before asking. I can tell it's not a recent photo from the models of the cars parked in the lot. I wonder what it looks like now.

"That's not far," I say. "Will there be volunteer efforts to help build it?" It's barely a question. Of course there will. There's nothing congregants of Heights Above like more than a charity photo op.

Ruth smiles. "Yeah," she says, her tone lighter and less bored. "There are some old buildings on the property, but they need to be demolished before new work can begin. My aunts are coming down when the first wave of construction starts. I wish they were already here."

I totally understand why. Ruth's aunts are from her mother's side, and they're great with kids. If they were here, we wouldn't be balancing this busywork with babysitting three kids under five. Ruth always has so much more free time when her family visits. They haven't been by as often since her mom died after complications with Esther's birth. Ruth has never said it outright, but it's pretty clear they blame Pastor David for her death. After the twins, Grace was warned that another pregnancy could put her body at serious risk, but they still conceived Esther less than two years later.

"Is he almost here?" Ruth asks.

I pull out my phone, but Andrew hasn't texted since he said his bus arrived. "I don't know," I admit. I type out an arrival estimate request and pocket my phone. "Thank you again for letting us meet here."

"Anytime," Ruth says without looking up from her folds. "Well, not really, but you know what I mean."

"My parents would be furious if they knew I was meeting with him."

"I mean..." She expertly piles her pamphlets. "We still don't know if he's involved."

"The police cleared him," I argue. "I saw it on the news." My parents haven't told me much of anything about Sutton's case since she came home.

"But he had your sister's car."

"For two days," I confirm. The police department only released her Jeep from evidence yesterday. It was weird walking past it when I left for Ruth's this morning, particularly knowing Sutton won't be driving it anytime soon.

"That's not good," Ruth says. "I don't need true-crime YouTubers to tell me that."

"You know what's worse than a suspicious boyfriend though?" I ask. "A team up. Sutton's hiding something. If anyone knows, it's him."

"*If* she's hiding anything," Ruth says.

I haven't told Ruth about finding Sutton's old laptop—or Natalie's idea that something on it may spark her memory. Ruth comforted me when I had to give up my Ivy money to replace it, but I don't think she truly believed the story as I told it to her. You'd think she would understand how vindictive older siblings can be, but maybe brothers are kinder than sisters. Or at least less pathological.

If I could unlock the laptop, maybe it would contain clues that could help me. I just need to figure out the right password. I've tried half a dozen options already and nothing has worked.

"I know she is," I insist, but I duck my head to focus on my stack of pamphlets instead of pressing it further.

> Located inside the city limits of Willow Bend,
> Rise Above for Youth's convenience will reduce
> transportation time and costs for parents. At the
> intersection of...

My pocket vibrates, and right after, the doorbell rings. "That has to be him."

"Who is it? Who is it?" Esther asks. She starts to stand, pushing her half-finished plate precariously toward our stacks of paper.

"It's probably the mailman," Ruth says, gently guiding her back to her seat. "Casey's gonna go see, and we're gonna stay right here. Aren't you still hungry?"

"Yeah," Esther admits. I slip out as she sticks her finger in one of her sandwich pieces to scoop out some jelly.

Before I've reached the door, Ruth has texted me. Talk on the deck. I don't want the girls to see him and tell the nanny.

I reply with a thumbs-up.

Andrew stands on Ruth's porch, hands clasped behind his back. His outfit isn't much better than at the search. The hem of his T-shirt is starting to fray. His shoes are muddy. I ask him to take them off before he follows me across the house.

We slip out onto the back deck. Summer has definitely begun. The sun reflects off the man-made lake connecting the Heights family's home to their neighbors. I lean against the railing. He moves to follow my lead but doesn't say anything. I'm unsure of how to proceed. Should I start? I've never done something like this before. I don't know how to confront anyone other than Sutton, and that's always been less calm conversation and more furious screaming.

He makes the choice for me. "Thank you for meeting with me," he says. "I've been trying to contact Sutton ever since she got back."

"I know," I say. "I've heard my mom complain about it."

He pulls at the hem on his sleeve. "I'm sorry."

It doesn't sound fake. His face carries more emotion than Sutton's has since she returned. I step back, putting more space between us. It's weird to see him so broken over someone who hasn't mentioned him at all—even though I'm looking for answers from him about their relationship before, when he was all she cared about.

"I can't imagine how awful this has been for all of you."

I nod. I almost thank him, an instinctual response to the hundreds of empty condolences I've received since Sutton didn't come home that day, but then I remember: I don't have to console him. I didn't invite him here to patch his wounds.

He owes me answers.

"How is she?" he asks at the same time as I say, "Why did you have her car?" He lets out a pained half groan like he really may throw up.

"She lent it to me," he shares in a breathy rush. "We texted each other." He digs in his baggy jeans for his phone. "I showed them to the police."

"Then why didn't they find her Jeep for two days, Andrew?"

He deflates. His knuckles go white as his hand clenches his phone. He rests his arms on the deck railing as he stares at the water like he wishes it would swallow him whole. "I was scared."

He speaks so quietly, I can barely hear him.

"I was scared," he repeats. "I didn't know what they would do if they found me with her car. I had to get rid of it."

I suppress a chill that has nothing to do with the warm breeze. "Why?"

He lifts his gaze from his self-imposed punishment to look at me. "I didn't hurt your sister."

"I didn't say you did."

"Sutton loaned me her car to go to Seattle and meet a loan officer. She's been trying to help me—trying to help my family—with a financial issue." He looks down at his phone. Sutton smiles up at him from his lock screen. "She'd been trying for a long time."

"Here," he unlocks his phone and hands it to me. It's already open to their last text thread, like he'd been reading it when he last used his phone. "I realized I wasn't going to make it back to town in time to meet when I promised, so I texted her."

JUNE 13, 7:15 AM

Sutton: I'm outside. You wanna drive?

11:15 AM

Andrew*:* It's almost time for my meeting. Parking is free. I got it validated.

Sutton*:* YAY! I'll see you after school. I hope it goes well.

2:00 PM

Andrew*:* It's going great. We called my parents to discuss details and he's going to start working. My dad is heading to the credit union to get some of the documents he needs.

2:30 PM

Andrew*:* Running late. Should be leaving soon.

3:15 PM

Andrew*:* I don't think I'm going to be there on time. I'm just leaving. I'm probably going to get stuck in rush hour traffic.

3:50 PM

Andrew: Babe?

Are you getting my texts?

4:43 PM

Andrew*:* I'm at The Garden. Where are you?

I'm sorry I'm late.

Please answer your phone. I'm really sorry.

5:15 PM

Andrew: Sutton please

SUTTON ANSWER YOUR PHONE

7:26 PM

Andrew: Sutton please call me back. Tell me this is a
joke.

Where are you? I'm really worried.

"I showed all this to the police. They said she was last seen that afternoon around three. By the time I left Seattle, she was probably already gone."

"The meeting was your alibi," I confirm. He couldn't have taken or left with Sutton. I think of Dad telling me the story of our ancestors, how the daughter accused of killing their plantation owner was proven innocent because she was out of town at the time the crime occurred. *Justice was done in our favor then, and it will be done again*, Dad said. *No matter what.*

I hand Andrew back his phone. He scrolls through the thread one last time before dimming the screen. "She never got my texts," he says. "She didn't know I wouldn't be there in time. Maybe if I had..."

It wouldn't have made a difference. She was gone an hour

before they were supposed to meet. Whatever happened to Sutton didn't involve Andrew.

Unless she'd intentionally planned for him to be cleared of any suspicion.

"Why didn't you tell the cops about the car at the beginning? Why wait?"

He laughs. It's a dark melody, cold. "Are *you* really telling *me* I should have called the cops? You?"

"You had to have known how it would make you look."

"Of course I did!" he yells. "Of course, I knew how it would look for my rich, pretty girlfriend to disappear the same day she conveniently lent me her car. Two other Black teen girls have gone missing from Bend's End. I knew the police weren't going to take me at my word. Like I told you, I was scared. I ditched the car. The police found it on their own. I regret that, but I was scared."

"Wait—others have gone missing?"

"Yes, one two weeks before Sutton and another three weeks before her," Andrew says. "Sutton knew about them. She didn't seem scared, but that's why I was nervous to leave her without her car. Still, I thought—I thought she was safe. I thought she'd be okay. Your side of town usually has more security. I still don't understand. Why her?"

This is the first I'm hearing of other missing girls. No one mentioned this in Sutton's coverage. A pattern like that makes Sutton faking it seem less likely, unless she knew her disappearance could be blamed on whoever took those girls. But no one seems to have made the connection.

"Do you think the person who took the other girls is also behind what happened to Sutton?" I ask.

He leans against the railing again, his expression more pensive than self-hating. "I don't know," he finally answers. "I wish I did. How is she? Is she doing okay?"

Okay is a pretty open-ended term. "She doesn't have nightmares, but she hasn't talked about any of it. She basically watches her fish."

"Her fish?"

"We got her a goldfish. His name is Juliet."

"Has she asked for me?" he asks. "Do you think I could see her?"

I shake my head. "She doesn't ask for people." Except me. "She claims not to remember anything that happened. Or anyone from before." Except me. "Our parents have taken down all the photos of you in her room too, so I don't think she'll get a spark of recognition anytime soon either."

Andrew grimaces. "I guess your mom got what she wanted. She never liked me."

That surprises me, though I'm not sure why. It makes sense. She's always been protective of Sutton—and her reaching her goals without distraction. I want to ask what makes him so sure of that, but Ruth texts me again. The nanny called. She's ten min away, her message reads. He has to leave before she gets back. You should go too.

"We gotta go," I tell Andrew, showing him my phone. "Come on, I'll walk you to the bus. I need to order my rideshare anyway."

He toes out of his shoes for the journey to the front door. As I lock and close it behind me, he reaches into his jean pocket. I brace for him to show me the texts again. Desperation to be believed pulses from him like lights at a rave. I know all that happened must be much harder to deal with when he isn't allowed to talk to Sutton, but I can't fix this for him. My parents have a valid reason not to trust him.

I'm still not sure if I do.

"Can you give this to her?" He hands me a folded photo booth strip of him and Sutton. Her hair is in its typical flat-ironed style, and her smile is small but unguarded. He looks so much healthier than he does today. The photo is wrinkled, seemingly from living in his pocket. "I want her to have something of us. In case it helps her remember."

"Okay," I concede. I don't think it will shift anything, but it's easier to take the picture than to convince him of that.

"Maybe—" he hedges as we walk away from the Heights house. "Maybe you could help us see each other? Briefly? Not today, obviously. It doesn't even have to be soon, but if you could..."

I don't see Andrew getting an invitation to the house at any point in the near future, but he looks so dejected, I say, "Maybe."

He needs something to look forward to.

THIRTEEN

When my rideshare drops me off in front of our house, Mom and Sutton watch me from behind the trimmed hedges. Mom waves.

They're kneeling in front of Mom's neglected flower garden. Sutton squirms, wiping her bare legs where the grass touches it and pulling on her shorts to cover more skin. It's a useless effort. None of Sutton's summer clothes were chosen for modesty. Even the casual T-shirt she's wearing (that I assume Mom picked out) is practically open shoulder.

Sutton starts to stand, but Mom stops her. "You don't need to get up. Casey will join us," she tells her, though Sutton didn't ask, and I never offered. It reminds me of Ruth translating what her younger sister meant this morning. I guess with enough practice, a good caregiver can anticipate common requests. Mom has always been quick to adapt and understand people's needs. In her career, it's crucial to staying relevant and keeping an anchor seat. At home, her skills don't always transfer as well, but I guess it's been a long time since she was a teenage girl.

She turns to her monogrammed garden tote to pull out another pair of gloves. I'm not as allergic to dirt as Sutton has always pretended to be, but I already feel sticky after several hours with toddlers. Layering a new coat of mess in the growing afternoon heat was not how I planned to spend the rest of my day.

But as Sutton's smile reminds me, Mom's statement was not a request. She stares at me with satisfaction, daring me to resist.

I don't get to say no.

I accept the gloves and sit on Sutton's other side, cushioning her between Mom and me like the filling of a sandwich. She is the most crucial component after all.

She's humming the song from our ride to the pet shop again, but this time she adds lyrics to the melody. Despite her obvious discomfort, she returns to tending the blooms Mom assigned to her as I slip on my gloves. Her voice is soft and slightly uneven. She was never the best vocalist, but she doesn't seem to care.

"*The riverbed makes a mighty fine road,*" she whisper sings. She pats mulch around pink daisies and hands me the trowel Mom passes her without pausing. "*Dead trees will show you the way.*"

"What is that?" I ask her. This is the second time I've heard her repeat this melody.

She smiles up at me, the afternoon glow illuminating the auburn in her dark curls. "What?"

"The song, Sutton. You were singing it again."

Her contentment fades. She stills, gloved hands half buried in mulch. Like she's buffering, waiting for the right reaction to load.

Mom pauses for her response.

Sutton doesn't move for so long, a passing butterfly lands on her exposed shoulder. It settles and opens its metallic-blue wings, nearly brushing her ponytailed ringlets. She doesn't even notice. She seems preoccupied with how to talk her way out of this.

"Mom," I say. "You heard it, right? She was singing that song from the car. Tell me you remember."

But Mom has stopped listening. She's shed one of her gloves to use the camera on her phone. She has it pointed at the two of us but mainly Sutton. "Don't move, sweetie," she says quietly. "I want to get a picture of the butterfly on your shoulder. You both look so beautiful."

At the mention of the butterfly, Sutton jolts her shoulder to shake it off. It launches into flight, fluttering in front of her face for an extended breath, almost like a stare down. She glares at it. Her hands flex in the dirt, but before she can lift them, the butterfly takes off. Sutton returns to the daisies.

"There goes a family Christmas card opportunity." Mom attempts to laugh it off, but I can tell she's disappointed. "We'll get some photos of you both soon. It's so special to be together again."

I hear what she leaves unsaid. That having a few family shots to share when she returns to work will be a good way to thank the community that rallied around us while Sutton was gone.

Sutton would have never willingly ruined a photo opportunity like that before. The Sutton of before never ruined anyone's day but mine. She was always game for the perfect photo, whether a candid or carefully staged "spontaneous" shot. Mom and she would trade phones to make sure they had the best angle on their selfies. She always helped me if I asked, though I rarely did.

I've long been a lost cause for Mom's posturing and planning. I'd never intentionally sabotage her efforts, but I don't get into creating these photo-perfect moments. Not like Sutton. They bonded over preparing for Mom's promotional shots together and attending family-centered events Mom was assigned to cover. The network didn't usually need more than one kid to showcase, so I didn't often have to beg out of her camera-ready commitments. After a while, her employers stopped requesting that I join.

Sometime after my kindergarten cheeks slimmed out of age-appropriate cuteness and the melanin in my skin didn't fade in the winter, one Cureton daughter was enough to cement Mom as the most comfortably "woke" family-friendly reporter in the Pacific Northwest. Hip enough to be married to a Black historian, but white enough to keep senior audience numbers steady in western Washington's urban liberal paradise.

Sutton is lighter-skinned. She can tolerate the time it takes to flat iron her curls. She's older. She's more *acceptably* diverse. It made sense.

I never blamed Mom for not pushing harder to include me in her career. I didn't want in.

Sutton did.

Now she doesn't.

I wonder how Mom feels about that. I know she cares how we look to the outside world. She knows the power of the media. That was the entire reasoning behind the Home Again Narrative. *It's not enough that they know she's missing,* she said. *The community has to know* her. *They have to care. They have to love her like we do. Or she'll disappear all over again.*

Does she still want the world to care about Sutton now that she's back? Or does she just want Sutton to care about being back? Mom has never had to work this hard to keep Sutton's attention or get her to agree to anything, even small tasks.

They rarely fought before. But they must have fought over Andrew, or he wouldn't have been so certain that his absence pleased my mother.

Sutton was always the perfect daughter. What would my mother do if Sutton strayed from that path? I watch Mom lift a manicured hand, still ungloved, toward Sutton's hair. Sutton shakes free of her touch before she can smooth any strands. Mom retreats, putting on her glove and picking up the other trowel to loosen the dirt around her rosebush.

"Mom?" I ask. "Did you know two other Black girls went missing before Sutton?"

Mom turns to face me so fast, a scoop of dirt slingshots at

Sutton, hitting her square in the chest. Mom scrambles forward to help her brush it off, but Sutton sees the dirt and screams.

It's a not a shocked shriek of surprise. Nor is it a cry of disgust. It's a full-bodied, breathtaking bellow of terror. In my worst nightmares, I never envisioned my sister capable of a wail this unsettling. Mom stops like she's been slapped.

Sutton's cry ends and is followed by shuddering gasps. She shakes as she drags her still-gloved hands down her chest, streaking her top with dirt. "Get it off! Get it off!" she repeats. "Get it off! I can taste it."

She pulls and rips at the fabric of her shirt. I can see the star pattern on her Victoria's Secret bra underneath.

"I can taste it," she sobs, clawing at her neck, her gloves painting her collarbone an even darker brown.

"There's no way you can taste it," I try to point out. "It hit your chest. None of it is on your face or your mouth. You can't taste it."

She grabs my wrist, her hold unexpectedly strong. "Casey," she pleads, her eyes brimming with tears and terrified. "Help me. Please."

Mom scoops up Sutton from behind, lifting her from under her armpits into a standing position. "It's okay," she soothes, leading her back to the house. "Everything will be fine. Let's get you inside. I'm going to help you wash off the dirt. We don't have to do that again. How is that, Sutton?"

At the threshold of the door, Sutton turns back to me,

abandoned in the garden. Mom squeezes her shoulders in reassurance, but she doesn't look at me. Sutton is still shuddering.

"I'm fine," I say. "Go with Mom. Let her help you clean up."

They leave. I take off my gloves. I can still see the imprint of Sutton's grip around my wrist. The phantom of her fingers slowly concedes to my normal complexion. I can't tell if it's going to bruise.

I want to wash today away too, but it's more than the lack of hot water they're certainly using up that's delaying me. Nothing about today has gone how I expected.

Or how I wanted, if my mind were clear enough to actually know what that is.

Andrew was broken. I had known he would be. He was fragile while Sutton was missing. I never thought he'd admit to hurting my sister on Ruth's deck, but the reality of him disappointed me.

The missing car threw me, but Andrew always seemed incapable of hurting Sutton. From the start, he was the one destined to be destroyed by their relationship. Every version of their story could only end with him wrung dry and forgotten, even if she had never gone missing. I just didn't realize that would be the literal outcome.

I get up and drag myself to the house. I hope I've given them enough time to get upstairs and run the bath. I don't want to trigger Sutton's clinginess at the sight of me again.

My hypothesis is correct. The living room is clear of everyone but Dad and a pile of books. He's at the dining table again, wearing Mom's favorite sweater-vest of his—proof he has not stepped outside our air-conditioned house today.

He doesn't hear me come in. His hands are on his keyboard, but his eyes are on the stairs, not his laptop screen. Sutton's outburst was a disconcerting distraction for all of us.

"Hey, Daddy," I say as I slip into one of the chairs. I pull the least ancient-looking book from his piles toward me, taking care to open it gently. *African-American Slave Medicine*, the title page reads.

This definitely isn't more family photos for the heirloom table.

"Good afternoon, baby girl," he says, refocusing. "How was your visit with Ruth?"

"Fine." I flip to the table of contents. It's not a very long book when it comes to Dad's typical research tomes. It's barely one hundred and fifty pages, two hundred if you count the appendixes. "She said she's looking forward to coming over here when we're comfortable having visitors."

Dad makes the effort to look me in the eye when he talks to me. "I think that would be great," he says. "Hopefully we can plan something soon."

I nod but don't ask about a specific date, despite the fact Mom had no problem making time to invite Sutton's friends. I know that in our current state, the idea of making plans is more comparable to a wish than a map anyone could actually follow.

"What are you working on?" I ask. "Is this for the genealogy company?"

"Nah," he says. "I'm on family leave from consulting at Familiar Roots. I technically don't need to be working on anything, but—"

"But you like to keep busy," I finish for him. He smiles at me. I'm happy for it. His attention doesn't come with strings, doesn't tie me in any complicated emotional knots. It's simply love. Uncomplicated. Unconditional. Mine. I don't have to share.

At least not right now.

He lifts from his chair and leans over to point at the table of contents I have open. Each chapter title bears a different focus on the medical practices of and for African American slaves during the era around the Civil War, but Dad's index finger points at the fourth section. "Conjuring and Hoodoo," the chapter heading declares.

"I'm considering pitching a new course to the university on hoodoo magic during slavery and its ties to modern-day African American spirituality," he says as he returns to his seat. He picks up one of the older books and starts to extend it toward me but pauses. "Can you be careful?"

"Yes," I promise.

He hands it to me. I can feel its age before I open it. It smells divine, that perfect scent of old paper mixed with a spicy herbal overtone like it was steeped in Ma Remy's kitchen.

"This belonged to Henny," Dad says.

"Mima's mother, right?" I clarify. "The one she drew." The sketch is hard to forget: Henny's intense gaze and that scar across her face, creeping into her shaved hairline. I've gone back and forth on asking Dad if he knew what injury caused it, but I'm not sure I truly want to know.

"Yes," he says, his smile growing wider with pride. "Your fourth great-grandma. This was her medicine book, though it was mainly written by her grandson while she dictated what to include. She could read some basic words but was never taught how to write, so this book was put together long after they finally found their freedom. I'm using it as a starting point, then will cross-reference it with my more modern academic sources. If I know what slaves at the time were using certain treatments for, I can avoid repeating misinformed interpretations that other historians may have claimed."

"You mean lied about," I say.

"Casey." He tries to scold me, but I can hear his amusement. "Most accounts outside living history must deal with healthy debate among qualified historians, but that doesn't mean any one interpretation is untrue. One must be extra careful when examining material that had important spiritual meaning."

"And this is spiritual?" I ask, setting Henny's book back on the table. I don't know if I should be touching anything sacred. My track record for good luck—let alone miracles—is sorely lacking.

"No," Dad says. "It's a plant book. It shares the most common remedies slaves on her plantation used to treat illness and injury when their masters couldn't or wouldn't help. It includes drawings and some pressed clippings of their most common herbs too. It's not a prayer book. It was never professionally printed or even submitted to a publisher. I'm only using it to check a direct source's perspective on some of the things suggested in my later academic sources."

"Against the hoodoo," I say. "The stuff that isn't real."

"The rootwork. The conjure," he says. "It's not about whether I believe or not. I'm not trying to prove or disprove that. That's not what I want this curriculum to be about." He straightens a lop-sided pile of library books near the edge of the table. "My mama believed in this stuff. Well, some of it, you know."

I laugh lightly. Oh yeah, Grandma Remy was definitely superstitious.

"Your grandmother wouldn't want me to make money on our ancestors' rituals, even if it is to paint a more factually correct account of what those rituals may have been truly for."

"What do *you* want, Daddy?"

"The documents I'm gathering and the interpretation I hope to share—I mean, what I hope potential students will take from this course—is that these practices gave slaves power. Rootwork and conjure gave our ancestors a source of hope during a time of great helplessness. These practices were believed to ease their suffering." He clears his throat again and gently lifts Henny's book before placing it near him. "I believe there's a connection to modern Black spirituality and civil work in faith and worship."

"I think it's a great idea," I tell him. "I think the university is going to love it."

Grandma would too.

FOURTEEN

Andrew's gift is burning a hole in my pocket.

I'm not even wearing my jacket anymore—it's hanging on my chair—but I can still feel the photo paper between the pads of my fingers. I've been trying to distract myself, mindlessly watching old tour clips of Ivy James on my laptop, but I can't stop peeking at it. Checking on it like the photo strip is going to climb out of my jacket and walk to Sutton's room all by itself.

She has nothing of him in her room. I keep thinking about how she lingered on that picture of the two of them on my phone the other day. The ghost of her, of who they used to be to each other back when the worst thing that had ever happened to her was being my sister.

If she's truly faking, she probably misses him a lot. But if she's faking, why should I ease her suffering? If she's putting us through this hell on purpose, the last thing I want is to make it easier on her.

No one has tried to make any of this easier for me.

But if she isn't faking...

If what happened to her was so horrible, her mind erased everything that came before...

I don't even know where to start processing that. Yet she remembered the bracelet. There was no hiding that.

I'm not going to let Andrew become my problem. I slide my computer off my lap and hop off my bed before grabbing the ragged print from my jacket. If this memento gets anyone in trouble, it won't be me. Maybe being caught with it and yelled at by our parents will trigger some memory in Sutton, and all our problems will be solved.

As I approach her door, she's humming her song again, sitting in front of Juliet's tank, which seems to be her new hobby. She's wearing cloud-patterned pajamas and Mom's best robe, but her hair is still wet and dripping down her back.

"Why isn't Mom helping you with your hair?" I ask her. I'm a little shocked she'd leave Sutton alone with soaking hair. With all this babying, I half expected Mom to be pressed against Sutton's back, sectioning out her locks like she did when we were kids. Sutton and I used to trade off the torture of wash day, sitting both smug and sympathetic in front of the other while Mom re-created the protective styles Ma Remy taught her.

Sutton liked to make a game out of handing Mom hair bands and other decorative elements like ribbons and beads. Before she started middle school and decided she was old enough to do her own hair alone, Sutton would create secret codes with her choices that I would spend the next week trying to decipher.

"I don't like it when she touches me," Sutton says, still staring at the fish tank but dipping her chin toward the rug. If I didn't know better, I'd call it shame.

"You can't sleep on wet hair." She must know this, amnesia aside. It's obvious she does because I've walked past her bedroom around this time of night several times since she returned—neither Mom nor Dad closes her door when they leave her room, and Sutton doesn't seem to care about her privacy anymore. If she weren't concerned about damaging her hair, she'd watch her water-locked friend from the comfort of her duvet.

I sigh. I'm already regretting it as I open my mouth, but the gods of natural hair care would smite me if I didn't ask. "Do you want me to help you prep it for bed?"

She smiles at me, teeth on display like a wolf post-kill. "Yes, please."

"Wait here," I instruct, though it's not like she's going anywhere. I slip back into my room to grab my styling kit, then I sit behind Sutton, in the spot where Mom should be, and hand her the jar of miniature rubber bands, the rattail comb, and my best curl cream to hold while I work. Her hair won't be completely dry when I'm done, but if I braid it at least it won't tangle.

Then, before I can talk myself out of it, I also give her Andrew's photo strip.

She carefully nestles the products between her legs so she can properly examine the print. She leans forward to look at it, but my hands are already in her hair. "Sorry," I say, "but I need you to stay still for me."

"I trust you," she says.

I bite back the instinctive urge to reply, *Don't.*

She lifts the strip to examine it. The glow of the tank casts it an almost clinical light. She stares at it for the time it takes me to section off her entire head of hair. I'm unfurling the first section to braid when she says, "I know him."

"Yeah," I say. "I showed you a picture the other day. Hand me the comb."

She lifts the comb, careful not to move her shoulders or neck with the gesture. "No," she says. Her thumb rubs at a discoloration on the edge of the strip. "I know him." I can see her smile in the reflection of the aquarium glass. It falters. "What's his name?"

Oh yes, the first question of someone who *definitely* remembers the boyfriend they repeatedly abandoned me for.

I pull tight as I use the comb's edge to create a part. Sutton doesn't flinch. "His name is Andrew," I tell her. "He's your boyfriend."

"Rain or shine," she says.

I have no idea what that is supposed to mean.

I hand the comb back to her. "Open the curl cream and lift it so I can scoop it." She sets the picture on the floor so she can use both hands to unscrew the lid of the tub. She holds it like anointing oil above her head. I dip in two fingers and scoop out enough to moisturize this section. "You can place it back down for now." I begin to braid.

After returning the cream to its spot, she starts to reach for the strip again but stops herself. There's no product on her hands—though mine will need a thorough rinse when I'm finished—so she has no reason not to touch it.

"Sutton," I begin, though my gut churns to even ask this question. "Did Andrew hurt you? Or..." I lean forward to grab a few rubber bands, not wanting to distract her while she thinks about her response. "Do you think he might have hurt you?"

"Before?" she asks.

"When you were gone," I confirm, sealing off one braid and starting another.

"No," she says with the same certainty she had about Grandma's bracelet. "I think he made me happy."

Okay. Well, that's reassuring. I'm not sure I can trust much of what she says if she's really traumatized, but I trust she's telling the truth about that.

We fall into silence. I watch Sutton watch Juliet. In the reflection of the tank, she catches me looking at her as I begin the third section of braids. Her dark pupils seem like the entrance to an endless cavern. Is my sister really in there?

"I don't think they liked him," she says. "Before."

"Who?" I ask, though I think I know the answer.

Sutton doesn't elaborate. She doesn't look away from my gaze in the glass either.

"Are you talking about our parents? Their feelings for Andrew are separate from their feelings for you. Did they—Do you think they hurt you?"

My mind spirals. *Did Mom hurt you? Is that why you won't let her touch you?* Mom can be short-tempered about petty, shallow things, but I don't want to believe she could ever—no. She couldn't. She wouldn't.

Sutton finally breaks eye contact. "I think I hurt them," she says quietly. She touches the photo again, but she doesn't pick it up. "Can I keep this?"

My plan had been to give the picture to Sutton and let her deal with the consequences alone, but I forgot how entangled we've become. Her hair suddenly feels like vines creeping up my arms. If I leave this with her and our parents catch her with it, she won't go down alone. They'll know it wasn't something she found in her desk, that it came from outside—and that will lead directly back to me. Maybe they'd get mad at her, but I'd be the one they would punish.

"Can you keep it a secret?" I ask her. It's a risk, not only because the Sutton I know would jump at the opportunity to get me in trouble, but this Sutton is unpredictable in her own way. Still, I don't want to take it back, and the only other choice is to destroy it. Something about that feels wrong, even though it's probably the safest option.

Sutton nods, pulling the hair in my hands with the movement. "Sorry," she says, straightening.

I tighten my grip on her roots. "This is serious, Sutton," I say. "You can't tell Mom and Dad. Do you understand?"

She doesn't move. Neither do her eyes in the tank's reflection.

"If you can keep this between us, maybe I can figure out a way you can see the real Andrew." She can't help but sit up at this possibility. I press her shoulders down again. "But if you tell on me, you will *never* see him again."

"I can do it. You can trust me." She picks up the photo once more. "Rain or shine," she repeats.

"Uh-huh," I say, unconvinced. I return to braiding. Soon, she starts to hand me rubber bands without prompting and lifts the curl cream to help me prep a new section as soon as she feels the weight of the last rest against her neck. I catch her eyes every now and then in the distorted reflection. She smiles at me again but in a different way than she has before.

It feels less stifling, less predatory. It's calm. Content.

"This is good, right?" she asks.

"What?"

She lifts the photo strip, pointing at Andrew. "If I start to remember, everything will get better. They won't be so sad."

"No," I agree. "They won't be sad. But they will be pissed if you show them that. Maybe you should try to remember something about our family before sharing this newfound *progress* with them. Something a little less...romantic, maybe."

"I'll try," Sutton says.

I stifle the urge to roll my eyes. I won't be holding my breath.

FIFTEEN

My hands still smell like coconut after I wash them twice.

My own scalp itches, neglected, as I head from the bathroom back to my room. Sutton is still awake as I pass hers; she's watching Juliet from her bed with her new crown of fresh braids.

I crawl under my own covers as soon as I close my bedroom door behind me. Despite my exhaustion and aching hands, sleep eludes me. I shift and shuffle countless times. I will my mind to shut down behind my traitorous eyelids, but my thoughts blare like the green charging light on Sutton's old laptop, glowing from underneath my bed like a monster waiting to devour me.

I slide off my bed to the cold floor and pull it out. I unplug it as I flip it open. I know it's fully charged. It's been doing nothing but charge for days now.

I've tried every password I could think of. Sutton's birthday, Romeo's birthday, Romeo's adoption day, the day she got on the cheer squad—every relevant date I could think of, and several more I figured out by studying her social media timelines more intensely than I ever wanted. I've tried nicknames from her comments. I tried the name of the restaurant that seems to be her and Andrew's favorite—the Garden, a small diner in Bend's End. No luck.

I even tried my own birthday, that's how fruitless my attempts have been.

But her comment about the photo strip repeats like an Ivy chorus in my mind. I've never heard her say that before.

I type it slowly, careful around the missing keys: rainorshine

The password field shakes. Another wrong answer, but I know I'm close.

I try it again, changing the capitalization: RainOrShine

No.

Okay. Maybe she used some numbers. I replace the *O* with a zero, first all lowercase and then with two variations of capitalization. No. No. No.

I try replacing the *I* with a one.

Nothing.

A few more tries, and then I'm looking at her desktop wallpaper, a photo of Sutton and the squad holding a hand-painted WILD WILLOW CHEER sign. I feel so victorious, I can almost hear them shouting in my ear like I've scored a touchdown. I did it. I finally unlocked the laptop.

I stare at their motionless excitement for a full minute before the screen starts to dim with inactivity. I'm finally inside her laptop, and I have no idea what to look for.

I move a finger across the touch pad to keep the screen open and peruse the icons on her desktop. In the corner, minimized, is one of the applications she must have opened when she last used this computer.

I don't know how relevant it will be, as the cracks crisscrossing the screen remind me that she hasn't touched this in months, but it's a start.

It's a video-playing software, paused halfway through a clip.

I pull the cursor back to the start, lower the volume, and press play.

Sutton looks at the lens straight on, her face taking up most of the frame for the first minute or so as she adjusts the camera. She steps back to judge her handiwork, revealing she's in the school gym. After a few more adjustments, she seems confident in her work and walks onto the mat.

She's wearing red lipstick, a crop top over a sports bra, and school uniform shorts. She tightens her straightened hair, which she wears in a high pony, and begins to stretch. Slowly, other teammates arrive and join her, but I keep watching Sutton.

Even from a distance, I can see her smile. She laughs at something one of the other girls says. I assume it's their captain, based on the deference the others give her and the authority that reminds me of the leader at the yogurt shop. The captain shakes her head in disbelief at whatever Sutton says. My sister grins wickedly and jogs to the farthest corner of the gym.

The squad clears out, moving toward the periphery of the room. Sutton starts running, then tumbles through the air. She cartwheels across the gym three times before she stops, once flipping without even touching her hands to the ground. The team whistles and yells their support the entire time.

The captain half-heartedly dismisses them, but she doesn't seem annoyed with Sutton. They break into smaller groups, and some start complicated lifts, while others repeat choreographed dance moves. Sutton is in one of the dance groups, but it's clear she's also watching one of the other groups. She gets called out on it twice.

The second time, Sutton struggles to return to her assigned task, especially when Coach McCoy shows up. Her teammates all rush to greet him, but she holds back. She stands at the back of the crowd while he finishes a call, something about personal training at a corporate retreat. When he releases her teammates to start the next stage of practice, she comes back to where she left the camera.

For a moment I think she's going to turn off the camera, but she doesn't. The view falls into darkness—covered by her sports bag?—and I hear her muffled steps. I'm not the only one who thinks she's leaving.

"Cureton!" yells Coach McCoy. "Where do you think you're going?"

"Nowhere, Coach," Sutton says. "I'm moving my bag closer to

the mat so I can get at my water easier." She places her water bottle close to the lens when she moves away this time. It blocks the view of half the gym, and I can't see her through the tinted plastic as she returns to her group.

The only people visible are those in the pyramid and Coach McCoy. The girls are all dressed similar to Sutton, but their coach looks...kind of half-assed, to be honest. He's wearing the expected school logo jacket and sweatpants, but his shoes are rather dirty considering they aren't outside, and he keeps checking his watch like he's bored. Like he's not being paid to be there.

I can't see Sutton for the next five minutes, and I'm close to fast-forwarding until I hear her addressed again.

"Cureton!" Coach yells. "This isn't some urban step team. Get your head in the game and memorize these moves, or give your spot on the mat to someone else."

"Sorry," Sutton says. The captain's voice chimes in to tell their coach she also had to remind Sutton to stay on task before he arrived.

"Three times?" he asks Sutton, but it doesn't feel like a question so much as an insult. I wish I could see her face. She must be raging. "What's going on with you today?"

"I—" Sutton starts and stops, but Coach makes a "hurry up" gesture, so she continues, "I'm distracted by the pyramid."

"You're not in the pyramid."

"I know—"

"I'm not gonna put you in the pyramid if you can't manage basic choreography."

"I'm not asking to be in the pyramid."

"Then why does it have your full attention?"

"I'm worried for Natalie. I feel like she could get hurt."

Now that she's mentioned by name, I recognize Natalie and her strawberry-blond locks in the group assigned to the pyramid. Natalie doesn't have her cast in this video, so I guess Sutton was right to be concerned about her. Was this stunt how she got injured?

"That's not your job to worry." Coach McCoy dismisses Sutton. "It's mine. Keep your mind on your own responsibilities if you really want to avoid people getting hurt."

"Yes, Coach," Sutton says. "Sorry, Coach."

I watch for another five minutes, but nothing interesting happens. I skim through another ten minutes of footage and even less happens. Then the battery on her camera must've run out because the recording stops.

It's weird to see Sutton not excelling at something. Her flips at the start were impressive to a complete cheer virgin like me, but I barely know what to call the stunts they were practicing, even after years of overhearing sport talk on the way to and from school, practice, and the competitions I was forced to attend with the family. And I certainly had no idea about the social politics on the squad.

I didn't join the marching band because I was nervous about being critiqued in front of others. I don't like crowds. I don't like admitting my mistakes. I could never put myself on display in front of hundreds of people, asking them to pick apart everything from my stance to the perkiness of my smile. Sutton's been learning how to play a part for far longer than I ever realized.

I poke around the laptop again, but she didn't have other applications open when she shut down the computer last, so I start digging for useful information.

Her Notes app seems like a good place to start, but it's pretty boring and stereotypical. Her most recently edited note is literally titled Wishlist for the next Sephora sale. In addition to obvious homework notes, she also has files for Andrew money ideas, Cheer scouting, and Low-income homeowner programs.

I'm about to give up on this avenue when I see Birthday ideas for Casey.

I can't help myself. I open it.

- Money
- Driving Lessons
- Record Player (and Ivy vinyl to start her collection)

My birthday was two weeks after she broke this laptop. She got me a gift card to Starbucks. I'm pretty certain it's not because she couldn't remember her original ideas. She didn't even bother buying a card to go with it, obviously still angry about Ma Remy's bracelet.

Still, it's unsettling to find proof of what she thinks about me. That she has kind thoughts, that she listens enough to consider a thoughtful and generous gift idea, even if she didn't follow through.

I close out the Notes app. I've seen movies and crime dramas. I know how to find useful information about someone from their electronic device. I need to stop messing around with stuff that isn't going to help me.

I open the browser and click into her search history. My sister had an obscure password, but—thank God—she's not smart enough to erase her search history.

The last page she visited is from the same day she tossed the laptop from the railing. It's timed an hour after we all came home, probably minutes before she came to demand the bracelet back.

search results 1–20 for "talking to your sister when you have a bad relationship"

I know that has nothing to do with why she went missing, especially since it happened months before, but my stomach tightens all the same. That's the only web page she visited that day.

The previous few weeks are similarly useless: lots of YouTube binges of other cheer teams' performances and makeup reviewers, nothing incriminating or noteworthy. Not until I'm a month into her search history do I find something interesting.

Fire Text | Send Messages in Secret

I scroll down to the beginning of that day for context to what led her there. It starts out fairly innocent, with searches on what I can do to help fix gentrification followed by gift ideas for boy-friend, but three hours later, it takes a hard turn.

search results 1–20 for "Do adults use WhatsApp"

search results 1–20 for "parents WhatsApp"

WhatsApp Safety: a how-to guide for parents—
    Internet Matters

search results 1–20 for "message someone privately
    without WhatsApp"

search results 1–20 for "burner phone app"

I open the Fire Text web page. It's an app for having pri-vate conversations without interference. I don't understand why Sutton would ever need such an app though. What happened after searching for gifts for Andrew that could have possibly led her to this?

I guess your mom finally got what she always wanted, Andrew said at Ruth's. Could Mom's disapproval of their relationship really have pushed them this far? What could they have needed to talk about that they didn't want to risk our parents reading if they broke into Sutton's laptop or phone—a privacy invasion they have never once exercised?

The images and potential texts my mind cues up as explana-tions are so gross, I have to suppress a gag. I'm not sure I want to see what they worked so hard to hide. But if those messages had anything to do with her disappearance...

I have to look.

I open the Fire Text app online since I don't have access to Sutton's phone. There's another password lock, but luck is on my side this time, and it's the same as her laptop.

There's only one chat thread, which reinforces the Secret Boyfriend Sexts theory. I hover above the link for a long moment, dreading opening it. The contact she's texting is labeled Hard End. Ew.

You don't have to read everything, I remind myself. I can skim—really, really fast—and look for parts that seem relevant to what happened to her. I pray there are no pictures.

There aren't. At least not among the most recent messages, which were from the week leading up to the afternoon she disappeared.

There's something much worse.

JUNE 4, 3:43 PM

Hard End: We'll meet tomorrow?

Sutton: Tomorrow. Alone.

JUNE 6, 9:05 PM

Hard End: I have everything for Friday.

10:27 PM

Sutton: Great. See you then.

Hard End: You bitch. You lied to me.

Sutton: This is over.

Hard End: No, it's not.

Sutton: Stop texting me. You know better. Or do you
    want everyone to find out about this too?

Hard End: I don't give a shit anymore.

I'm not kidding.

I will end you.

SUTTON

THREE YEARS BEFORE

I would rather die than be here right now.

The darkness of the Heights Above church during Sunday sermons seems counter to its name. You'd think they'd want to flood the congregation in light, a blessing from actual heights above, yet the only light from heaven is focused solely on Pastor Heights on the stage. His haloed image echoes on the huge screens behind him, broadcasting his face twice as large as he stands tall to the congregants in the farthest seats of the amphitheater.

"It warms my heart to see so many families here today," Ruth's dad bellows into his microphone on the stage. I don't know how he can see any of us through the spotlight illuminating him, but who knows—perhaps God granted him vision to see each of us in the crowd and those watching the live stream or replays at home.

Casey isn't sitting with us today. She's in the front row with

Ruth, her mom, and the other Heights kids, like they're her actual family. Mom and Dad are on either side of me. I don't want to be here, but I take one of their hands in each of my own and squeeze to remind them that I am. I'm sitting here with them like a proper daughter should. I'm not even on my phone. I wish I were.

I was not given a choice about attending today. I would much rather have stayed home alone or visited Ma Remy. She knows better than to step foot inside this place. *I don't need a shelter to find my spirituality*, she'd say. *My lord is in you.* I wish I could go to the church she describes from growing up. I bet her church would have bright windows. I bet it would be bathed in color, as joyful and alive as her treasured gospel records.

At least I have Sunday dinner at her place to look forward to in exchange for sitting through this.

"I've been thinking a lot about families lately," the pastor continues. "Especially local ones here in our beautiful Willow Bend. I know we come here to replenish and rejoice in the Lord and all the incredible blessings He has bestowed upon us, but sometimes we must also come together to discuss hard truths. To face hardships even if we feel they don't apply to us. But the suffering of those around us is as important as our own. Remember, we are commanded to love our neighbor as ourself."

Some of the adults sitting around us shift in their seats, like several of them realized they were sitting on their keys or their phone at the exact same time. Mom and Dad don't move like the others, but Dad squeezes my hand tighter on the armrest.

THE SHADOW SISTER

"'Carry each other's burdens,' says Galatians 6:2, 'and in this way you will fulfill the law of Christ.' Many of our neighbors are feeling a burden that I know from personal experience can be all-consuming. The terror of poverty was designed to eat at your faith as surely as it devours everything else in your life. A threadbare body with an empty stomach hungers for earthly desires more strongly than it craves divine sustenance. It is harder to submit to the Lord in moments like these, but it never more important."

He looks down with a pitying smile at someone in the front row. We're not seated so far from the stage for me to recognize the recipient, but I bet even those in the very back can tell he's looking at his wife, Grace Heights. She's nine months pregnant with their seventh child, so she doesn't stand for the camera, but she lifts a hand before pressing it to her heart in support.

"There is a lot of blame being thrown around as to the root of the suffering in our town. I am not here to relitigate that." The anxiousness of those seated around us eases, but I only grow more restless. "Fear of change is natural. To try something new after years, perhaps decades, of routine is justifiably daunting but also an incredible opportunity."

I don't quite understand what the pastor is attempting to get at until Dad scoffs under his breath next to me. Mom sighs at him. "Behave, please."

"Sorry," Dad whispers. "I'll let him get back to defending the causes of the Great Migration."

"Isaiah," she tries, but she stifles a laugh. "It's not the place."

185

Dad nods and refocuses his attention, but his comment recontextualizes the entire sermon for me. His last book was on the Great Migration, a period from soon after the turn of the twentieth century until just before Dad was born in the seventies when millions of Black Americans moved from the South to other areas of the country. Ultimately, the results of this mass relocation were positive in many cultural ways, but Casey and I walked the journey with him as he explained his research while writing. It wasn't all good news.

Most people who left the areas they called home their entire life did so because they couldn't afford to live there anymore, both financially and socially. They didn't really have much of a choice. The uncertainty of the future was better than the reality of their present.

"The world we live in now likes to demonize those who seek to improve their lot and provide for those they love, when the truth couldn't be further opposite. God rewards his most faithful. Faith is the strongest currency we have. Trusting in Him is the best investment anyone can make."

Pastor Heights keeps talking as church staff walk down the aisles, passing collection plates down each row. "You should never feel guilty for doing what is best for your family," he says. "The housing issues in our town are not the consequence of prosperity rightfully earned through hard work and dedication like I know lives in this congregation. If anyone should be blamed, it should be our local government. But that doesn't mean that we can't help."

He smiles down at Grace again. "I'm honored to announce a new outreach initiative in which we would love your support. We are scouting real estate opportunities to begin work on Rise Above, a camp for at-risk youth in our community. We hope to offer it at an extremely discounted rate or even free, if we can raise enough to cover the costs."

Applause breaks out all around us along with the sound of shuffling purses and wallets opening to contribute to the shining copper collection plates glittering in every direction. I think of the families in Dad's book, leaving everything they knew behind to move north to places like Willow, just to face a similar ultimatum generations later.

"You okay, darling?" Mom asks.

"Yeah," I lie as the pastor continues to preach.

"Faith has always had its cost..." he says.

"I think I'm getting a headache," I tell Mom. "Can I go to the bathroom?"

"Of course, hon. Hurry back."

I flash her a smile, then I maneuver my way out of the row. But as soon as I'm in the clear, I sit on a bench in the hallway and take my time to bask in the small miracle of silence instead.

I didn't think anything could be worse than the pastor's sermon, but after almost forty-five minutes of my parents' "quick goodbyes," I'm mourning the time I was at least sitting down while I suffered.

"Where's Casey?" I ask no one in particular. More than anything else, it's an attempt to remind my parents I'm still here.

"I don't know, baby girl," Dad says. He makes a gesture like he's holding a golf club, slowing his imaginary swing while a white guy with a thick salt-and-pepper beard watches thoughtfully. "Probably with Ruth still. Do you want to go get her?"

"If I do, can we go home?"

My parents and their friends laugh like I've made a great joke, but they nod before resuming their conversations. I will take that as a binding contract.

Dad's likely right about Casey's location, so I head to the large group in the slowly thinning lobby crowd. If Casey is still with Ruth and the rest of the pastor's family, they'll be at the center of the conversation.

I weave through the congregation like I'm parting my own Red Sea.

As if to mock me, I find Casey and Ruth right in front of the door. I can see the parking lot from here. I'm so close to salvation and yet so, so far.

"Hi, Sutton!" Ruth smiles as brightly as her multicolored braces. I don't comment on how her new lisp messed up my name.

"Hi, Ruth. It's nice to see you," I say. To my sister, I get straight to the point. "Casey, Mom and Dad sent me to get you. It's time to go."

They frown at each other as if they won't be together literally tomorrow at school. Middle schoolers are so dramatic.

"Do you want to come over to my house for the afternoon?" Casey asks Ruth. "We can drop you off at home on the way to Ma Remy's for dinner."

"Case—" I start, but Ruth replies before I can shut them down.

"My dad probably wouldn't like that, it being Sunday and all." She frowns. "But I bet if we ask my mom instead, she'll say yes!"

The two of them dive back into the crowd before I can say anything. I follow their path of giggles and sprinkled *excuse me*s. They only stop when they reach their target.

Grace Heights holds a more captive audience than her husband. She glows even with the shadows of sleep deprivation under her eyes. Mothers gather around her, interacting with Ruth's two-and-a-half-year-old twin sisters, who are in their stroller, happy for the attention.

"I'm officially due a week from Wednesday, but Esther could come any day now," Grace tells her congregation. "Do you hear that, angel girl?" She addresses her belly directly. "Mama says it's time to get out!"

Everyone laughs at that, even Ruth and Casey. I smile.

"Should you even be here today?" asks one of the mothers. "I know your pregnancy with the twins took a lot out of you."

Understatement of the century. Three separate sermons in the final months of that pregnancy were little more than hour-long prayer sessions for the continued health and safety of Grace and her baby girls.

"I want to be here," Grace promises. "I enjoy supporting David and seeing all of you. I know I'll probably miss a few sermons once Esther arrives, so I'm trying to take it in, you know?"

There's murmured agreement among the adults before one of them asks about her plans for the actual birth. I press at Casey's back, urging her and Ruth to ask their question before this group gets carried away in conversation, but my sister twists her head to glare at me—her beaded braids twirling in judgment like Medusa's snakes—before returning her attention to Grace.

I'm never gonna leave this place.

"We're actually planning a home birth this time," Grace says.

That must be a very interesting topic for middle-aged moms because this single sentence sets Grace's audience alight. They have tons of questions and anecdotes to share. Lots of opinions too.

"My cousin did a home birth with her second, she said—"

"I'd never. I mean, even if I could get my house clean enough, my kids would be such a nuisance—"

"I've read some really inspiring articles on how home birth is a much more biblical way of—"

I have no idea what they're talking about. I only took sex ed last semester, and it didn't really teach me much. Mom tried to fill in the gaps, but that was even worse. I feel small and uninformed. Cheer has taught me more about my body than anything else, mainly because it's helped me figure out what I can and cannot handle physically. I assume preparing to have a baby requires a similar personal journey of exploring your body's limits. I don't know. I don't plan to find out for myself for a quite a while.

The women all talk over each other until one of the ladies asks a pointed question.

"Are you sure that's safe?"

It comes out more like an accusation than a curiosity.

In the silence that follows her words, the woman adds, "We worry for you, Grace. We know you'd never risk any harm to your sweet babies, but I just hope you are valuing your own health too."

"You have a servant's heart, Bellamy," Grace says. "Thank you for your concern. You know, I wasn't entirely sold on it at first, but David really wants us to take this path together. My last pregnancy put us through many trials, especially at the hospital during the birth. Like you said, April, there are interesting writings about the biblical benefits of home birth. David has been studying it a lot from that perspective."

"But David isn't the one giving birth," I interrupt. Casey spins to glare at me again, but everyone is looking at me now, so she's the least of my worries. "Pastor Heights isn't the one carrying your baby, Mrs. Heights. If you aren't sure about having the baby at home, that should be your decision to make. Not his."

No one speaks for a long moment. I try to think of a way to fill the silence, but nothing I can think of would make the moment less awkward.

Grace simply chuckles and says, "From the mouths of babes," and all the adults laugh like I'm a toddler trying to have a Grown-Up Discussion.

Grace shifts the conversation, finally acknowledging her child. "My dear Ruth," she says.

"Hi, Mama. Could I go over to Casey's this afternoon? She said they can bring me home before dinner."

"Of course, sweetheart," Grace agrees without argument. "If you help me get the littles in their car seats, you can leave with them after. Okay?"

"I'll get started right now," Ruth says, taking the stroller with both hands and maneuvering it toward the exit.

"Thank you, Mrs. Heights!" Casey smiles at Grace before grabbing my elbow and pulling me away. Her kind expression disappears as soon as we're out of Grace's earshot.

"I can't believe you did that to me," Casey says as we make the trek back to our parents. Her tone is so heated, it could power Hell entirely on its own.

"Did what to you? I wasn't even talking to you."

"You humiliated me. You had no right to criticize Mrs. Heights like that."

"I wasn't criticizing anyone." After a second, I rephrase myself. "I wasn't criticizing Grace. I don't think her husband has the right to make decisions for her. That's all."

"No, you think she should listen to you instead."

"That's not what I'm saying at all."

"You think because you're a freshman that you know everything, but you don't. You don't know anything at all."

I grab her arm to stop her. "That isn't fair. I was trying to look out for her."

"No, you weren't." Casey tears her arm out of my grasp. "You can't be happy unless you're ruining things for everyone else."

"Casey!" I try.

She ignores me. She plasters on another fake smile for our parents and leaves me behind.

SIXTEEN

Sutton keeps her promise.

Every morning I brace for the storm clouds to open and drench me in my parents' fury that I've had contact with Andrew, that I've mentioned him to Sutton, but it never comes. Days pass, but Sutton keeps silent. She's offered countless opportunities to rat on me, and hiding the photo strip is difficult with her nonexistent privacy, but she keeps our secret.

I'd be grateful if Sutton's silence weren't the only positive change. She hasn't remembered or recognized anyone or anything else from her life. As the days drag on, she seems to be regressing instead of improving.

For once, I don't blame her. I *also* feel like I'm losing my mind.

I can't stop thinking about those "Hard End" texts, and I don't know what to do about them.

I will end you.

I should tell someone, but don't the police already know? They have her other laptop. They probably requested her text logs from our service provider. They have to know, right? Surely they would do something if they knew someone was threatening her. Just because Sutton is home, it doesn't mean her missing person's case is closed. Or does it? What about all these unanswered questions?

The police never mentioned any threatening messages. That seems too big of a lead for my parents to keep from me. It's not possible that I've put more work into investigating my sister's disappearance than the authorities have. Right?

"Casey," Dad says, in a tone that implies it's not the first time he's tried to get my attention. "I thought you were sorting."

"I am," I say, though it's obvious my body has been as still as my mind has been active. I survey my section of the dining table. The heirloom pieces take up less of the space as Dad grows increasingly more interested in the new curriculum he's developing for the university.

It would probably be more useful to have me help research for his lessons instead of thumb through photo albums and journals, but he'd probably be twice as annoyed at my disassociating while doing that work. This is busywork. But I'll take what I can get if it means I still have a chance to get my Ivy tickets.

"I'm kinda out of old stuff," I tell him. I like the mixture of photos and items in the current display, like Mima's portrait of her mama next to the bag of pressed herbs. I have selected several photos of young Ma Remy and Grandpa Booker. It would be cool to pair them with mementos. "If I only add pictures, it's going to be boring."

"Pictures aren't boring." Then Dad pauses. "I may have some old movie tickets and things in my office. You can go look if you want. They're in a box beneath the window."

I can tell that it's an invitation to get out of his hair. I scoot my chair back, careful not to knock anything off the table as I leave.

My phone is out of my pocket before I've reached the hallway. Andrew is at the top of my messaging app, though I haven't texted him since our meeting at Ruth's. He texts me a new question every day. He makes it no secret how desperately he wants to see Sutton.

Andrew: Did you give her the photo strip?
Has she mentioned me?
Do you think I can see her soon?

I can kind of see what Sutton saw in Andrew. He's not that different from her. Like Sutton, he knows when to use fragility and vulnerability to his advantage. I think back to our conversation at Ruth's. All my questions for him evaporated, despite the fact he'd used me as a shield with the press while knowing I was clueless about his ties to her missing car.

I believed him. I pitied him. I trusted him.

And now I don't know what to think at all.

I text Andrew as I let myself into Dad's office. I know about the burner app. I saw the other texts.

I flop into Dad's big orthopedic chair and wait for him to respond. I stare at my phone for several minutes, flipping between my message to him and Sutton's conversation on the burner app, which I installed on my phone hoping some new message will come in.

Hard End hasn't texted since his final threat the day she disappeared. Andrew was worried, scared in the messages he showed me from the day Sutton disappeared. But if this is a secret app and Hard End assumed no one would ever find this conversation, who was she texting? Was it Andrew? Did he know about this?

Shit.

I just told Andrew. Maybe that was a mistake. Those messages and the vitriol inside them don't match what I've come to learn about Sutton's boyfriend, but I don't really know him at all. I'm starting to wonder if Sutton ever truly knew him herself.

I refresh my screen, but my text is marked as delivered, not read. What if he's at work and doesn't respond for hours? For a moment, my mind entertains the idea of an *Ocean's Eleven* heist at the golf club to grab his phone and delete my message before he reads it.

I was not built for detective work. I am no good at this.

If Andrew is a monster and responsible for what happened to Sutton—and if I showed my hand by admitting I know the secret he was keeping, or at least part of it—then there's nothing I can do.

I should tell *someone*.

But who? I have no idea how far off the course of normal thought processes I've fallen because I don't have anyone to talk to about this. I don't have anyone to validate my concerns or walk me back from the edge. I can't tell my parents. I still don't trust Sutton, and besides, she knows less about her life than we do at the moment.

Ruth has been so supportive, but it's different for her. She won't say it, but I can tell she judges me for my continued suspicion. I should be grateful Sutton came back to me. Ruth would give anything to have her mom here, no matter what.

Maybe my fellow Jamies would believe me, but something keeps me from sharing this part of my life with them. Several have texted me, concerned about my absence in our group chat, but a part of me doesn't want to combine my worlds. Ivy has always been my sanctuary. Her music, the fandom community—I need it to stay pure.

I need at least one thing to stay the same.

But this is the first solid proof I have that Sutton was keeping secrets. *I will end you.* Given all that happened, it seems as if someone made good on that threat. Sutton's messages are as concerning.

Her messages are seared into my mind. *This is over. Stop texting me. You know better.* And the most damning: *Do you want everyone to find out about this too?*

She had a plan for the day she disappeared. She'd made several plans over the course of that week. I don't know what she did or who with, but loaning Andrew her car wasn't the only thing outside her routine before she vanished.

I don't even know if Hard End is Andrew. It could be anybody.

If Andrew didn't hurt her, he'll surely confess what else he knows to prove his innocence. It's my only chance to discover how these messages are tied to what happened. I have to wait for him to read my text. I have to take a chance that this lead will pay off.

I set my phone on Dad's desk and slide out of his chair to open the box under the window. I may as well do what I told Dad I would. I unfold the flaps of the cardboard box and find a few journals inside, as well as an old wooden trinket box. I go for the box first. Like Dad promised, there's a pair of movie tickets to *Jaws* from 1975. That's cute, but it probably doesn't have much relevance to our family legacy.

A familiar green hue peeks out from under the tickets. It's another pendant like the one on the bracelet Sutton stole from me. This one is different though. It's on a frayed string, not a silver chain, for one. It's not as well-kept as my bracelet. The insides look different too. There's no white flower, and the green is muddier.

It's still pretty though. And I no longer have Ma Remy's bracelet. I think it would make a good addition to the display table, so I set it aside to take back with me.

The rest of the box is filled with newspaper clippings and old coupons mixed with rusting earrings and costume jewelry from the seventies. I reach down for the journals.

I remember what my dad warned about Ma Remy's unapologetic horniness in the diary he took from me, so I flip through the pages quickly but try to make sure I'm not missing anything important. The other notebook is thicker. It's tied closed with an old ribbon. I gently pull at the knot until it comes undone.

The book springs open like a jack-in-the-box. Polaroids spill from it in every direction, and there are flowers pressed between pages. Old news clippings are taped amid the entries. I try to tuck the memories back where they belong, but in doing so, the truth of what I'm holding becomes clear.

This isn't a diary. This isn't a collection of items to add to my family history. This *is* my family history.

Ma Remy's delicate handwriting fills every page of this journal with the life histories and proudest moments of family members I know and many more I've never heard of. There are so many pictures and details.

From these pages, it's obvious Ma Remy inspired and fed Dad's obsession with history. This should be his most cherished keepsake, not some book forgotten in a box. Why has he never shown it to me before?

A picture of Dad as a baby peeks out from the back. I flip to the page it's tucked in. He sits in Ma Remy's lap, but she looks more like Mima or Henny. She's dressed like a slave, and she looks radiant. She holds the pendant with the flower in her hand, while Dad reaches his tiny fist toward it.

I read the entry.

September 13, 1976

I went back to the Civil History Center today. The last time I went, I brought Mima's drawings and some other documents to prove to them that items in their slavery exhibit belonged to her. Belonged to us. They didn't care. They wouldn't give them back.

I don't have the money to hire a lawyer again. We are comfortable with the family income from the construction business, but I can't risk bleeding our coffers dry to get back some sketches and faded cloth. I can't do that to my brothers, not after all they've done to help me since Booker passed.

But...today they were having a reenactment event.

I spent the past fortnight sewing. Isaiah got lost in the petticoats. I could hear his little giggles under the cotton. When I had to take the seam ripper to one of the hems, he furrowed his little brows in an imitation of my concentration and moved his fingers along the edge of the fabric to "help" me. He's darling. And I finished just in time.

I put on the dress I made and walked right into the building. No one looked twice at me. I blended in with everyone in their period attire, their big hats, and working replica rifles. So many men were dressed proudly in gray uniforms, their wives looking on fondly and their children running around unaware of anything but the treats and excitement.

The white people ignored me like their ancestors would have, and as they streamed out to the lawn for the start of the reenactment, I crept to the back. The Ladies Auxiliary volunteers, who usually watch visitors like plantation overseers, were all preening in the sunlight, playing their roles as Daughters of the Confederacy.

Mima's things sat there: sketches of Henny and the landscape of their plantation, old embroidery with the same detailing as I have on a family handkerchief, and the pendant. The pendant I've been searching for forever. The one I've been trying and failing to re-create. It called to me. Even if I hadn't recognized her artwork, I would have known that green teardrop belonged to our family.

They didn't even have it locked up. I raised the glass top on the display and held it. I almost cried. Then I closed the lid and put the pendant in my pocket, leaving everything else behind. I walked right back out the doors, past the very same lady who refused to relinquish the items last month. I looked her dead in the eye like a dare. She didn't recognize me. She didn't remember me at all.

Now I have the cornerstone of these stories and our history I'm gathering for my boy. This pendant kept us together before and now it's gonna bind him to our future. Booker is gone, but his son will never lose another part of our legacy. I will make sure of it.

So that's why I've never seen this journal before. Ma Remy didn't simply *find* the pendant after it was lost to the family. She stole it back.

I guess she and Dad kept secrets too.

My phone vibrates. I glance over.

Andrew is calling me. He's never called me before.

"It's not what you think," he says when I answer.

"You have no idea what I'm thinking."

"It's not me," he says. "She wasn't texting me on the burner."

"Then who was she talking to?" I ask him. "Who could it be if not you?"

"Her coach. Hard End is her cheer coach."

SEVENTEEN

We're all waiting on the couch for Dad. It used to be that Sutton took the longest to get ready to leave the house.

When Mom tries to tuck an errant ringlet behind Sutton's ear, my sister glares and jerks away from her touch.

The entire strand of hair comes off in Mom's fingers.

Mom's hand shakes. She set the thick lock down on the heirloom table, patting it as if she intends to save it like the clipping from a first haircut instead of the latest proof of Sutton's deteriorating health.

This isn't the first time this has happened. Sutton's hair is shedding much more than it should. It started a few days after I braided it, and I almost blamed myself, worried I was too rough on her scalp. But Sutton used to color and flat iron her hair all the time—things she doesn't have the patience for anymore—so it's likely delayed product damage.

The transition from using harsh products to natural hair care is not always smooth, at least from what I've heard. I made an oath to Ma Remy when I was little that I'd never use relaxer or otherwise intentionally damage my hair, and I'll help Sutton repair hers. I'm the only one who can. She still refuses to let Mom or Dad touch it. She doesn't like them touching her at all.

The only other family member she's warmed up to is Romeo.

He paces in front of her, circling our feet. The two are nowhere near as close as they used to be, but they have some sort of unspoken truce. He tolerates her presence now.

"Okay, my lovely ladies," Dad says as he enters the living room smelling of pomade and beard oil. "Are we ready to go to church?"

I straighten in my sundress. We haven't gone to weekly service at Heights Above since Sutton came back, but the church organized an event to welcome Sutton back to the congregation and community this evening. I'd rather sit through a long-winded Bible study than an entire evening of our neighbors praising my sister like she's the second coming, but I haven't seen Ruth in person since we babysat together.

Sutton isn't as excited. "No," she says, though she's as dressed up as I am. More so, because Mom forced her to sit still long enough for me to pin back her hair and apply some lip gloss to her cracked lips.

Mom ignores her. She stands. "We're ready, baby."

"No," Sutton repeats. The venom in her voice is matched in her stare, which she turns on Mom alone. "I don't want to."

I bite the inside of my cheek, suppressing a sigh. Of course, she does this the one time going to church is literally all about *her*. Sutton never liked church. She tolerated it. She'd skip weekly service sometimes, but social nights were a safe bet. Sutton always loved a party, no matter the purpose.

"It'll be all right, honey," Dad tries. "I know seeing a lot of people may sound overwhelming, but everyone will understand your limits, and we don't have to stay the whole time if you don't want to."

Sutton turns the same icy look on him. "I'm not going," she repeats.

Mom turns to me, accusation and pleading on her face like I'm responsible for causing and solving this. I shrug, tossing my hands up. This isn't my fault.

"Sutton," she says. "We have to go. The church worked so hard to help find you. They donated their time and money because they love you so much. They want to welcome you home."

She squeezes Sutton's knee. Sutton rests her hand on top of Mom's, and for a half a second, I think she's about to give in.

Then she shoves Mom's hand away and says, "I don't care."

Mom recoils. "This is for you!" she yells. "This night is about *you*. These people are here for *you*. Everything we've done, it's all for you! Why won't you see that? We invite your friends over, and you won't talk to them. The church organizes a reception for you, and you won't go. Can't you just be grateful? Can't you pretend like you love us for one goddamn night?"

"Madison!" Dad shouts.

"I'm sorry," Mom says, her jaw tense. She turns to Dad. "I'm sorry," she repeats, then again to Sutton and finally me. "I'm sorry. I didn't mean that."

Sutton's expression hasn't changed. "I'm still not going."

Mom closes her hands into fists at her sides. Dad reaches for her shoulders and pulls Mom into a hug. "That's fine," he tells Sutton. "You don't have to."

Mom starts to push herself out of Dad's hold. "Isaiah, we have to go. We have to show our appreciation—"

"You go," Sutton agrees. "Casey will stay with me."

"What?" I say. "No! I want to go. I'm tired of being trapped in this house. I'm ready. I already told Ruth I'd be there."

"We can't leave your sister alone," Dad says, but it's a lie. She's done nothing to hurt herself. She's not the baby they're pretending she is. She would be fine alone. They just don't *want* to leave her.

"I'm not a babysitter!"

"That's not what—"

"Mom's right!" I say. "Everything is about Sutton! And I've been so good about that. I haven't done anything to make this about me. I've listened and I've helped. But it's all her, every time. I want to go tonight. Please don't make me stay home."

"Casey," Dad says. It's worse than Mom's outburst. He doesn't cushion it with an affectionate *baby girl* or even the slightest hint of begrudging understanding. He's not on my side. There's no argument to be had.

"This is such bullshit." I push past both parents and this predictably Sutton-controlled scene out to the backyard. Romeo toddles through the patio door I leave open behind me. At least I have one ally in this house.

I kick off my sandals and dip my feet in the pool. Romeo investigates, but he doesn't trust the water and walks over to me for reassuring belly scratches. I know when Sutton has come outside by how he tenses under my hand.

I'm not coming tonight, I text Ruth with my free palm. Sutton is ditching and dragged me down with her.

> **Ruth:** I'm sorry. So you're all staying home?
>
> **Me:** No. My parents will be there.
>
> **Ruth:** My Dad will be happy to see them.
>
> **Me:** He's back?
>
> **Ruth:** Yep! :)
>
> **Me:** Don't worry about tonight. There's always next time.

"Leave me alone, Sutton," I say without looking to see if she's within earshot. She must be. She's attracted to me like a moth to a flame, a pest I can't get rid of.

She ignores me like I knew she would. She sits across the pool from me, submerging both legs in the clear water without even taking off her shoes. Her yellow flip-flops slip off her feet, bobbing to the surface. They crawl toward me with the current.

She sticks her hand in her cleavage and pulls out the photo strip. I almost laugh. Ditching church to lust over her abandoned boyfriend. A true heathen indeed.

Romeo leaves me to chase bugs along the garden bed.

I'd almost gotten used to Sutton's new form of manipulation. Guilting our parents, making them work for every scrap of affection or acknowledgment. I don't understand her motives but I'm learning to live with them. Everyone has their role. Mine is to be the reminder of before.

We're never allowed to forget, not for a single moment, that everything has changed. Mom was right. Sutton refuses to pretend. It's like she doesn't even want to get better.

I wish they saw her like I do.

She caresses her little love souvenir. I want to light everything on fire.

I look at my phone resting on the grass and tap it to wake the screen. No further texts from Ruth. She'll be distracted, like my parents, until the church social ends around eight. That gives me hours. It's barely five.

I try to think of a silver lining to staying home, but other than avoiding a night of Sutton worship, I come up with nothing. All I can think about is Sutton and her reasoning to stay home. That useless photo strip of a boy she can't even remember, one who refuses to share her secrets with me even if it could help solve what happened to her.

He said those texts were from her cheer coach, but when I pressed for proof, Andrew said he'd show me in person. He'd show me and Sutton both, if I agreed to let him see her.

I can't believe I ever thought Andrew was too good for her. He's as manipulative as she is. They're made for each other.

I open the messaging app and click Andrew's contact. You still want to see your girl? I ask him.

I don't even have to wait five minutes. Yes.

And you'll tell me the truth?

Again, immediately. Yes.

If you can get to our house in 30 minutes, she's yours.

It's barely an offer. I know from Sutton's complaining that the bus from Bend's End to the city common is as slow as watching paint dry, and our gated enclave is even farther than that. He won't arrive in time, but maybe I'll still let him in.

I'm tired of this game. I'm going to expose her tonight. It's my turn to be in charge.

The doorbell rings less than twenty minutes later. Romeo races out of the roses and through the open sliding door like he's breaking past a finish line, barking in excitement the entire way. Sutton looks up but doesn't move. I follow Romeo inside.

My wet feet squelch against the hardwood with every step.

When I open the door, Andrew stands there wearing his busboy uniform from the golf club. I'm surprised they didn't find some half-baked excuse to let him go when suspicion fell on him. That lessens the distance he had to travel, but it still doesn't explain his speed. "I ordered a ride," he says, shaking his phone. He runs his palms along his thighs like he's waiting for me to invite him in.

I don't step back to let him through. He's going to have work harder than that.

Romeo doesn't get the memo though. He recognizes him instantly and squeezes through my legs to give Andrew the welcome we all expected him to give Sutton. He hops around like he's been zapped with a taser and then takes off for the backyard to alert Sutton like in the old times. I wonder if he'll come back to us when he remembers he doesn't like her anymore.

"How did you get past the gate?"

"Sutton gave me the code," he says. "Before. It hasn't changed."

That sort of defeats the security it offers, but the gate is for our entire neighborhood, not only our house. I know my parents changed the codes for our property, but it makes me uneasy to know that anyone who had the code before Sutton disappeared could still get to our house.

But Andrew didn't show up at our doorstep uninvited, despite all his pleading and obvious desire to see her again. He waited for permission.

He doesn't seem like a secret monster. But what if he wants me to think his patience is proof of innocence? Sutton has always been patient and cunning to get what she wants.

"We'll have to change that."

Andrew sighs deeply, trying and failing to hide how he keeps glancing over my head, looking for my sister.

"She's not there."

Anger flashes through his general state of grief. It reminds me of Sutton when I asked her what happened to Ma Remy's bracelet.

"She's in the backyard. But you can't see her until you tell me the truth."

"I can do that," he says in a single breath. He lifts his phone.

"Texts aren't gonna be enough. I saw what you showed me last time, but the burner texts go on after you said you last spoke with her."

"I know," he says, scrolling on his screen. "Because those texts weren't from me. They were from her coach."

"You knew, and you were okay with that?" I am unable to suppress the accusation in my tone. "Your girlfriend was texting her much older cheer coach about things that had nothing to do with practice, and that was perfectly okay with you?"

"Yes—I mean, no, of course not. But it's not what you think. Look, if you check the phone number, it's not even a Washington area code, right?"

I begrudgingly unlock my phone to double-check. He's right. Hard End's number starts with an area code of 986.

"That's an Idaho area code," Andrew says, peeking over at my screen. "That means the owner of the number either bought or registered their phone there originally, no matter where they live now. I've never been past the Cascades. I've never left the state. It couldn't be me."

"Okay," I say. "Let's say it's her coach. Why is she talking to him outside of school and practice? Why is he angry at her?"

"Well, he's a dick, first of all," Andrew says. "He doesn't need a reason to be an asshole. That's his default personality. He's a bad coach. He's classist. He's also *such* a racist. Once he told Sutton—"

"Andrew," I interrupt. "I get it. But what did she want from him?"

"Right." Andrew shows me his phone again. He has a video paused on the screen. I can't tell what I'm looking at because the frame is so dark. It must have been taken at night. "This would be easier if your sister could explain. She had more of the evidence than I did. She was filming their practices."

"I saw that," I say. "It was on the computer where I found the burner texts. Her teammate told me she was recording practices because she was worried about her skills, but it looked more like she was focusing on everyone else instead."

"Sutton wasn't taking the videos for herself. She was filming his coaching. She felt like he was neglecting safety policies to attempt more impressive stunts."

"Sutton went ballistic when Natalie got hurt. She knew it would happen. That's when she got the burner to confront him. She thought Natalie's injury would get him fired, but it didn't."

"Why would she care so much?"

Andrew's nose scrunches. "Do you know your sister at all?"

My grip on the door tightens. "Yes," I bite out. "Just because she was nice to you doesn't mean that's how she is with everyone. Maybe this was a mistake." I start to close the door, but Andrew sticks out his foot to stop me.

"I'm sorry. Forgive me. I know you two haven't always gotten along, but your sister does care. I promise you she does. And besides, his negligence was a clear danger. Cheerleading is a dangerous sport. His mistakes could have gotten one of her teammates killed."

He can't bring himself to voice the ultimate conclusion, but I hear it anyway: her coach's actions endangered Sutton too.

I look toward the backyard. I can't see Sutton from this angle, but Romeo hasn't returned to me either. "So she knew what those messages would imply," I say.

"Yes," Andrew confirms. "That was the point. He's disgusting, so she knew it wouldn't be hard to get him to incriminate himself. She wanted the proof of him cutting corners and it hurting the team to be enough, but this was Plan B. She wanted video of him meeting her after hours to pair with the texts if he didn't follow through on what they'd agreed."

He presses Play on his phone. It's still dark, but I watch as a streetlamp brings the subject into better focus. Sutton has one of Dad's golf clubs, and she's swinging it into the taillight of a dark-colored van.

"Are you out of your mind?" her coach screams from out of frame, but he reaches out to grab her.

"Keep your hands off her!" Andrew yells. The camera jostles as he runs. "I'm filming all of this, you pervy shitbag!"

Coach McCoy takes a step back with his hands up as Andrew gets him fully in frame. "I should've known," he says. "You fu—"

"Yeah, you really should have," Sutton says, twisting the club in both hands like she's primed to strike again. "Maybe if you thought with your head instead of your dick more often, the squad wouldn't spend so much time benched with avoidable injuries. But I can let this go." She lowers the club in a half surrender. "I can make it all go away if you do what I say."

"I'm not agreeing to anything with that," the coach says, pointing at the camera.

"It's okay, baby," Sutton tells Andrew. "You can turn it off."

The video ends. "She used him to set up the meeting with the loan officer for me. He does a lot of personal training outside the school, so she had him pull a favor to connect us with a client. And then she sent her videos of the practices to the school board anyway."

"But not the texts," I confirm.

"Nobody knows about the texts. No one except me and you."

"You didn't tell the cops?" I ask him. "This makes him a better suspect than you."

"No," he says. "It makes her look like she was hiding a relationship. This was the nuclear option. She knew it would be as awful for her if the texts got out, but she wanted him gone. It would have gotten him fired, but it would have ruined her too. She said some of the girls had told her about weird things he'd said or suggested to them, stuff they'd laughed off. She thought leading him on like this might distract him from acting on anything real with one of her teammates. I didn't want her to do it."

He looks like he's going to throw up. "I told the police about the videos she took in the school gym," Andrew continues. "But this would have given them a reason to discredit her. One of the missing girls in my area lost local help and support when it was rumored that she once texted nudes to her boyfriend. I couldn't risk that. I couldn't do anything that would hurt Sutton's chances of coming home."

I don't know if I agree with him, but I step aside to let him in the house. He's not going to hurt Sutton, but I'm not sure if he's done enough to protect her either. He kept her secrets even when it hurt him. Now the only one they can hurt is me. The more I learn about Sutton's lies, the less I feel I ever knew her at all.

In the backyard, Andrew turns to me. "Thank you so much for this."

"You can't stay for long." I look around. The yard is empty. "Sutton?" I call. "Romeo?"

Romeo peeks out from the side of the house, then gallops over to us. We head toward the garden bed.

Sutton is standing with her back half turned to us. Resting on her palm is yet another blue butterfly. They're both unnaturally still, like a snapshot in an old history textbook.

"Wow," Andrew says in reverence like he's the one attending church. "A butterfly. It must be so cool to hold one."

"There's been a lot of them around here lately," I say. "Sutton doesn't really like them that much though."

As if in response, Sutton closes her fist around the butterfly in her palm. She squeezes so tightly, her entire arm shakes with the pressure.

"NO!" I scream and lunge at Sutton. I pull at her clenched fingers to free the innocent bug, but it's far too late. Its ocean-blue wings are creased and ripped. It doesn't flinch or flutter in panic. In a small mercy, the poor creature met a swift end. It's gone.

I feel a complicated urge to bury it.

I look back at Sutton. She shows no remorse.

She's noticed Andrew. She smiles, uncaring about the corpse in her hand or the apprehension on his face. "Rain or shine," she says.

"Yeah," Andrew releases in a choked breath. "Rain or shine."

"I'll give you some privacy," I say, sweeping Sutton's kill into my own palm. Maybe this wasn't a good idea after all. I never expected a body count from Andrew's visit, and I could be next if he's here when my parents come back. Even if she is more herself in his company, they would know I was the one who invited him.

I take the butterfly to the plants by the pool and scoop out a small hole. The butterfly is beautiful even in death. I cover it in soil. "I'm sorry," I whisper.

I rinse my hands in the pool, scraping the soil from my finger-nails. Romeo returns to me. He sniffs the grave.

I check my phone. It's not even six thirty. My parents won't be back for at least another hour. What else could Sutton do by then?

Andrew joins me ten minutes later, much sooner than I expected. Is he ready to leave? Sutton is still at the garden bed, but the butterflies are giving her a wide berth now.

"You don't have to go yet," I say, even though I want him to.

"I'm not comfortable staying." He looks back at Sutton.

"My parents don't know you're here," I assure him. "They won't be home for a while. You're fine to stay a little longer."

He shakes his head. "Something is wrong with her."

"Yeah, obviously." I thought bringing him here would force some clarity, but Sutton is always one step ahead of any plan I can think of.

"No," he says. "She's not the same."

Oh. I almost feel bad for Sutton. After all that begging and worrying over her, he can't take the reality of this either. I guess it's harder to pretend nothing happened with her in person.

Unlike us though, he has a choice. He has a way out. He can run. I'm jealous.

"I guess she doesn't care as much as you thought anymore," I say. "Can't say I'll miss you texting me."

"No," he repeats. "That's not it." His blue eyes bore into mine, searching. "She's not here. That isn't Sutton."

Of course it is. Who the hell else could it be?

EIGHTEEN

I wanted life to go back to normal, but this wasn't what I meant.

Apparently, one is allowed only so much time to grieve when one's child isn't really dead, so both Mom and Dad return to work. Or attempt to. Dad has fully devoted himself to his new curriculum. He's returned to his office with a new open-door policy that means anyone on the first floor of the house can overhear his dry lecture recordings and Civil War documentaries he's using for his research.

He relieved me from my assistant duties, claiming he needs to focus on the new study. I should be happy because he promised to buy my Ivy tickets anyway, but I liked helping him. I'm not sure what I did wrong other than not telling him I found Ma Remy's story about the bracelet.

But if he doesn't know I read her journal, that doesn't have anything to do with his decision. I think. He's so hard to read. He keeps everything bottled up.

Mom is also being private about her assignments. Sutton is in no way ready for cameras, but the price of all the media attention Mom sought has finally come due. She does not leave her door open at any time. I tried to interrupt her once, to let her know dinner was ready, and her office was double-locked.

I understand her apprehension, but it still seems extreme.

Keeping us shielded from the world and the news will only help for so long. Once the summer ends, at least one of us will have to go back to school. Even if Mom wanted to, neither of my parents' careers is suited to homeschooling us. I could maybe see them hiring a tutor for Sutton, but that feels like a final admission that our lives will never be the same again.

We aren't allowed to answer any unrecognized numbers— even on our cell phones—after Sutton accidentally picked up the landline when a rival news station called. "There's supposed to be a level of respect," Mom said about her coworkers, but trust is clearly nonexistent both at work and at home. We aren't allowed to answer the doors by ourselves either.

I'd think the new rules were punishment for having Andrew over, but neither of my parents have mentioned him.

If they knew what I did, there's no way they would ever let Ruth come over today, even after days of begging. I'm pretty sure they only agreed because they felt guilty for making me miss Ruth at the church event. Or guilty and embarrassed.

Mom's sudden reclusiveness is probably connected to her outburst.

I burrow deeper in my comforter, cocooning with my laptop. The internal fan works on overdrive, but the base of my computer is warm where it sits on my chest. I double-check that I'm in a private browsing session and then type my search term:

missing black girls Willow Bend, WA

Sutton is the entire first page of search results and all the images featured at the top. At the end of the second page, I find a link to a social media page that mentions a different name, but the results past the third page become more disjointed and irrelevant.

I adjust my search: missing girls Willow Bend

More Sutton, but also some white girls who ran away and a domestic murder case of a husband killing his wife like three years before I was even born.

I try again: missing Bend's End

Jackpot. Almost. It's more like winning $15 on a scratch ticket than winning the Mega Millions lottery, but the results don't center on my sister. Well, not entirely anyway.

The name from the first search repeats a few more times, along with a second name. I open every link in new tabs.

The first girl to disappear was Tamika Horn. She went missing on a Friday at the beginning of May. She was last seen leaving the Boys & Girls Club near Willow Middle School. She'd walked her thirteen-year-old sister there but never returned to walk her home. She was fifteen.

The second girl was Imani Brenton. She was older than both Sutton and I, almost nineteen. This must be the girl with the nudes that Andrew mentioned. Her last known whereabouts are less clear than Tamika's. It took an entire day before anyone noticed she was gone.

That hasn't stopped her family from searching for her. Though Tamika has been missing for longer, Imani's name shows up wherever Tamika's does, even if it's only in the comment section.

Most of the comments come from Nia Brenton, who seems to be Imani's mother. It's hard to tell because her profile picture on both social media sites I find are of Imani's missing person flyer. Nia is young herself in the hand-filmed clips she shares for her three hundred followers, but the lines on her face are too deep-set for them to be sisters. If she's Imani's mom, she must have been my age when she had her.

Her desperation is intimately familiar.

> **@NiaBre89:** Two months without Imani. I know she's out there. Please share the attached photo far and wide. You could be the key to bringing her home. #ImaniBrenton
>
> **@NiaBre89:** @BroadcastPNWW there's more than one missing black girl in Willow Bend, though you

wouldn't know it by watching your coverage. RE-
TURN MY AND @findtamika EMAILS AND CALLS!
#ImaniBrenton

Tamika's parents are less technologically inclined, but they
look to have their hands full from the family photos they shared
publicly. Tamika is the oldest of five. Her youngest sibling couldn't
be older than Ruth's sister Esther. They've relied a lot on their
community to help search for Tamika.

Like our church, there was a neighborhood search effort just
days after Imani disappeared. Despite the combined resources of
two families, it didn't get a fraction of the coverage Sutton's search
did. No leads were found.

There hasn't been another big search since, though they've
tried.

@findtamika: Does anyone have the contact information for Heights Above Church? It looks like they're
organizing a rescue effort for #SuttonCureton and
I thought maybe we could donate the #FindTamika
army. What do you think @NiaBre89? #ImaniBrenton
#TamikaHorn

@NiaBre89: @findtamika Don't bother. I already
tried the numbers and email addresses on their
website. They said they'd "get back to me" like I
was offering a pie for a bake sale.

@findtamika: @NiaBre89 Won't hurt to try again. We both know what the first week of this is like. I'm sure they'll be open to help, especially if it benefits all of our girls.

@NiaBre89: @findtamika They only care about that light-skin girl and her white mom. They don't give a shit about any other black girls in Willow.

@findtamika: @NiaBre89 I'm still gonna try.

I want to believe none of this is related. I want to hope Tamika and Imani were unlucky in a similar but unconnected coincidence. It's wrong and I know better, but facing the alternative unlocks a level of guilt I'm not prepared to face.

I hated Mom's Home Again Narrative. All the posturing and pretending like we were a happy family. Like Sutton was kind and generous, so loved and needed. No swearing. No risqué photos. Definitely no hidden sexual texts with her cheer coach, ulterior motive or not.

I don't want to believe Mom knew about Tamika and Imani's families reaching out to the church. It's likely she had no idea. The church board handled the community outreach for the search. But if she had known, would she have let them in? Would she have invited their terrified mothers to join her media crusade? Were they the "right" type of people or another potential stain on our family like Andrew?

She worked so hard to make strangers care about Sutton.

Could it have worked for these teens too? Mom acted surprised when I mentioned them in the garden. But was it shock or shame? Sutton's disappearance was all-consuming for Mom. She might not have had any brainpower to think about anyone else. In fact, I know she didn't. I ceased to exist to her while Sutton was gone.

But if she did know about them... If she knew about Tamika and Imani and the lack of media attention and resolution, maybe that's why she painted Sutton in complimentary brushstrokes. Would anyone have cared about my sister's return without the nonstop coverage? If someone really took her, it's possible the attention scared them into releasing her. Maybe Imani and Tamika could be found too if more people knew their names.

Or maybe we would never have found Sutton if the world knew how imperfect she could be.

Mom raps on my door twice before opening it. "Ruth is downstairs."

I slam my laptop closed, my heart jackhammering, but she doesn't comment on it.

"Do you remember what I said?" she asks.

"Um..." I hedge as I tuck my computer under the blanket and slide off my bed. "Maybe?"

"I need you to be mindful of your sister's limitations while Ruth is here, or we won't have visitors."

I nod as I follow her out the door, but she isn't done yet. "No TV. No watching videos on your phones. No talking about things that could upset her."

LILY MEADE

"I get it, Mom," I say. "We'll finger-paint with her."

"*Cassandra*," Mom warns.

I lift my hands in surrender. "Kidding!"

She shakes her head, adding that she'll be in her office if we need her. *Don't need me*, is more implied than outright stated.

Staticky orchestral music plays from Dad's office when I reach the foot of the stairs. My father sits in his leather chair while reading at his big desk. His own laptop is closed, the music coming from speakers on the bookshelves behind him.

"Daddy?" I inquire. I'm used to hearing facts recited by monotone old men, but this is a new addition. "What are you listening to?"

He looks up and takes the ballpoint pen from between his teeth. Then he gestures wide across the desk. "Negro spirituals and folk songs. Research for the course."

I nod. "Should I shut the door? Ruth is here, and Sutton and I are going to hang out with her in the living room."

"No, your mother wants it left open." He pauses. "In case you need me."

Mom wants this, huh? Mom, who double-locks herself away to check her emails. She asked Dad to leave his door open for us. Right. Sure.

"Okay," I say. "We'll let you know."

He gives me a soft smile. A long-dead woman crows about forgiveness. "Sounds good, baby girl."

Ruth is caressing the remote control when I enter the living

226

room, eyeing our flat-screen like a starving desert traveler looking at a feast.

I pull the remote from her manicured hands. "No TV," I say. "No phones either. Mom's orders." I work hard not to look directly at Sutton, but she can tell it's her fault. She makes a weird face like she's gonna apologize to Ruth, but Ruth replies first.

"So HBO is off the table, then?" she jokes, flopping down on the couch next to Sutton. "And here I thought I left the parental controls at home."

"I'm not sure where that leaves us either," I admit. The music echoing from Dad's study changes to a jaunty jazz number not unlike a circus theme.

"We could do board games," Ruth says.

"Yeah!" I open the bottom cabinet of the entertainment center. All our games are covered in a thin layer of dust, but there are a couple of options. "We've got Life, Monopoly, Clue, and Scrabble."

"Clue," says Ruth at the same time Sutton says, "Scrabble."

Ruth snorts. "No, you're right—let's do Scrabble. Scrabble is good."

I pull out the box and set it on the coffee table. Sutton scoots forward to the edge of the couch. Ruth watches me unbox the board and various pieces. "Can't believe I suggested Clue," she mouths at me when I've completed the setup.

I rest back on my heels. Sutton runs her finger along her letter tiles. "Are there rules about who goes first?"

"Probably," I admit. "The instructions weren't in the box." We likely lost them years ago. "I only remember that each player gets seven letters, so that's what I gave each of you. Don't worry, I didn't look at them."

Ruth makes an exaggerated "mm-hmm" and playfully drags her letter stand away from me.

"You go first," Sutton decides.

I'm not going to argue. I consider my options.

"A-C-E." I punctuate each letter with its proper tile. "Ace."

"Starting with the big guns," Ruth says.

"Let's see you do better," I challenge.

"You're talking to a Scrabble champion here," Ruth replies. "Show some respect."

"You play against grade-schoolers."

"Don't know why I even came over here," Ruth mumbles as she lays down her wooden tokens. She adds a second *E* above mine, then adds an *R* on top of that, and a *T* on top of the *R*.

"Tree," I read. "*Wow.*"

"I know," Ruth says, leaning back. "I'm a prodigy. Your turn, Sutton."

Sutton wastes no time making her play. She adds a single letter to my original word. RACE.

Dad's music shifts. A warbling voice blares across the house like a glee club ghost. "*Swing low, sweet chariot, coming for to carry me home...*"

Ruth's eyes flicker between me and Sutton as the song

continues. She fiddles with her tiles to busy herself, struggling to maintain composure. She's reaching to refill her tiles when Sutton cracks.

She laughs.

Sutton giggles without restraint, bubbling over and melting the tension as the somber music continues. *"If you get there before I do,"* the singer drawls, *"coming for to carry me home. Tell all my friends I'm coming too, coming for to carry me home."*

Sutton laughs so hard, she starts snorting like a pig, and I can't help myself, I give in too.

"Your dad really knows how to set an upbeat mood, doesn't he?" Ruth says between bouts of her own laughter. "What is he listening to anyway?"

"Negro spirituals and folk songs," I quote when we calm down. "It's for his new course."

Sutton's shoulder brushes some of the errant curls spilling from my messy bun as she leans across me to grab a new letter. I move the bag to a more central location while I consider my next turn. I add to the *R* in Ruth's TREE. RUN.

"How old does a song need to be to qualify as a spiritual?" Ruth asks.

"I don't know," I say. "Why?"

"I was just thinking," she says as she swaps tiles in front of her to compare choices. "I feel like there are newer songs to add to the canon."

"Like what?" Sutton asks.

"'Say My Name' by Destiny's Child."

I start laughing again, but she doubles down. "You can't tell me it hasn't had an impact on the culture! It's older than we are, and it still hits!"

"That's not what defines a spiritual," I say, trying and failing to stop smiling. "Dad says they came from a specific time and grew into gospel or other important cultural meaning. Lots of them started as work songs or even directions for the Underground Railroad."

"I dunno," Ruth says. "I feel like it still counts." She surveys the board. "Is it too soon to swap my letters?"

"Yes," Sutton says.

I laugh.

"Cureton girls ganging up on me already. Who says things aren't going back to normal?" Ruth's mouth stays open as if freezing could rewind time for her to swallow her words. Her playful shock mutates into embarrassment.

"Speaking of normal," I segue. "How's your house? You said your dad is back?" *Take the out, Ruth*, I plead in my mind. *We don't have to get stuck here.*

"Yes," she breathes. "Yes. He's been back for almost a week, but he's barely home. He says he's catching up on everything that fell behind while he was gone."

"I thought it was a planned trip," I say.

Ruth plays a letter. "It was planned, but he stayed longer than any of us thought he would. I'm just glad he's home. He's picking me up tonight."

We settle into a comfortable silence for the next several rounds. Our focus is necessary. It turns out amnesia did nothing to curb Sutton's competitiveness. I quickly remember why our games were abandoned: I got tired of losing to her. She isn't playing complicated head-scratchers that require a dictionary, but she's very deliberate in her choices. Her talent for utilizing a triple letter score is unmatched.

Just past sunset, I catch her singing her song again as she tilts her head to study the board. *"Follow the drinking gourd,"* Sutton sings. *"For the old man is waiting to carry you to freedom. Follow the drinking gourd."*

Ruth hums along too. It throws me for a moment until I understand how that's possible. Ruth has never heard my sister sing this song before, but she doesn't need to in order to follow the tune because Sutton isn't singing along to a melody only she can hear this time.

She's singing along to the music coming from Dad's office.

"The river ends between two hills," Sutton serenades as she places a letter. *"There's another river on the other side. Follow the drinking gourd."*

"Is this where you learned the song?" I ask her. "From Dad?"

Sutton frowns, like she's annoyed with me for asking. "It's your turn, Casey."

I make a random word plural. Ruth mocks me as she plans her next move. I don't care.

I never thought Sutton's song was the key to an elaborate

charade or unlocking her memory—I never assigned it that much importance—but this mundane and obvious explanation weighs me down more than I expected.

She learned it from Dad. She probably heard it when he was working at the table and memorized the lyrics while Mom tried to get her to remember old baby pictures and I drowned them all out with Ivy in my bedroom.

It wasn't a hint to the secrets she keeps because the truth of it was nothing at all.

She wasn't hiding anything. She really doesn't remember.

I feel like I've lost even though I'm only six points behind Sutton.

What was she winning by dragging this on? my mind scolds. Nothing. At the start, her caginess may have had a purpose, but this extended recovery has benefited no one. Her cheer friends have stopped calling. Her hair is falling out. Her boyfriend even ditched her.

She would never let her life fall apart like this if she had a choice.

"I got it!" Ruth says. She adds to Sutton's BRACE. "Bracelet! That's a big one. What's my score now?"

Sutton doesn't even bother looking at the scratch pad. "Still third place."

The doorbell rings.

"That's probably my dad," Ruth says. "Rematch next time?"

"Don't answer the door!" Mom calls from the second floor. "Wait for me!"

Dad stops his music but doesn't come out.

"David!" Mom says from the entryway, confirming our suspicions.

Ruth stands, careful not to knock the board askew with her knees as Mom comes in with Pastor Heights. He looks exhausted. The bags under his eyes could qualify as gym weights. I guess travel and then returning to parent seven children is not easy.

Ruth rushes to hug him. She's barely been here four hours, but I can't blame her for soaking in the parental affection she missed. I'd do the same with my dad.

"Is this our girl?" the pastor asks with a tone of mock incredulity. He squats to look Sutton in the face. His sandy five-o'clock shadow ticks deeper on his chin as he scrunches his lips. "Sutton Cureton," he says. "Returned to us. God is truly just."

He stands. I move to do the same so I can greet him properly, but Sutton grabs my wrist and roots me into place. I try again, but she tightens her grip. Her nails dig into my bare skin.

I give up and stay put. "It's nice to see you, Pastor."

"David," he reminds me. "We're so glad to have you back, Sutton. I've been praying on you every day."

Sutton's clenches her jaw. The pastor waits a moment for her to warm up to him, but it never happens. She doesn't move an inch, her eyes watching him unblinkingly until Mom finally breaks the silence.

"We appreciate that so much, David," she says. "Again, I'm sorry the girls couldn't join us the other evening. Sutton's been having trouble with crowds and strangers—not that you're a stranger, of course. She's just so attached to her sister nowadays. Did you want to say hello to Isaiah before you go?"

"Oh, absolutely," Pastor David agrees. He tosses Ruth his car keys. "Let yourself in, sweetheart. I'll be right out."

She nods as he and Mom head to Dad's office. I try to stand again to hug her goodbye, but Sutton's nails dig into my bare skin with every movement. "Sorry I can't get up," I say.

"Don't worry about it," Ruth says, bending to embrace me. She moves to do the same for Sutton, then seems to think better of it at Sutton's posture.

Sutton doesn't relax until they both leave. She won't let go of me, but her hold loosens. She pushes the letter bag toward me with her free hand. "Your turn," she says. "Unless you want to stop?"

I want to snap at her for monopolizing me in front of my friend. But if I shut her out, she won't have anyone else.

We finish out the game.

She wins.

NINETEEN

'm sorry my sister was so weird to your dad," I tell Ruth on the phone later that night. I drag out my bath basket from under my bed. My hair supplies are dwindling quickly with Sutton using them too, but I should be good for at least one more wash day. Maybe two if I'm conservative with my product. I never am, but it's the thought that counts.

"Don't worry about it," Ruth says from the phone pressed between my shoulder and my ear. I shut my door behind me and pad softly across the hallway, careful not to wake anyone. Sutton's door is open, but I don't see her inside. Romeo is taking advantage of her absence, curled in a ball on her bed. The aquarium is the only sign of movement in her room.

I hope she's not in the bathroom. She's been somewhat okay

today—if you ignore snubbing the pastor—but I want a little alone time. Some solitary self-care for once.

"No one blames her," Ruth continues as I let myself into the bathroom.

No sign of Sutton.

I set my basket and the phone on the countertop. I tap the speaker button in time to hear Ruth's next sentence. "Honestly, my dad was giving me a weird vibe too. Hold on. There's a noise in the driveway."

The sound on her end goes clunky for a moment, like she's moving around. "What is my dad doing out there? I see him unlocking the car from my window. The headlights are on. So much for not ditching me again."

"I'm sorry," I say.

Ruth doesn't even acknowledge it.

I unwind my hair from the messy bun I twisted it into. It falls around my shoulders in waves with uneven volume. I fluff it with my fingers, but there's no way I can push it to another day of acceptable viewing. Though that only matters if I plan on going somewhere. If I were *allowed* to go anywhere.

"Ruth?" She doesn't respond. "Are you still there?"

It's quiet for a long moment before she replies, "I'm here."

"Are you okay?"

"I'm just frustrated," she says. "I don't mean to bother you with it. You have enough going on."

"You never bother me," I promise. "It's totally okay to be

annoyed at your dad. He could be running an errand," I offer. "Heading to the grocery store or something."

"It's ten o'clock at night. And he didn't even tell me he was leaving. But maybe," she admits. "I'm probably being a baby. I'm tired of having to do everything alone. I miss my mom. It's nothing. I'll talk to you later."

"It's not nothing," I insist, but Ruth cuts me off with a quick goodbye and hangs up before I can wish her a good night.

I look back at the lion's mane on my head. I don't really want to tackle taming it. It's so late. I don't have time to air-dry, so I'd have to blow-dry it enough to sleep on. I pull a satin hair tie from my basket and pile my hair high on my head.

I'll just take a bath tonight. I can deal with my hair tomorrow.

The shower curtain hides the width of the tub. I grab an edge and tug to open it, leaning down to reach for the faucet.

My body stops before my brain can process the sight in front of me.

My ears ring, and I grab the tub's edge, then plunge my hands into the water. It's ice cold.

I grab Sutton. She lies underwater, fully clothed. Her eyes are open and unmoving. No part of her is moving. She's so still. Too still. There aren't any bubbles.

I pull. When Sutton's face breaks the surface, she takes a gasping breath and blinks.

I let go of her in shock.

She doesn't slip back down. She stares at me like I'm the most unexpected part of this. She doesn't shiver as the water drips from every inch of her, including the fresh braids I helped her with yesterday. I can't stop shaking.

"What—" My throat closes. I can't breathe. I can't remember how. Sutton stands in the tub. Her pajamas are skintight. She lifts a foot from the water and then the other before crouching to approach me. I scurry back until my spine hits the closed door.

"What were you doing in there?" I finally manage.

"I can't remember," she says.

"You can't *remember*?" I spit. "Can you think? What would've happened if Mom found you like that? Dad? Do you have any idea what that would have done to them?"

What about what it did to me? *Does she even care?*

"If I say I believe you, will you stop?" I beg her. "We can't keep living like this. I believe you. You don't have to prove it anymore. I understand something awful happened to you. You don't have to be okay, but please—"

"Casey, I'm sorry." Sutton pulls me into her freezing arms. I let her hold me, even though her cold embrace zaps the warmth from my bones. "I'm trying," she pleads in my ear. "I'm trying to remember. I'm trying to fix it."

"You don't have to fix it, just please, please—"

She squeezes tighter. "I remembered more about Andrew after my shower the other day. I thought the water would help again." She lets me go. I sink back against the door. "It's not working. I'm trying, but nothing helps. I feel like I'm running out of time." She looks back at the tub.

I reach for her hand. Her skin is so cold. She wipes at her eyes with her free hand. I'm crying too.

"You aren't running out of time," I say to reassure her. "But you have to *stay*. I'm sorry I blamed you for all that happened." *Please don't go. I won't survive it a second time.*

Sutton nods, but she doesn't look like she believes it.

"Maybe you don't need to remember," I say. "I've been looking into what you were doing before. Your coach was pretty mad at you. Do you think he might have something to do with what happened?"

Her brow furrows. She's so quiet, I can hear the water dripping from her pajama pants. "My coach," she repeats.

"In cheer," I clarify. "You suspected he was hurting your teammates."

She stiffens at that. "Yes," she says. "No one else can get hurt. I want to protect them. I want to protect you."

"Okay," I say. "We'll tell Mom and Dad tomorrow. They'll tell the cops. We'll get help."

She nods. "I'm sorry I got you all wet."

I laugh. I can't help it. I try to stop, but that only increases the pressure inside. "You're soaked," I point out, the words filtering out through giggles.

She doesn't laugh with me, but her frown lessens. "So much for not sleeping on wet hair."

"You've ruined all my hard work," I agree.

"Sorry," she repeats.

I lift a hand to the doorknob and pull myself up. "One night with wet hair won't kill you, but you should try to wring out as much of it as you can. Give me your clothes to toss in the dryer while I get you some dry ones."

"Okay," Sutton says, almost relieved.

I don't know if I'll ever get used to having an older sister who listens to me. She starts to strip before I've opened the door, so easily vulnerable in my presence. Eventually, this will fade. As she heals, she'll pull away from me again. She'll stop relying on me, trusting me above all others.

I know that's what I should want. I should be happy about that.

I take our clothes downstairs and toss them in the dryer before setting it on the longest setting. I head back upstairs. Sutton's already in her room. She got herself fresh clothes without my help, and she's sitting in the spot Romeo vacated. He's on the floor now, watching us both. I get a shirt from my room, then loop back.

"Did you dry your hair?" I ask.

"As much as I could," she says. "It's still damp near the roots."

"I'll grab a towel for your pillow." I don't know how else to be useful, but I don't want to leave her and go to bed yet. I'm afraid to go to sleep and see her in the water again—or worse. I'm not going to admit that out loud though.

"Climb in," I instruct when I return. "I'll set it down before you lay your head so you don't mess it up moving around."

She grabs my wrist as I tuck her into bed. "Can you stay with me?"

I nod.

She scoots back to make room and lifts her blanket. I tuck in, the little spoon to her tall frame. Her arm rests over me, heavier than it should be but not suffocating. I'm transported back to movie nights on the couch and dragging one of Grandma's quilts over my face during the scary parts. Sutton would tighten her hold until the villain went away, letting me know once it was safe to come out again.

Romeo waits until we're both settled before making his nest at our feet. I listen to them both breathe against me in the dark. The only other noise is the whirring of Juliet's tank.

I don't intend to stay all night, but I fall asleep before I can catch myself.

When I wake, I know there's no point in trying for a clean getaway. The sun shines strong through Sutton's window, clearly several hours past sunrise. Romeo's weight has disappeared from my feet. Our mother stands in the doorway. She's crying. Like Dad, she's tried very hard to hide her sorrow from either of us, leaving for her office at the slightest hint of emotion since her outburst. She looks directly at me, making no attempt to hide her tears.

I try to untangle myself from Sutton, but her grip is somehow tighter when she's unconscious. "She asked me to stay," I attempt to explain. "She wanted me here. I didn't—"

Mom shakes her head. "Casey—Casey, stop."

241

She comes into Sutton's room and squats beside me. She tucks a wayward strand of hair from where it escaped my half-hearted updo last night. Her hand rests on my cheek.

"This isn't about your sister," she says. She blinks hard, like whatever she's keeping from me is causing her physical pain. "I'm so sorry, honey."

"What happened?" I ask.

"Pastor David called. Ruth has gone missing."

SUTTON

FIVE YEARS BEFORE

I wish Ruth would go away.

Casey took *her*. She went to the Ivy James concert with her instead of me. I'm her sister! Ruth has siblings of her own. But they treat each other like sisters more than friends.

I don't have anyone else. I only have Casey.

Ma Remy presses an edge piece into the puzzle on the table. The edge of the picture is almost complete. She says that's the best way to solve a puzzle quickly. I'm supposed to be sorting the other pieces by color, but I don't think I'm doing it right.

I scoot my chair closer to the table. The beads in my braids hit the rim of the dining table. Ma Remy reaches out and tucks my hair behind my shoulder. Her hair is short near her head, her small salt-and-pepper curls popping out in all directions.

"What's wrong, baby girl?" she asks.

"Nothing," I say. I look at the image we're supposed to re-create on the box. It looks like Ma Remy's garden. There are so many flowers and colors. Mom has started planting in our yard too, but nothing has grown yet. This morning, before Casey and Mom left for the concert, Grandma told Mom she'd give her some lessons and clippings. I've never seen Mom so excited. She loves Ma Remy and always glows for days after she includes her in stuff or compliments her.

"Doesn't sound like nothing," Ma Remy says.

"All the *sounds* are at the concert," I mumble. I push a yellow-gold piece into my light pile.

Grandma sticks her finger in my dark pile and swirls it around, screwing up my system. She finds another outside piece and picks it up between her long red nails. The pendant on her silver bracelet trails through the cardboard cutouts.

I try to fix the mess she made. I'm no good at this. This puzzle is a thousand pieces. It's too complicated, and the colors are so similar. I couldn't possibly make enough piles to organize them all. "We're never gonna finish this before they get back."

"We don't have to," she says. "We've got time."

"Hours and hours," I agree. "They're gonna spend all day in Seattle, I bet." That's what we did with Mom the last time Ivy came to Washington. We left early and went to the pier for lunch and ice cream before heading to the arena. I can still remember the look on Casey's face when the men at the market tossed fish at each other with their bare hands.

I wonder if they'll bring Ruth there too. They could be there right now. Casey's probably having more fun with my replacement.

"I thought you were happy to spend the day with me," Ma Remy says.

"I am!" I flex my hands again, admiring my matching red nails. She did such a great job on them. I'm much better at nail polish than Casey is, but my left hand is still too shaky to paint my right one perfectly. Ma Remy is so good, she even painted a tiny rose on both of my thumbs. "I just..." I tap my fingers on the table.

"You what? I'm not a mind reader, darlin'."

"I don't understand why she left me behind."

"Your sister?"

As if I could be talking about anyone else.

"She took Ruth to go see Ivy James. She didn't even ask me!"

Grandma doesn't look up from the puzzle when she responds, "I thought you didn't want to go to the concert." She ruins another one of my piles searching for another edge piece. "You've been telling anyone who asks that you're too old for Ivy now."

"I am," I say.

"Then I don't understand why you're upset," she replies. "If you wouldn't have enjoyed yourself, doesn't it make sense she invited someone who would?"

I don't know how to explain that you can be too old for something and still like it sometimes. Ivy isn't cool anymore, so I can't talk about her at school, but that doesn't mean I forgot the lyrics to her songs. It's not like I would have seen any of my friends at the concert. Besides, it's not about Ivy. I want to be Casey's first choice.

"She still should have asked me."

"You two haven't been getting along lately," she says. She finds the final outside piece, so she presses it into place and leans back, smiling at me. She looks so proud, as if we don't have the rest of the picture to fill in. "Aw, baby," she says at my frown. "It'll be okay. There will be other concerts."

"I don't know how we're supposed to start liking each other again if we never hang out." I try to connect two pink pieces from one of my piles, but they don't match. "I'm trying to be the mature one. I'm older. I can't expect her to understand."

"Maybe you should ask Casey to join you on one of your activities instead."

I snort. "That's different. I can't do that," I tell her. "Grandma, I'm *twelve*. I'm in middle school now. It'd be social suicide to invite an elementary school kid to hang out with me and my friends."

Ma Remy nods, her face very serious. "It seems you're at an impasse."

I don't know what that means, but I nod too. "Yeah."

Grandma pulls the empty chair between us next to hers and pats the seat. I slide out of my spot at the head of the table and go where I'm told. She leans across our makeshift bench, then hooks her arm around my shoulder. She presses me against her.

"Sutton," she says before kissing the top of my head. "Your problem is not gonna be fixed today. It's probably not going to get better tomorrow either. Or the next day or the next day. But it will get better eventually."

I push out of her hug. "How can you be sure? You never had a sister. You only had brothers. You don't understand."

"I don't need a sister to know what I'm saying is true," she says. "You haven't stopped being sisters. You never will. Family isn't something you can ever truly lose, even if you can't see what connects you in this moment. And you will be friends again. Closer than that. It just takes time."

"I don't see how." My voice is so low, I don't know if she can even hear me. "Every day we get madder and madder at each other. It's like she wants us to hate each other." I start to slide off the chair to go back to my multicolored piles. Ma Remy stops me, turning my shoulders so we're facing each other instead of flush together.

"I promise you she doesn't," she says. "But my certainty doesn't come from your sister's changing whims. It's more powerful than that." She takes both my hands in hers. "Can you keep a secret?"

"Yes," I say immediately. "Tell me."

"Our family has a surefire way of keeping our loved ones together."

I open my mouth to ask what that is, but before I can speak, she's undoing the clasp of her bracelet. The silver chains pool together in her wrinkled palms. She gestures for me to open my own hands, and when I do, she carefully places the bracelet there, the shiny pendant resting on top.

"This pendant has been with our family for many generations," she says. "When we were torn from our homeland and brought to this land as slaves, we weren't allowed to bring mementos of home. Memories, bonds of blood were actively discouraged. Families were broken apart and sent to different places: husbands and wives separated, mothers ripped away from their children."

"We had to rebuild our concept of beloveds in this new world. We had to find new brothers and sisters in our new homes. No one looks out for you like family, so we remade ours from scratch. But the plantations were like the ships. They didn't care about keeping people together. They'd take our new families and crack them open too."

"I'm sorry, Grandma," I say. "I guess I have it pretty good now. Casey isn't going anywhere."

"*Chile*—" Ma Remy warns. "I'm not done with my story. Hush."

I press my lips together.

"This pendant was made by a member of one of those new families," she continued. "Sick and tired of being separated, she took many herbs—"

"How do you know it was a girl?"

She gives me her look. "What did I just say?"

"Sorry!"

"She—or he, or whoever—took many herbs and ground them. Each of the plants was chosen for its special ability to bind people together. Now, understand I was told this by my papa, who heard it from his mama who heard it from hers, so I don't know all the plants inside. I tried to figure it out once. There is ivy, used in marriage wreaths and to bless luck upon people. And cleavers, a plant with tiny hooks that cling to all they touch."

I turn the pendant over in my fingers. I saw it hanging from Ma Remy's wrist my entire life, but I never thought about what made the green coloring. Looking closer now, I can see the small specks locked in the teardrop. The smooth polish on the pendant doesn't seem old enough to match her story, but I don't dare interrupt again.

"They wore this mixture in a small bag tied around their ankles so the slave master didn't see it. They poured all their love and hopes for reunification inside. And somehow, despite the auction block, they were brought back together."

"Every time?" I ask.

Grandma lifts the bracelet from my hands. She closes her fist around it, as if drawing energy from it. Hiding it. Protecting it. "Not always," she admits quietly. "Sometimes people are lost from you, no matter how much you wish they weren't, and before you can even begin to know how big of a hole they'll leave behind. But our family was reunited more than anyone else they knew. They believed in the power of these plants so much, they sealed them inside this pendant so our family would never lose what binds us."

"And you think it could help me and Casey?"

"Well, you said your problems aren't as serious as our ancestors'," she says. "I don't see how it could hurt."

She opens her hand again. At the center of the pendant,

pressed against the top, small white petals open like a butterfly spreading its wings to soak up the sun.

"What do I have to do?" I ask.

"You have to believe. You have to trust, with everything you have, that the love you and your sister share will be enough to bring you back together. Even when you're mad at her. You have to believe your sisterhood is stronger than your anger. No matter what. Can you do that?"

"Yes," I say. "I promise I can. I will."

"Good," Ma Remy says. "You also have to give it something."

She takes my thumb and pricks it with the hook of the bracelet's closure. I pull out of her grasp and suck at the wound. She doesn't apologize. She tugs on my wrist until I give in, and she squeezes a fresh drop of blood to the surface.

I pull away again. "I can do it myself."

"Okay." She holds out the pendant for me. I press my thumb to the flower at the center and then put my finger back in my mouth. The white flower looks pink under my red thumbprint.

"Is it mine now?" I ask around my thumb.

Grandma hooks the bracelet back around her wrist. "Not yet, sweetheart. I still have a lot of family I need to reunite with myself, so I'll hold on to it for now."

I frown. *What was the point of this, then?*

"Don't worry," she says. "I'll keep your sisterhood safe with the others. Just keep your faith."

TWENTY

After Mom wakes me with the news, her phone rings from where she left it downstairs, so she steps out to let me wake Sutton myself.

Climbing out of Sutton's bed is enough to rouse her, but I don't have to tell her that something is wrong. She comes to consciousness like a computer turning on, asleep one second and alert the next. This time I'm the one who can only stare at her in a weighted silence, lost in a world I don't recognize anymore.

"Another girl is gone," she says without lifting her head from the pillow. It's not a question. "Just like me."

"Ruth," I manage to choke out.

She sits up and moves like she wants to hug me. I back away—no, I flee from her to the safety of my room. I don't lock my door behind me, but she doesn't follow. I stay that way as time distorts and breaks around me. I hear Mom getting terse with whoever called downstairs, but her voice bleeds in and out of memories I can't help reliving. Ruth downstairs losing at Scrabble. Ruth here in my bedroom with me, listening to Ivy and painting our toenails bright colors her dad would find far too "worldly." Ruth listening to me complain about Sutton. Sutton, Sutton, Sutton. My sister before. The bane of my existence. The worst thing that ever happened to me.

The worst thing that ever happened to *her*. I think of Sutton now, sitting alone in her bedroom as shattered as I am. Not even smoke left of the fire she once was.

I can't begin to imagine Ruth like that, but the alternative is worse.

"Isaiah!" Mom snaps from downstairs, loud enough to register through my closed door and scattered mind. Dad's voice is muffled through the distance but even more upset than hers. I move to my door and crack it a little to eavesdrop on their conversation downstairs.

I can see Sutton hiding in her doorway too.

"I'm not doing it!" Dad says, his voice echoing through the house. "I won't. I can't."

Mom's reply is either nonexistent or too quiet for me to hear. I look to Sutton unashamedly sitting in her doorway and move closer to the stairway myself. Romeo follows me, but I grab him before he can head downstairs and blow our cover.

"You know I'm not happy with them either, right?" Mom

says. She's not matching Dad's volume yet, but I can hear her anger.

"*Happy* doesn't belong in my vocabulary anymore."

"Baby, baby, babe," Mom says, attempting to soothe. I hear her bare feet pad across the hardwood. Dad doesn't speak, but a grunt of refusal turns into a loud sigh.

"I don't want—"

"I know," she says. "I *know*. It shouldn't have been our responsibility. We should never have had to go on camera every day to shame them into doing the bare minimum. They should have organized a search themselves. Our friends shouldn't have had to pay for it. We pay their salaries. They are supposed to work for us."

"It's a power move. It's not about the money. It doesn't matter how much we make. It doesn't matter how hard we work to rise above. None of it fucking matters, Madison."

There's a loud thump I can't identify. Romeo tenses in my arms with an anxious growl. I hold him a little tighter.

"I thought it wouldn't happen here," Dad continues. "I hoped they'd care about her because she was yours. I thought maybe if I stepped out of the spotlight and let you take the lead, they would want to return our baby to us. I didn't want to be a distraction."

"You could never," Mom says. "This is not your fault. Don't tell me that. None of the police's failures belong to you."

"Our baby girl was found naked in the street. Alone in the dark. Traumatized. And they blamed *her* for it. Tried to convince us she was on drugs, even though the tests were clear. I can't even say they gave up on her because they never tried at all. It's been almost a month since she came home, and how many times have they called us with an update on her case?"

It seems like a rhetorical question, but Dad must be waiting for an answer, because after a long moment, Mom says, "Once."

"I can't do it," he says. "I can't go to that station and nod politely while a bunch of white men promise they'll bring Ruth home after they've done nothing to find out who hurt my daughter. They let it happen again."

"That's why we have to go," she says.

"I know. For Ruth."

"Ruth," Mom agrees.

"But I'm not bringing our girls to the station," Dad declares. "If they want to talk to them, they will come here. It's on our terms. We're in control."

"Absolutely. I'll make the call. Do you want to tell the girls?"

I don't hear his reply because Sutton and I are too busy scrambling back to our bedrooms before he can reach the stairs.

The detectives arrive an hour later. We're prepared for them. Sutton and I are on the couch in front of the heirloom table. Dad told us we didn't need to dress up, so we're still wearing our pajamas from last night. He didn't take his own advice. He's in his nicest button-down, usually reserved for church. Mom is in a simple but expensive sundress Dad bought her for their fifteenth anniversary trip a few years ago.

As Mom answers the door, Dad moves the second armchair closer to the coffee table so it's clear where he'd like the police officers to sit. Mom takes her time showing them in.

"This is from the second time Isaiah hit the bestseller list," she explains from the hallway. "It was his first time at number one. We don't bother framing those accomplishments anymore. We'd have an entire wall filled if we did!" She laughs at her joke until the cops contribute their own chuckles, and then she guides them into the living room.

They're the same detectives we met at the hospital when Sutton was found. I recognize Brendan and his patchy goatee. His partner is clean-shaven but still as blank-faced as he was that early morning.

"Hello," Dad says. He gestures at the armchairs and sits in the loveseat. Mom joins him. We're all circling the heirloom display. Dad points that out while Brendan's partner opens his briefcase. "I've been working on a project showcasing some of our most meaningful family heirlooms. It follows our ancestors from slavery to more modern accomplishments."

"Wow," Brendan says. He leans forward for a better look. "Your people—Your family has overcome a lot of adversity. That takes strength."

Henny's portrait stares at him until he covers her with a manila folder.

Brendan looks to my parents, ignoring Sutton and me. "We were hoping to speak to the girls separately. Privately."

Mom smiles. "No. We'll do this all together."

"Okay," Brendan accepts, like he had expected as much. Then he addresses us. "Good afternoon, girls. We've met before, but I'm Detective Brendan Sorno, and this is my partner, Detective Micheal Pace. We're here today to ask some questions about your friend Ruth."

"Is she still claiming memory issues?" Detective Pace asks my parents.

I glare at him before I can stop myself. "She's not *claiming* anything." While I had my own suspicions, no one questions my sister like that.

"I apologize for my partner," Brendan says. "He didn't mean to phrase it that way. What we mean to ask is has Sutton's memory improved?"

"She's doing the best she can," Dad says. "It's hard to make meaningful progress in recovery when you have no updates or closure about what happened to you."

Brendan ignores the insult. "Sutton," he says. "Have you remembered anything new? Anything at all."

Sutton looks at me. She bites her lip. I can tell she's considering telling them about Andrew. I squeeze her hand in support.

"I remembered my boyfriend," she admits. Mom tenses next to Dad like someone poked her with a tack.

Detective Pace smirks. "That's not exactly what we're looking for."

Brendon opens his folder and spreads photos on the table. They are shots of some outdoor locations, taken at night with a flash camera. An intersection, with evergreens on one side and a small red building on the opposite street.

The building looks familiar, but I can't place it. It's too old and abandoned to be from our town. Still, I know I've seen it. Though maybe without the boards on the windows. I don't remember when or why. *Where is it?*

The street signs read 113TH and JERICHO.

"No!" Mom stands and slides the photos into a pile before Sutton or I can inspect them closer. "We did not agree to this. I told you on the phone, nothing from that night."

"Mrs. Cureton, we are not seeking to retraumatize your daughter, but if there is a connection between these cases, Sutton's memory of the when she was found could help us find Ruth."

"I don't remember what happened," Sutton says. "I remember after. Pain. Cold. Lights. Casey."

Brendan glances at Pace. "All right," he says, patience obviously wearing thin. "Casey, what can you tell me about Ruth's temperament?"

"Her temperament?"

"How was she feeling? Not only last night, but overall. Has she been stressed lately? Upset for any reason?"

"Um." I stall for time. I focus on Detective Brendan to numb the overwhelming urge inside me to look at my parents. Their anguished voices from this morning ricochet in my mind like a pinball machine. Every question feels as if it's seeking blame, not resolution.

Something happened to Ruth, and I want her back more than anything. I also know that if I tell the truth about how she's been feeling lately, they could think she ran away.

But I don't really have a choice.

"She's been stressed," I admit. "Her dad is our church pastor, and he's been out of town a lot to raise money for a youth camp. She has younger siblings, and she had more family responsibilities while her dad was gone."

I dip my head when I finish. I look at Dad, but he doesn't see me. His elbows are on his knees, his chin resting on his folded hands. He's watching the detectives with fire in his eyes, like this is a football game that isn't going well. It's like he knows what their next move will be before they even set up the play.

"Was she mad at her father?" Brendan asks. "Has she ever left without telling anyone before?"

Dad leans back, palms dropping, defeated. Mom takes his hand in hers and straightens her posture.

"Why are you asking me this?" I ask.

"Ruth's phone was found in her bedroom. It was turned off. Her bike was gone. You're her best friend. You probably know her better than anyone else. Can you explain that for us?"

"No," I say. "I mean, yes. I can explain it, but it's not what you think."

"What do we think, Casey?" Detective Pace asks.

"Ruth would sometimes leave her phone at home so her dad couldn't track her through parental controls, but never at night and never without me. She's not a troublemaker. She's not rebellious. Her father can be really strict and conservative, and we're fifteen, okay? She isn't into anything bad, I swear—"

Brendan cuts me off. "We didn't say she was. We're trying to figure out what happened last night. When we looked at her phone, it told us you were the last person she called before she disappeared. In that conversation, did Ruth seem angry at her father?"

"A little," I admit. "Her dad was going somewhere, and she felt like he was ditching her again. But I told her he was probably going to the store, and she seemed to accept that."

"Yes. Mr. Heights told us he went for a late diaper run last night. We've seen the receipt," Brendan says. "He said when he returned, he went to check on all his children and that's when he discovered Ruth's absence. Do you think it's possible Ruth left on purpose, maybe to punish her father? To make him feel abandoned, like she felt?"

"Ruth's not like that. And she wouldn't run away." But I know that's how it looks. I know they won't believe me.

"Is there anything else Ruth was keeping from her father?"

I won't answer this. Ruth hasn't come out to her dad. I'm the only person she's told that she knows in real life. The only other people who know she's a lesbian are our friends online, our fellow Jamies. I won't break her trust.

"Why are you acting like Ruth is a runaway?" Dad asks the cops. "She's a pastor's daughter. She spends all her time at church or with my girls. You did the same thing when we reported Sutton missing. Ruth running off on her own doesn't make any sense, especially after her best friend's sister just returned from a traumatic abduction. She's a smart girl." He points at us. "All of them are. Someone is clearly targeting Black girls in this area."

"Mr. Cure—" Detective Pace starts, but Dad won't let him finish.

"Maddie," he prompts Mom. She nods and gets up from her seat to grab something from the kitchen. She returns with printouts of her own and slides them on the table, right where Sutton's crime scene photos once lay. "Ruth is the fourth Black girl to have gone missing in Willow Bend in less than three months."

Mom's printouts are missing person flyers. It's the girls from Bend's End: Tamika Horn and Imani Brenton.

The police are not happy about this ambush. "Mr. and Mrs. Cureton, I understand you are concerned and upset about what has happened to your daughter and family friend, but this is not the time to bring up unrelated cases. We must focus on Ruth."

"Unrelated?" Dad snaps. "Have you looked at these?"

"We are very aware of the Horn and Brenton cases. They are ongoing cases, but we have no reason to believe those disappearances are related to either Sutton or Ruth's."

"I don't see how that's possible," Mom argues.

My parents' fury makes an encore presentation. The

detectives repeat themselves in an attempt to regain control of this conversation.

The four of them are so preoccupied, none of them see Sutton pull one of the flyers closer to her.

She looks at Tamika Horn's picture and runs her finger along her pixelated hairline. Tamika is wearing the same type of braids Sutton is right now, though Tamika's hairdo is in better shape than Sutton's growing frizz. Tamika's head is tilted against one of her hands, almost embarrassed, like she was surprised by the photographer and wasn't sure how to pose. On the wrist of that hand, Tamika wears a beaded friendship bracelet spelling out her name. It doesn't seem like the sort of thing a teenager would make or wear for herself, but I remember she has multiple younger siblings from the posts I saw. One of them probably made it for her. I think of tiny Esther, who practically sees her big sister as a surrogate mom. The twins and her older brothers, they all adore Ruth, and she, them. If she came back like Sutton...they couldn't handle that.

If she comes back at all.

Mom pulls the flyer from Sutton's hand. "No, darling," she says as she gives the papers to the detectives. "You don't need to worry about that." She joins us on the couch, folding Sutton into her arms. She turns back to Dad with a pleading look.

The tension deflates, the fight going out of my parents.

I try to help. "Have you spoken to Sutton's cheer coach?" I ask. "Sutton felt he was ignoring safety rules and putting her teammates at risk. She reported him to the school board." I don't mention the texts or what she did to his van, but I shouldn't need to. This should be motive enough.

"How do you know that?" Mom asks me at the same time as Dad asks the detectives if what I'm saying is true.

"Yes," Brendan admits. "We are aware of Sutton's complaints against her coach, and Mr. McCoy was once a person of interest in Sutton's case, but we don't believe he has anything to do with Ruth's disappearance."

"You never told us there were any additional suspects since you cleared her boyfriend," Dad says. "Why did you keep this from us?"

"We weren't intentionally keeping anything from you. Lots of people are investigated in cases like this, and we didn't want to worry you without certainty."

"We asked you to tell us everything," Dad says.

"We begged you," Mom adds.

"We know he's not involved. He's in custody for a separate issue with his personal training business. I can't disclose any information, but he was in the county jail last night and couldn't have been involved with Ruth's disappearance."

"But what about Sutton?" Dad asks. "What about my daughter? What did he do to her?"

"We are still investigating her case," Brendan claims, "but Ruth is the one we need to focus on right now."

Mom redirects the conversation. "You talked to Pastor David? What does he think about your theories on Ruth?"

Brendan breaks eye contact with Dad. "He's been very helpful with our investigation. He understands we must consider and eliminate multiple possibilities in order to find her as quickly as possible."

Dad nods slowly. "Absolutely. Just like you found Sutton. I think we're done here."

He walks away without a goodbye.

TWENTY-ONE

'll walk you out," Mom tells the cops. Detective Pace lingers as his partner seals the briefcase, watching Sutton. She matches his intensity and doesn't blink until he turns away.

She lets go of my hand as they leave. "I'm going to get Romeo," she says. "He's tired of being locked upstairs. I can hear him whining."

I don't hear anything, but I let her go.

I don't know what else to do. I tried to be honest with the detectives, but it seems to have backfired. They dismissed me outright, and I upset my parents at the same time. I didn't mean to make things worse.

I just want Ruth back. She needs to be okay. She has to come home.

Good luck with that, my traitorous mind scoffs. Tamika and

Imani's faces flicker in my mind. Four girls in less than three months. We were beyond lucky to have one returned home safe, though I wouldn't qualify Sutton's condition as *sound*.

If she didn't run away, the odds of Ruth coming back are astronomically low. And I know she didn't run away. She'd never leave like that. Not without telling me. I check my phone again, but I have no new notifications from Ruth since our call last night.

I follow Dad to the backyard. He's pacing the edge of the pool. The collar of his dress shirt is unbuttoned, and he swings his hands at his sides, squeezing them in and out of fists. I don't try to hide my approach, but he's so in his head, he doesn't notice me until I'm right in front of him.

I smell the salt of his unshed tears as I hug him. He squeezes me so tight, I almost go airborne. When we part, I don't move away. We sit together at edge of the pool. Dad trails a finger along the surface of the water, creating his own current.

"I'm sorry, baby girl," he says. He flicks the water. "It's my job as a father to keep you both safe, and I failed."

"No." I scoot closer to him, putting my hand on his knee. "You haven't failed anyone."

"I can't help but think that if your mom married someone else..." He looks away from me before continuing, "If you girls were white, maybe we wouldn't have to fight so hard to be taken seriously. Maybe this wouldn't have happened to Sutton."

"Dad," I say. He doesn't move. "What about Ruth?" He grimaces. "What about the other girls? Tamika? Imani? You had nothing to do with their disappearances. Their families didn't fail them. You'd never say the pastor failed Ruth, right?"

"No, I wouldn't," he agrees.

"If Mom had married somebody else, Sutton and I wouldn't be the people we are. Even if she still had two daughters, they wouldn't be us. I'm who I am because of who made me. You *and* Mom made me. Grandma Remy made me. The people whose stories you've collected in our heritage table made me." I pause, considering whether I really want to rock the waters further with my next sentence.

"Dad," I say, "I found something in your office."

He waits for me to continue.

"I found a journal full of stories about our family. And what really happened to the pendant. I read the entry Ma Remy made about how she got it back."

Dad sighs. "I didn't want you to know about that. I don't agree with what she did. I don't condone stealing. We could have gotten it back another way."

"Could we really though?" I ask. "Maybe now, with the access and experience you have. But you're here now because of how deeply she cared then. It said right there in the book that she tried to go about it the right way, but they wouldn't listen to her. She wanted to hire a lawyer, but she worried about finances after your father passed."

The father you never talk to me about, I leave unsaid.

"I understand now why she did it," he says. "She was in so

much pain after my father died. I never saw it because she wouldn't let me see her suffering, but my uncles told me how devastated she was when I was young. She thought they were going to have the rest of their lives together. He died before I ever got to meet him, and she could never let that go. She felt robbed."

"How did he die?" I ask.

I can tell this is the last thing he wants to talk about when he's already upset. I open my mouth to take back my question, but he starts speaking.

"After he came back from Vietnam, he was very disillusioned with what he'd experienced and what life was like back in the States. He wanted better for Mama and him, so he got involved in some activist groups and attended a lot of protests. He felt the Civil Rights Movement still had a long way to go—and he was right, of course—but things weren't always *civil* at protests, and he was shot at one."

"He died trying to promise you a better life."

Dad shakes his head. "His death denied me a life. I was so angry with him for a long time about everything I never got from him. For how we struggled in his absence. How Mama mourned him in a way I could never comprehend because I never got to love him at all."

"But you do love him," I argue. "You wouldn't have been so mad if you didn't care."

"I thought if I avoided conflict, if I worked hard and rose above, that I wouldn't end up like him. I hated him, baby." He looks at me with tears in his eyes. "I was so mad he left me behind. I never wanted you to feel that way. But it didn't matter. Despite my education and our money, Sutton still got hurt. I couldn't protect her. I let her down. I let you both down."

"Daddy, it's not your fault." I lean forward to hug him again. "What happened to Sutton had nothing to do with you. You couldn't have prevented it, and you've done everything possible to support her. To support us. You haven't let me down. You can't. I love you."

"I love you too," he says. "But you shouldn't have to give me a pep talk. That's my job."

"Maybe I'm angling for a promotion," I joke when he lets me go. "Instead of being listed on the dedication page of your next book, maybe I'll start demanding royalties. Emotional support and all that."

Half a laugh slips from his lips.

"Like you said before," I remind him. "Against all odds, justice was done for our family before, and it will be done again. No matter what."

"No matter what," he agrees. His face wrinkles again, but it doesn't look like anguish this time. It's almost embarrassed, like he's biting back an uncomfortable truth.

"Dad?"

"I discovered some alternate perspectives in my research for the spirituality course," he admits. "Diary entries from another relative that shed new light on the case of the slave master."

"About Mima and Henny?"

"Apparently," he says, dragging out the word like it should be taken with a grain of salt, "other members of their family believed Mima really did kill their former owner. Family gossip in these writings say Mima was certain the slave master had murdered Henny."

"But he didn't," I say. "Henny came back. Didn't that help her case?"

He shakes his head. "These entries are years after the legal battle. This family member—an aunt through marriage—claims Mima refused to believe her mother would have tried to escape without her, even to try and secure a future for them both. This aunt was of the opinion that Mima killed the slave master and that her innocent nephew was married to an unrepentant sinner."

"But she was acquitted, right?" I ask. "They let her go?"

Dad nods. "Both Mima and her mama had a long and prosperous life afterward, as good as could be had in that time. Mima had a son with her husband, and that son had another son, and so on to the eventual daughter who had me. Ma Remy. If Mima did kill him, she got away with it."

"What does this have to do with your new class?"

"Henny was referenced in a few conjure documents from the time period," Dad says. "I thought it was because of her plant book and medicine work on the plantation, but it turns out the slave master accused her of cursing his crops right before she escaped. All the plantations in that area were suffering from a bad harvest that year, but it might explain why Mima would think he killed her. Why she might have wanted revenge."

"Okay, let me get this right: A racist lost all his money and then died?" I ask.

"It's not that cut-and-dried, baby."

"I don't know," I argue. "I get you're upset that the perfect legacy you've grown up on may be a little darker than you thought it was, but this still sounds like justice to me. A man who owned us was murdered—maybe by our ancestor!—and now we're alive, and he's bones in some forgotten cemetery. I don't feel bad about it. He can rot. Literally."

Dad's laugh is loud in the open air. He pats my shoulder with the mirth of it. His laugh sounds just like Sutton's. I miss it. I lean into him, letting his big arms embrace me again.

I know that, like Mima for her mother, I'd do anything for him. I'm the one who should be worried about failure, not him. I'm the one who should be scared to disappoint my parents, not the other way around.

Sutton's not the only one who has a long road to recovery in front of them. Her absence shattered us all in different ways, and picking up the pieces after her return comes with new cuts. No one deserves this.

I have to find Ruth.

TWENTY-TWO

mani is calling for me.

I run after her, yelling her name. She needs to know people are looking for her. Her mother misses her. She turns her head without stopping and frowns at my inability to keep up. I push harder, but it the distance between us seems to widen.

"Come back!"

My legs give out. I hit the road hard and roll onto my back before running my hands over the gravel embedded in my knee-caps. "Come back," I plead again, but Imani is too far gone.

A hand reaches down to help me up. On the wrist is a beaded bracelet with letters that spin, as if on a slot machine continually spelling new words. Tamika.

"They're looking for you too," I say as she helps me stand.

She doesn't respond.

We're no longer on a road. The shade of a willow tree chills my bones, but Tamika doesn't react to the cold. She sits in front of me, watching, as her features shift. Her braids become longer. Her face gets leaner, slightly older. Her skin lightens as her hand reaches out for me again, the bracelet on her wrist shedding its beads like a snake sheds its skin.

It glitters in the filtered light. Silver, with a single green pendant.

Sutton.

I reach for her, but she pulls out of my grasp. I step back and sink into the dew-covered grass. By the time I find my footing, she's far ahead of me. Running. Just like Imani.

I yell after her so hard, my voice cracks and dies with the effort. My sister ignores me. She races toward a pier on a lake with no signs of stopping. I run faster, but she dives into the water before I can catch her.

I dive after her. My momentum stops. I blink in the dark, but the murky water doesn't get much clearer. I kick deeper while looking for Sutton. I can't see her. I can't find her. She's gone.

My chest spasms from lack of oxygen. I have to surface in order to keep looking. I try to propel myself upward, but nothing happens. I look down to see my foot entangled in a weed. A bubble escapes my mouth as I struggle to free myself. Pulling at it only makes it worse.

I start to sink.

I push up with the last of my energy. It's no use. As the weeds wrap around my flailing arms, I finally see my sister next to me.

Except... It isn't Sutton.

Ruth's body floats next to mine. Waterlogged and long, long dead.

The last of my air escapes in a scream.

I wake with a gasp, panting.

I try to fling the covers off my sweating body, but Romeo won't move from his perch at my feet. He's standing at alert, staring at the door. All the lights are off, so I can't tell what he sees, but I follow his line of sight anyway. I blink several times as my eyes adjust to the dark. Finally, I see it.

Sutton is sitting at my open door, watching both of us.

I flick on my bedside lamp. She tilts her head.

The dim light only makes her look worse. Her eyes are bloodshot and seem sunken into her skull. They're bordered by dark circles almost the same shade as her pupils, like she hasn't slept in weeks.

"I remember the bracelet," she says.

I lean back against my headboard.

"When I was younger, I was mad at you," she begins, as if that doesn't describe almost any day. "I was spending the day with Ma Remy, and nothing she did cheered me up. I couldn't put it into words. I couldn't explain why you'd upset me so much. I felt like making up with you was hopeless. Impossible. Grandma disagreed. She explained the history of the bracelet. She promised me we would be close again, if I only had faith. But that wasn't all."

"You had to give it something." I can practically hear Ma Remy's voice as I say this. "She made you prick your finger on the clasp and drop the blood on the pendant."

Sutton nods.

"She did the same to me," I tell her softly. "On a day when I was upset with you. I got the same talk about family and loving each other. I bet she really laid on the guilt about how our enslaved ancestors suffered through things a lot worse than sibling rivalry, didn't she?"

Sutton smiles. Romeo lets out a contented huff, like he's satisfied the threat has passed. He hops from my bed and toddles over to sniff at Sutton, just in case. She offers him a belly rub as a peace treaty.

"Trust Ma Remy to convince us to trust a bracelet over simply talking to each other," I say.

"I know you want it back," Sutton says. "I don't know where it is. I've tried to remember. Are you still mad at me?"

"No." It's clear to me that Sutton didn't do this to herself. She didn't do this to me. She would never deliberately hurt any of us for this long. "I forgive you."

"I'm sorry," she says. She shivers in the air-conditioning. She's only wearing a thin tank top and sleep shorts.

I pull the rest of my covers off. "Let me help you back to bed."

She doesn't fight me.

"Is she okay?" my mother asks. She hovers in the hallway, looking as sleep-deprived as Sutton, when I close Sutton's door behind me. She spent most of the evening reaching out to her press contacts for coverage, this time to find Ruth. She was still awake when I went to bed.

I let go of the doorknob. "She's fine." I'm not sure how to explain what Sutton was doing. I have no idea how long she sat in my doorway before I woke up. "Nightmare," I say. I don't confess that it was mine.

"I thought it was you," she says anyway.

I pause midstep. Her maternal instinct has never been this on point.

"Y-you did?"

"When she was gone," she clarifies. "I thought you might have been involved. I thought you might have done something to her."

"Oh." I wait for emotion to hit me, any feeling at all. But no indignation, shock, or rage takes control—though a million contradicting emotions swim below the surface of my overtaxed mind. What am I supposed to say to that?

"I hated myself for it," she rushes to say before I can respond further. "You were always so angry at each other. So vicious. I would've thought the same of her if it were you who had disappeared." She takes a quick intake of air at the end. It feeds into a sob. "I'm so sorry. I'm so sorry."

"I didn't do anything," I say. "I didn't hurt her."

She closes her bedroom door behind her to avoid waking Dad. "I know," she says. "I knew it then too. It was a dark thought. But I should have never—I'm sorry."

"I had dark thoughts too," I admit. I don't tell her there were times I suspected her too. Or how long it took me to accept this wasn't all some elaborate scheme Sutton orchestrated to hurt us. But I do admit, "There were times when I didn't want her back. I'm sorry too."

Mom shakes her head. She opens her arms to hug me but stops. Is she afraid I'll refuse her?

I wrap my arms around my mother.

"You've been so good with her since she's come back. You're the one she turns to. She trusts you in a way she doesn't trust me anymore." She breathes in sharply. "Maybe that's what I get for thinking such awful things about my girls. All I want is to protect and comfort her. Both of you."

"Sutton thinks her presence hurts you and Dad. She's worried about disappointing you."

Tears spill down her cheeks. "She could never," Mom says, clinging to me. "*You* could never. I'm nothing without you girls. You could never let me down."

She pulls back from my embrace to rest her forehead against my own. She kisses my nose. "I'll love you through anything," she says.

She squeezes my shoulders, and I tighten my arms around her waist, breathing in the scent of her. It's been so long since she's held me like this, without rush or restraint. Dad's embrace has always felt secure, but I missed the primal relief of resting inside my mother's arms. "That's all I could think about with the detectives here today. You are *mine*. Nothing else matters."

No matter what. Nothing else matters. My parents think similarly, even when they've isolated themselves in their pain. I press tighter into my mom's embrace, finally feeling like her words ring true again. That I *am* hers, that I belong in her arms.

She squeezes me tighter. "I should have never let them in this house. After that look on your father's face, I wanted to drag them out. I want to scrub everything they touched. I'm disgusted by their lack of action. They won't fight for us like we will. Like we have to. For Sutton. For Ruth."

"For Ruth."

TWENTY-THREE

I wake to a series of thuds and grunts echoing from somewhere below my bedroom. Romeo scratches at my door, practically shaking to locate the noise. I let him out. He rockets down the stairs, but I follow slowly, still trying to shake the sleep from my head.

The noise intensifies as I reach the first floor, where nineties R & B cushions the dragging *clunk-clunk-clunk* of construction sounds. The coffee table base is leaning against the wall in the foyer; the television is in the hallway.

What is going on here?

I head toward the sound in the living room. Mom and Dad are moving furniture. The midday sun cascades through the open windows and glass patio door. Sunlight is all that illuminates the room. They've moved the table lamps. The entertainment center is against a new wall. The glass top and artifacts from the heirloom display are arranged carefully on the dining room table.

Mom slides one of the armchairs—on towels, so as not to scratch the hardwood. Her hair is in a ponytail, but several strands have come loose. One kisses her lips. She blows it away as she smiles at me.

"Good morning, darling," she says, then keeps pushing the chair toward the doorway.

"Good afternoon," Dad corrects with a smile. He's surrounded by packing material. He finishes cutting and pockets his box cutter.

"I woke up in the night and had a hard time falling back asleep," I explain. "What's going on? Are we moving?"

My parents laugh. Aaliyah's voice croons behind them. Her song ends and Faith Evans's "Love Like This" takes its place before they settle down enough to reply to me.

"We aren't going anywhere," Mom promises.

"We're redecorating," Dad finishes for her. "We bought new recliners. We're getting rid of the old chairs."

"Today?" I ask.

"Yes," Mom says. "We deserve a change."

Dad taps the headrest of a light-gray recliner. "The armrest has a drink holder *and* built-in USB charger for phones."

Very cool, but not at all Mom's style.

"You bought this?" I ask. "This morning?"

Mom laughs, but I'm not certain if it's directed at me. Her

eyes are still on Dad. He's smiling as he pats the fabric. "It was your father's idea," she admits. "I thought, 'Why not?'"

"You like this design, then?"

This time she looks directly at me, but there's no annoyance or judgment in her gaze. "They're perfect," she says. She looks as pleased as when she bought Juliet's giant aquarium for Sutton. All she can see is how happy this has made Dad.

Dad lifts some wrapping and hands it to Mom, who heads out the door to the growing trash pile in the yard. Romeo tags along at her heels. She nearly steps on him when she turns back. She ducks down to apologize to him with pets and a scratch behind the ear.

"You should take him out back," she says. "This is going to take a while. He'll be in the way." It's clearly a request, not a suggestion, but there's no frustration in it. Mom continues scratching Romeo's fur as she speaks, digging deep to help him soothe the never-ending argument he has going with the area just above his tail.

She scoops him up and hands him to me. "We picked up some snacks while we were out. There are muffins and bananas in the kitchen. Take one out to your sister. She's already outside."

She points the way like I need directions. The music transitions into a new song. Destiny's Child harmonizes in surround sound, and Mom forgets me entirely. Her eyes grow big. She spins away from me to face Dad. "'Say My Name'!" she gasps, waving her hands like she's not sure whether to clap or grab him with them.

"Of course," Dad says. "I told you I could be trusted with curating the playlist. Though this barely counts as a '90s hit. *The Writing's on the Wall* was released in 1999."

Mom doesn't care about the classification. She shimmies her way toward him, ignoring both me and the mess surrounding her. "You're so sexy when you get technical about music factoids," she says.

"Okay," I say loudly, reminding them I exist. "I'm going outside now."

I make my way through the maze, stopping in the kitchen to grab a muffin and banana for both me and Sutton. Romeo tries to reposition himself in my arms to steal the snacks, so I transition him to a football hold as I step outside. He kicks his little legs like he's running on air. I set him down.

I pull my phone out to text Ruth about my parents' grossness. She'll get a kick out of them being as obsessed with "Say My Name" as she was on game night. *You can't tell me it hasn't had an impact on the culture!*

I type half the message before I remember.

Sutton's sitting on the grass in one of my old Ivy James band tees and denim shorts. I hand her half my haul before sitting across from her.

The grass tickles my legs as I spread out.

Sutton peels her banana and breaks a small chunk off the top for Romeo. He attempts to get the same from me, but I won't share. His eyes narrow at me, almost closing. He looks back to

Sutton with an inquisitive look, like he's remembering why she used to be his favorite.

She offers him another chunk.

I don't care about the mutiny. Between Romeo's returning affection for Sutton and Mom and Dad's sappiness, it feels like we're getting closer to something resembling normal.

Though I don't see how that can happen without Ruth.

"What made you remember the bracelet?" I ask Sutton. "When you came to me last night, what sparked that memory?"

"The other girls," she says. Sutton breaks off another piece of her banana. She hasn't eaten any of it. She keeps feeding it to Romeo.

"Andrew told me you talked about the missing girls before," I say. "He said he was nervous about borrowing your car and meeting you at the diner because of them."

The corners of her lips flick upward at the mention of her former love. I feel a sudden wave of regret for bringing him up. He hasn't asked to see her since that catastrophic meeting at our house almost a week ago. He has messaged to ask how she's doing, but I don't want to lead her on with any false interest in meeting again.

Mercifully, she doesn't mention him when she responds.

"I looked at the posters, and I thought of you," she says. She doesn't expand any further. She feeds Romeo the last of her banana. He nudges at the wrapping of her muffin, but she doesn't give in, so he leaves us to chase butterflies again. They're starting to circle Sutton again, unaware it won't end well for them.

"That's it? That's what made you remember?"

She nods.

I think about the flyers and that photo booth printout, how Sutton hasn't had the opportunity to see anything that could spark more recent memories, good or bad.

I keep thinking about the crime scene photo that felt so familiar to me. I went over it again and again in my mind as I struggled to sleep last night. The old red building hasn't become any clearer to me. The intersection—113th and Jericho—is still a foreign destination on my internal GPS.

My tongue goes dry when I open my mouth. What I'm about to suggest could backfire in the worst way. I could retraumatize Sutton and erase the limited progress we've made. I don't want to hurt my sister, but I don't want Ruth to suffer like she has either.

I look back toward the house to make sure our parents are still preoccupied.

"Do you think you would remember more if we went back to where you were found?"

"Maybe," she admits. "They'll never let us go though."

That almost sounds like the old Sutton. I suppress a smile.

"Who said we were going to tell them?"

Sneaking out of the house after our parents fall asleep that night is the easy part. Not waking Romeo as we leave is much harder. Sutton hands me the keys to Dad's truck as I quietly open the front door. We would've taken her Jeep, but it's trapped in the driveway behind both cars because no one has driven it in so long.

I let her out ahead of me and close the door carefully.

I unlock the car manually to avoid the alert beep. "Don't slam the door shut!" I whisper yell to Sutton as I climb in the driver's seat. She mercifully obeys.

I transition into reverse without turning on the engine. I let gravity slide us out of the driveway before starting the car, and then we take off.

"Type this into the navigation system," I instruct and help her pick out the right intersection on the blue-tinted screen. It's almost twenty minutes away, barely in Willow Bend or Bend's End at all.

Sutton turns to the window like she did when we bought Juliet. There's not much to see in the midnight landscape, even in the yellow-gold glow of quickly passing streetlamps.

"If you want to stop or go home at any point, we can," I say.

"I'll be okay," she replies. The dark circles under her eyes are somehow more pronounced in the limited light. "You'll want to make a left at the next turn."

I look to the navigation screen, but it's still advising me to go straight. Sutton isn't watching it at all, her head tilted to the window. I keep going straight.

Two blocks later, the GPS says, "Make a left on Allyn Road."

After I turn, Sutton says, "Go right," two minutes before the navigation follows suit. This pattern continues until we reach our intended destination.

The red building from the photo reappears.

It's in even worse shape in person. I pause at the intersection though the traffic light is green. No one else is around. The entire area is abandoned. The other nearby buildings look to be in similar states of disrepair or are plastered with SOLD signs.

I still can't place it. I look to Sutton to see if she's doing any better. "Do you want to get out and look around?"

"No," she says. She's no longer gazing out the window. She's sitting upright, staring out the dashboard. "Keep going."

"Okay." We drive forward. Before we leave the last signs of civilization and head toward towering trees, we pass a final structure.

A church. It's as worn down and neglected as the rest of the area, but it unlocks something within me. My stomach knots.

I know where I first saw the red building.

Located inside the city limits of Willow Bend, Rise Above for Youth's convenience will reduce transportation time and costs for parents.

The pamphlets I folded with Ruth to advertise the new camp. The gas station was in better condition in the picture from the brochure. I could tell then that the photo was older. Now I know why they didn't use a more recent image.

"I remember the building," I tell Sutton, but she isn't listening.

"Pull over," she says. There's no rest area ahead. Only trees. I keep going, but she repeats herself. "Pull over." Her hand moves to the door handle, like she plans to open it whether I stop or not.

I slow down, trying to ease the truck into a safe spot on the shoulder of the empty road. Sutton opens her door and hops out before I've turned off the ignition.

She walks directly into the woods.

I hurry to follow her. She doesn't slow to wait for me, even as the low moonlight fades. All I have to guide me is her silhouette and the cracking of the underbrush breaking under our feet.

Eventually we break into a clearing bordering a swift-moving creek bed. The moonlight is brighter here. The ripples of the water are painted in an almost silver glow. A makeshift bridge sits precariously over the water, leading to another clearing on the opposite side. There's an old cabin there surrounded by building materials.

A light glows within. Could that be where Ruth is?

But Sutton doesn't cross the bridge.

She slows as she approaches the flowing water before dropping to her knees when she reaches the creek bed. There's something there. The ground has been disturbed. As I get closer, I see the soil has been tossed aside. There's a hole.

In the hole, a body lies in stagnant water.

I stumble back. *Ruth*, I think, but it can't be. Ruth has only been gone for a day. This body is badly decayed. It's barely recognizable as human. It looks like it's been torn apart. *From the inside out.*

The creek has started to reclaim the grave. Overflown creek water blankets the corpse. A few small fish swim around the maze of decomposing flesh. Sutton slaps at a trio of sleeping butterflies resting on what used to be a hairline.

The only identifiable thing is a flash of silver: a bracelet with a single green pendant I know by heart.

Grandma's bracelet.

"What is this?" I whisper.

"It's me," Sutton replies.

SUTTON

AFTERNOON OF

I pause before the crosswalk to tighten the laces of my running shoes. They're getting loose, and the heel on my right foot keeps slipping even when I'm not running. I double tie it, but I'm glad I'm not actually exercising today. The next time I sprint, my shoe's probably going to pop right off.

I pull my phone out as I cross the street to text Mom if we can get a new pair soon. I have enough to buy them myself, but if I go shopping with her, I can likely get a new sports bra and leggings too. She'll probably drag Casey along, but I can handle that.

I wonder if school will have hired a new coach in time for cheer camp. It's going to be hell getting back in the groove with someone new, but it will be worth it. I'm excited for us to take smart risks, risks that will challenge us to be better instead of sacrificing safety for show.

I press the wake button, but nothing happens.

I press it again.

A third time. The battery is dead.

I sigh. This isn't really a surprise. I almost always charge my phone in my car at lunchtime, but I couldn't do that today with my Jeep in Seattle. The last I heard from Andrew, he said he arrived safely and got his parking validated. I'm sure he's texted updates since.

The Garden is only three miles away. I'll ask one of the waitresses for a charger to plug it in when I arrive. There's no other solution for the time being. I really hope the meeting with the mortgage expert went well. The organization assured me when we spoke on the phone that they'd helped hundreds of low-income first-time buyers purchase a home, but I won't know if they were able to help the Prendergasts until he gets back.

If it doesn't work, we'll figure out something else. Coach isn't the only one with connections to real estate. Maybe Dad knows somebody. Or Mom. She doesn't love that I'm with Andrew, but it shouldn't keep her from wanting to help his family. Maybe she'd find an angle for a news story. We'll make it happen. Together.

I wonder if he's texted. I hope he doesn't think I'm ignoring him.

I walk along the road, and the closer I get to Bend's End, the worse the sidewalks become. There's only another hundred yards of paved walkway before the curb turns into gravel.

My fingers go to the pendant of Ma Remy's bracelet again.

The action should soothe me, but Casey's face replaces any worries I have with frustration. *I wish you were never born*, I told her last night. I feel bad about it, but she wished me dead first. I kicked her out of my room when it looked like she was about to cry.

I didn't want to piss her off.

She just refuses to understand.

All day I've wondered if explaining why the bracelet was so important to me would change anything. I know she thinks I'm a materialistic bitch, but maybe if I told her about the day Ma Remy promised me the bracelet, she'd understand. I could explain the story of our family. But would she even believe me?

Traffic roars beside me. I try to put more space between myself and the road, but it's a fruitless effort, like talking to Casey.

She hasn't trusted me in years. I could drop all my defenses and ignore every time she's screwed me over, and she'd recoil from me like a vampire from a cross.

There's no point in trying to explain myself. It doesn't matter.

Ma Remy willed the bracelet to *both* of us. I offered to share it; It was Casey who drew a line in the sand. She always does. There's no room for compromise with Casey. You either agree with her, or she thinks you're against her.

A red truck honks as it passes me, then pulls over. I can't see the driver but make out a decal on the back window. Heights Above Church.

Shit, shit, shit. I can't believe Casey enlisted Ruth to track me down. They don't even have their licenses! I'm pretty sure it's illegal for teens with only a learner's permit to drive with other underage people who aren't family. I tug my sleeve down to cover the bracelet.

I'm trapped.

The engine idles. I wait for Casey to jump out. She doesn't.

When the window lowers, neither my sister nor her best friend greet me.

It's Ruth's dad. "Sutton Cureton," he calls. "What are you doing on this side of town?" He punctuates the lighthearted scolding in his voice with his trademark smile, the same one plastered on billboards leading in and out of town.

I let out a relieved breath. I may not love Pastor David, but he's a far more welcome sight than his daughter right now.

"Don't you have a car?" the pastor continues, judgment in his voice.

It's going to take me even longer to get to the diner if I stop to chat with him, but I would never live it down if I snubbed him. I look both ways and cross the street.

I don't like David Heights. I never have. There's nothing wrong with him, but it feels like he has no personality outside praising God. Casey and I used to joke about it together, mimicking him, but Casey got more sensitive about criticizing him since his wife died.

Grace was incredible. She was the sweetest person and still had a backbone stronger than most bridges, especially against her husband. Most of the time. We never mocked her.

If anything, Pastor Heights's holier-than-thou attitude got

worse after his wife passed. He got more extreme in his preaching. The audacity of some of the things he felt emboldened to say stopped seeming like they were from the Bible and instead came from his opinions. I avoid church now more often than not.

"I loaned my car to a friend," I tell him as I lean against the open window. "I'm heading to get it back."

"Where?"

"The Garden diner in west Bend?"

His brow furrows. "That's a long walk."

"Not really," I say. "It's only a few miles."

He shakes his head. "You wouldn't know this," he begins conspiratorially, "because you're such a good girl, but this isn't the safest area." His tone is the same false disbelief he's perfected for his live streamed sermons. "There're a lot of people not living up to their potential. I don't know if I feel safe letting you walk alone. Let me give you a ride."

"I'll be okay," I insist.

"Can't you humor me?" he asks. "As a father? I don't know how I'd face Isaiah if something happened to you."

I begin to protest again, to assure him that I'm fine, but I can't quite get the words out. I remember Andrew's own apprehension about this part of our plan. He was worried about me walking alone because of other girls who disappeared from the area recently.

Tamika Horn and Imani Brenton. I met Tamika's mom before Imani's disappearance. Andrew and I joined the volunteer effort to put up missing person flyers.

I squeeze my phone in my pocket. I'd probably be fine if it were charged, but if something happened now, I wouldn't be able to call for help. Can you even track a phone if the battery is dead?

"You got me," I concede. I walk around the truck and pull open the passenger door. Climbing in, I say, "It's cheating to use my dad against me though."

"You could say I have a special connection with fathers." David winks and laughs at his own joke, and then he pulls back onto the road.

"It's good to see you, Sutton," he says. "I see your sister more often because of how close she is with my Ruth, but I've always known you girls to be smart. Kind. Respectful, you know?"

I nod, then mutter, "Yes. Thank you."

"You respect your elders. Not everyone does."

"Do you have a phone charger?" I ask.

He gives me side-eye for the interruption, but his perfect smile doesn't falter. "I'm not sure," he admits. "Ruth is always *borrowing* them, but you're free to look."

I don't see anything like a cord in the console or cupholders.

He continues talking. "Accepting assistance is an important virtue."

Nothing there. I check the glove compartment next.

"That's why God placed me here."

Nope. I move on to the pocket of my door.

"To help even the most sinful see the light."

No luck. I'm about to give up when I stick my hand in the

space between the seat and console. My fingers slide against the leather until they brush the carpet. Then I feel something.

It's thin. Like a small cord.

Yes.

I pull, but my joy is short-lived. It's not a charging cable. It's a beaded bracelet, like the kind kindergarteners make. The rope gets caught on the seat as I tug, and it breaks apart. The beads slip off the cord, but not before I read the letters falling from my fingers: TAMIKA.

The automatic car locks engage before I can move. I look up at the pastor, a single flower bead and the limp cord left in my palm.

His expression is almost sad. "I guess I was wrong about you, Sutton," he says. "Maybe you aren't the girl I thought you were."

TWENTY-FOUR

Sutton reaches toward the body and holds the decaying arm as she tugs Ma Remy's bracelet free. She slides it on her wrist and rubs the pendant with her thumb. Then she closes her eyes and bites her lip, taking a deep breath.

When she opens her eyes on the exhale, she looks directly at me.

I recognize the remnants of the clothes Sutton was wearing when she disappeared, floating in the decaying muck. I step back, reaching for something to stabilize me. I feel dizzy. My knees shudder under the weight of Sutton's piercing gaze. I should be used to her attention, but this time is different. She isn't studying me. She isn't watching my movements and decisions to mimic them, to understand me, to get ahead of me.

Sutton looks up at me like she knows me. And I know her.

"Casey," she says. Her voice is soft and raw in the same breath.

She says my name like a prayer. It holds the same intensity as her watering eyes, like I'm a freshwater spring after she's spent days in a desert. Like she hasn't seen me in ages.

It can't be.

"No." I take another step back, shaking my head. "No," I say again, and then again, and again, each time inching farther away. Sutton begins to stand, to move away from the thing in the dirt—or the thing moves away from Sutton's body. I don't know. I can't.

Please. Please, I just want my sister. I never wanted this shadow of my sister, this echo of who Sutton used to be. But she clawed out of her broken body and crawled back to me.

The imposter steps toward me. The moonlight glitters on Ma Remy's bracelet as she reaches for me, but the moonlight also illuminates something else in the grave. I recognize it with the same chill as when I saw its twin during the search effort weeks ago. The one piece of evidence recovered in the woods, the placement of which I questioned but the police disregarded.

Sutton's other white running shoe is half-submerged in the muck.

It's her. My sister is dead.

My sister is coming toward me.

I run.

"Casey!" Sutton yells after me, but I only sprint faster.

The moonlight disappears as I'm engulfed by the forest. The wind stings at my tearstained cheeks as I weave between the trees.

Sutton keeps yelling for me. I try to block it out. I try to ignore the desperation in her voice. The pleading. The pain. I stop and put my arms on my thighs, trying to catch my breath. I close my eyes, but I can't escape her.

I see her alone in the dark. My mind remakes her screams in a horrific watercolor behind my eyelids. I see her in the water, the dirt. I taste it in my mouth.

I start to run again and trip over a branch. I hit the ground hard, rolling into a bramble bush. The thorns prick every inch of exposed skin, but that isn't the agony that breaks my lungs wide open.

The truth hurts worse than any mortal wound.

The body in the waterlogged grave merges with my memory of Sutton submerged in the bathtub at home. *I'm trying to remember*, she said. The fish made a home around the corpse, like she made a home for Juliet. *Do you think they remember?*

Even the butterflies. Those beautiful bright wings that fluttered their way to wherever she was. They wouldn't leave her alone. It was like they were intoxicated by her. Swarming her. Feeding off her.

Ma Remy did this. Her bracelet. Her promises to keep us together as long as we trusted we'd be reunited. Generations of Cureton love and loss cast inside a single pendant. I knew she was superstitious, but I never believed in the conjure and rootwork outside of Daddy's academic interpretations. Herbs meant nothing to me beyond seasoning.

But I wanted Sutton back.

Even when I hated her, after I wished her dead with my own tongue, I needed my sister. I would have given anything to have her back. I would have traded myself. *No matter what.* Just like Daddy said.

Sutton finds me bloody and sobbing. She reaches for me, but I flinch away. "You died," I say. "That's you back there."

I can't see her face in the dark, but her silhouette nods. "Pastor David killed me," she says. "But I came back."

She attempts to touch me again. I don't have the energy to move. Her touch is warm, far different from the cold enveloping me as the truth of Pastor David sets in. I trusted him. He always treated me like another daughter—Sutton too. Until now. She rubs my forearm in a calming manner and says, "I remember now. I know why I returned."

"Why?"

"For you," Sutton says. Her tone is almost annoyed, like the answer should be obvious. She squeezes my arm, and the pendant slides down her wrist to touch the skin of both of our arms.

"He was supposed to give me a ride," she continues, "but when I got in his truck, I found the bracelet that belonged to one of the missing girls. He wouldn't let me go after that. He brought me here and..." She looks back toward where her original body lies.

The grave she crawled out of.

"I was so scared," she says.

"I'm sorry." I've been forced to say those words to her a million times, but I've never meant them as honestly as I do now.

"I wasn't afraid for myself," she says. "There was nothing that could be done to save me. But I couldn't stop thinking of you. When I was dying, it was *your* life that flashed before my eyes. I was gone, but you were still here. You were alive and in danger. Alone. You trusted him. My last thought was of you. I wanted to protect you. The next thing I knew was dirt and rain and lights and needles. None of it made sense. But then I saw you."

"And you remembered me."

"I love you," Sutton says. "I'm sorry it took dying for me to say it to your face."

I laugh through a fresh rush of tears. "I love you too," I choke out.

She takes that as a cue to hug me. I start sobbing again, my chest shuddering against hers as she squeezes me tight. "I'm sorry," she says, and I repeat the words. We stay like that for a few moments.

I tense, remembering. "Ruth."

Sutton lets go of me and stands. Then she offers a hand to help me up. I take it, wincing at all the scratches on my body. She releases me, but something is left behind in my hand.

I bring it closer to my face to inspect in the dim light. My heart sinks. It's Sutton's fingernail. The entire thing. I grab her hand to confirm. "Does it hurt?" I ask her, frantic.

Sutton shakes her head.

It's not even bleeding.

"Come on," she says, dismissing it. "We have to help Ruth."

She takes the lead as always. She retraces our steps to the clearing, her pace calm and determined. She doesn't look back to check on me or assure I'm still following. She doesn't waste any time.

How much does she have left?

This fingernail, Sutton's excessive hair loss, her tired sunken eyes... The bracelet brought her back, but can it keep her here? Is she going to leave me again? Will she die again permanently, disappearing when her original body finally returns to the earth?

I blink against the moonlight as I reenter the clearing. Sutton waits for me at the makeshift bridge. She doesn't look at her body.

"Do you have your phone?" she asks. "We should probably call someone."

I pull my phone out of my pocket, but there's no signal.

"I guess it's up to us then," she says.

She crosses the bridge and walks toward the lighted cabin.

I follow her.

TWENTY-FIVE

Yellow light glows through a single old window, half-frosted by time. The light flickers, likely from the fireplace slowly spitting smoke out of the chimney. Sutton reaches the building before I do, but she waits for me.

I rest my hand on the cold door handle and look back to my sister. The last time Sutton was here, she died. She never truly left. I'm afraid to open the door—not for myself but for what it could cost Sutton. Pastor David could be inside. I don't want to lose her again.

But I don't want to lose Ruth either.

The door is unlocked.

The pastor isn't here. An ancient oil lantern sits on a rickety end table, and a dying fire, nearing the end of its wood supply, burns in the old fireplace. In the corner, Ruth lies on a cot. Her body is still. Her hands are folded as if in prayer over a book perched on her chest.

I rush to her, trying to wake her, but she won't stir. I shake her again, and the book, a Bible, falls to the ground. I don't give it a second thought. I shake her again.

"Please," I beg. "Not you too."

"Stop," Sutton says, kneeling next to us. Her hand goes straight to Ruth's wrist to check her pulse. It's such a simple thought, but one my terrified mind was incapable of. "She's alive. Check for yourself." She replaces her hand with mine.

Ruth's pulse is strong. It thrums beneath my fingertips, even though her body doesn't react.

"He must have drugged her," Sutton says.

His own daughter. I lay Ruth back on the cot. My hands won't stop shaking. He drugged his own child. There's no evidence of food in this crumbling shack. She has nothing to sustain her but the fire and the brimstone of the Bible she trusts. I imagine her waking up here alone, knowing the man she trusted most did this to her.

Would prayer have been a life raft? She would have had nowhere to go. No one to turn to. What do you do when your support system is the cause of your trauma? How do you come back from that?

Wait... "The door was unlocked," I say at the same time Sutton asks me if I think we can carry Ruth out together.

She spins to face the door as it opens.

Pastor David smiles at the sight of us. He's carrying an armful of fresh wood for the fire. He bends to add some to the fading flame. "I knew you'd come," he says casually, as if we've all gone camping together.

I shift to put Ruth safely behind me. "I won't let you kill her too," I promise.

He twists his head from the fireplace to glare at me. "I never wanted to hurt my sweet girl," he scolds. His tone is disgusted. "You should know me better than that. I love my Ruth. I love you girls too."

"You killed me," Sutton says. She steps in front of me. I falter, wanting to pull her back and protect Ruth at the same time. "You killed me like you killed those other girls, didn't you?"

"You are too young to understand," he says. He stands, brushing soot from his pants. There's a knife holstered on his belt. "We are all put on this earth for a purpose. Mine has always been to guide the sinful, the inferior. I try to show them how life can be better, but they make it so difficult."

"Their life can't improve if you take it from them!"

Sutton looks back at me for a fraction of a second before returning her focus to the pastor. "When someone dies, they lose any chance to make amends."

"That's not true," says Pastor David. He shakes his head and steps back toward the door. Sutton adjusts her stance to keep him directly across from her. She's no longer in front of me. I can see the pastor in full view. He runs his hands down his face.

"What I did was a cleansing," he says. "I saved those girls. I gave them a new chance at salvation through atonement. They would not have made it to heaven if they'd stayed on this mortal plane—not with the choices they were making. But I cleansed them of their impurities. They have God's eternal love now because of me."

He points at Sutton. "You were different." His voice no longer holds his unshakable sermon authority. "You weren't like those troublesome girls. You were living right. You came from better stock. It wasn't your time. I admit my failure with you. That's why God brought you back. He brought you back because I made a mistake."

"If you made a mistake," I say, attempting to use his demonic logic against him, "you can rethink this. Ruth is far better than Sutton ever was. We all know that. Hurting her would be a far greater sin."

"The Lord is testing me," David says. "This is not my decision to make. I have no choice. It's like Abraham and Isaac. Sutton has left a hole in heaven. I have to sacrifice my righteous Ruth to fill the gap she left behind. It's the only way I can repent."

He frees his knife from the belt holster.

I won't let him. I lunge from my perch by the cot and grab the pastor around his waist, trying to knock him over. We both fall. I grab for the knife as I hit the dusty floor, kicking up dirt in my mouth and nose. My fingertips brush the knife handle as he regains his senses. He tightens his hold and rights himself before

I can sit up. He twists on top of me before pinning me to the ground. He fights my grip on the blade. It slices into my fingers, but I don't let go. Blood drips from my hand onto my face as I push up and against him. I had the element of surprise, but he's so much bigger than me.

He's going to overpower me.

"Casey!" Sutton screams. She kicks the pastor in the gut, forcing him off me. He drops the knife. I grab it and shift to lunge at him again, but Sutton has beaten me to the punch.

She straddles him, and before he can flip her, she grabs the oil lantern from the table and smashes it against his face. He screams as glass shatters and cuts his face, spilling liquid on him and the floor below.

Some of the fluid splashes the fireplace, strobing the cabin in a brighter glow. The fire is reflected in Sutton's eyes as she closes both hands around his neck and screams, "No one gets to hurt my sister but me!"

Sutton has never been so clearly otherworldly as while she chokes the life from the pastor. I feel a sense of shame for ever dismissing Ma Remy's superstitions as simply that because I see her in my sister now. I see myself and Mom and Dad and so much more in her unrestrained fury.

David is in pain, and he seems unable to retake control from my thin sister. His hands go to her arms, and when that doesn't work, he claws at her thighs, which are squeezing him flat against the floor. Nothing works.

Sutton is stronger than him.

Her voice doesn't sound human when she speaks again. "You are done hurting those I love," she says. "You have abused your power, so I will take it from you. My blood will outlive your blood. My body will outlive your body. My soul is stronger. *I will survive.*"

Pastor David stops struggling. His body stills.

My eyes burn, but I'm not sure if it's from a complicated grief for the man I thought I knew or the thickening smoke in the cabin. The fire is spilling from the fireplace. We don't have long before it spreads and lights the whole building in flames. I rush back to Ruth.

"Sutton," I say, struggling to loop my arms under Ruth's. "We have to go."

She looks up at me, still bathed in the flickering light. Her fury evaporates. She smiles the smile she gave me when she first returned and lets go of the pastor.

She stands to help me with Ruth, pulling slivers of glass out of her hand from the broken lantern. Each piece of glass is clean as it falls to the floor. There's no blood. She isn't bleeding from her cuts. I try not to think about what that means for how long Sutton has left on this side of life.

Together, we lift Ruth and carry her outside. A few moments later, the cabin ignites. The roar of the fire is louder than any wild creature, and we push to put distance between us and it.

We don't turn around until something even louder screams from within.

Pastor David is still alive.

He stands, his silhouette visible from the window, and moves toward the open door. Toward us. I tense, shifting more weight to keep Ruth upright.

Before he can reach the door, a shadow appears behind him. It's another person. A Black woman in an old dress. Her head is shaved, and she has a scar on her forehead. *Henny*, Mima's mother. She grabs him and starts to drag him back into the rising flames. He flails in her arms, but he can't overpower her. She isn't alone. Another woman steps out of the flames. She's dressed similarly to Henny but is clearly younger. It's not until a third woman joins them that I understand.

Mima helps her mama keep the pastor trapped in the flames. They don't move until he can't anymore.

The third woman comes to the window. The flames chase her but don't have any effect on her clothes or skin. She looks the same as she did in the photo with my dad from the diary I found, the day she reclaimed the pendant and bound herself to it again.

Ma Remy smiles at us as the inferno overtakes the cabin. She's come to protect us like Henny and Mima, the way she promised us our family always would. She brought us back together. She brought Sutton home.

Sutton gasps and drops her hold on Ruth's legs, causing me to stumble to the ground with her. I try to cushion Ruth from landing too hard, but I'm not successful. "Why'd you—" I start, twisting up to yell at Sutton, but she's not looking at either of us.

She's cradling her hand. It's bleeding from the cuts.

I look back to the cabin. Ma Remy is gone. They all are.

A moan of pain pulls my attention, but it isn't Sutton crying from her injuries. Ruth is shuddering, gasping for breath. The fall must have woken her. "Casey?" she asks, blinking.

"I've got you," I tell her. "We came for you. It's okay."

She blinks at the fire. "Is my dad in there?" We don't answer, but she doesn't need us to. She starts crying. "I followed him when he left again. He came here, and there was a body by the creek. Casey, my dad killed someone."

"He killed several people, Ruth," I say. "He was the one who took Sutton. She remembered, and he admitted it."

"I'm sorry," Ruth says, sobbing in earnest. "I'm so sorry."

"You have nothing to apologize for," Sutton says. Her injured hand is pressed tight against her chest. "None of this pain belongs to you. Don't let his rot claim you too."

A boom comes from the building, as some part of the structure gives way.

"Do you think you can walk?" I ask Ruth. "We have to get out of here and contact someone before that fire spreads."

"Yes, I can," Ruth assures us. Her body seems less sure. Her legs buckle under her weight twice, but she manages to walk by leaning on us. She doesn't speak again until we cross the makeshift bridge.

She stops at the edge of the clearing. "The body's gone," Ruth says.

She's right.

Sutton's grave is empty except for some water, the fish, and a single floating white flower. I turn to Sutton, who's staring at her wrist. On the wrist pressed protectively against her chest, the same flower glows in the moonlight, the only visible element of the rootwork in Ma Remy's pendant.

Sutton looks at me. We can't speak of it with Ruth here, but I know my sister is mine again. She's back for good. She won't ever leave me again.

"He must have gotten rid of it," I tell Ruth. She nods, sniffling.

We've almost reached the car when Sutton asks me, "Do you have any service yet?"

I pull out my phone to check. "No," I answer, my stomach clenching for multiple reasons. We have to call the police. We have to explain what happened tonight. If the pastor buried Sutton here, it's likely they'll find the other bodies nearby too. We probably don't need to mention Sutton's rebirth or our ancestors in the fire, but...*oh God.*

"We are so going to be grounded when Mom and Dad find out we snuck out of the house."

Sutton blows out a pained breath. "Well," she says, dragging out the word. "Technically, coming here was your idea."

"Wow," I say. "You're really gonna go there?"

"I'm traumatized, Casey," Sutton deadpans. "They won't blame me."

"I hate you," I say.

"No, you don't," Sutton says, laughing. Even Ruth chuckles a bit.

I have no comeback because she's right. I don't hate her.

I never could.

A NOTE FROM THE AUTHOR

Thank you for reading *The Shadow Sister* and getting to know Sutton and Casey as if they were your own sisters.

This book is ultimately about trauma and healing. Intergenerational trauma, in how today's Black Americans are affected by how their ancestors were treated. Family trauma, in the rifts that separate us from those we should be closest to. Personal trauma, as internal pain can compound, making healing on any level impossible until you face your own truth.

As someone whose ancestry is clouded by centuries of my family being treated as objects instead of people, reclaiming my history is important to me. My white grandmother was very into genealogy, so I learned a lot about my lineage on my mother's side through her, but my father's side has always been more murky.

The Cureton family surname is my father's. (I carry my

mother's maiden name.) I know that we come from slavery and that he got his last name from the plantation that enslaved our family. But I don't know who we were before then or much about where we came from beyond what a DNA test would share. I don't know many details about what happened to us after leaving the plantation either. Ma Remy and Isaiah's passion for legacy comes directly from my own. I wanted to redefine the history of a name that was branded upon us and rewrite what such a legacy means not only for this story, but for myself.

The magic in this book is inspired by hoodoo slave magic spirituality practices. Conjure and rootwork served as a way for the enslaved to address their powerlessness, to heal themselves, to seek retribution and some level of control over their suffering. It was important to me that all the elements of this story came from the bonds Black Americans made here in the United States, from the families and lives they forged after being stolen from their homeland. For me, being Black in America is an experience defined by both constant connection and division. I spent a long time struggling with my identity as a biracial person but finding my community and strength to embrace my full self has been an almost magical experience. Sacred, in a way.

The most interesting thing to me about history is how it impacts how we live today. Try as we might, we often can't help how our past influences our choices in the present. In this book, each member of the Cureton family is facing their own complex traumas. Sutton and Casey are both impacted by the rift between them, but also individually in how Sutton doesn't feel like she's Black "enough" to be taken seriously in her father's heritage interests and Casey feels like she's too dark to be palatable for her mother's journalism career. Isaiah and Madison struggle too. The abduction of a child is a unique and terrible trauma on parents, but their suffering is compounded by their inherited pain. Isaiah never knew his father because he was shot at a protest, so Isaiah spent his whole life trying to be a model minority to avoid losing anyone he cared about again. Madison married into a family that values familial bonds above all others, yet her returned daughter wants nothing to do with her—and her own siblings never even call her during the novel.

In order to help the Curetons confront what haunted them, I first had to heal myself. I was afraid to write this novel. I was afraid to center a narrative on girls who looked like me and weren't perfect. My experiences writing for publication as a Black woman had taught me that the only story I could tell that would be deemed worthy of an audience was a morality lesson. The only way my stories would be embraced was if they were based in trauma that cast us solely as victims of our racist world, the brutal reality of that injustice forever immortalized in the pages. That's not me.

I've always written to give myself the power that my everyday life has denied me. I come from extreme poverty and much personal strife, but I've always tried to live a "life inspired by fiction" that viewed hardships as obstacles in my journey to a happy ending. Writing gave me confidence that I could come through whatever I suffered and end up stronger on the other side, just like my characters.

When I began my journey toward publication, my writing became a source of trauma instead of therapy for me. I went through a lot of pain, partially because I didn't know how to stand up for myself and my stories. I was afraid of ruining what I thought could be my only chance at a career I'd worked for my entire life. I didn't start to heal until I embraced my writing without fear or shame.

With *The Shadow Sister*, I took that power back for myself and for Sutton, using my imagination to pull us both from the wreckage of our trauma and reclaim what we love most. With Casey, I regained my sisterhood of self, facing the fissures that broke us apart and healing them into a new unbreakable bond. I won't ever let us separate again.

ACKNOWLEDGMENTS

This is going to be extremely long and I'm not sorry in the slightest. Acknowledgments are the first thing I flip to whenever I pick up a book and I've been dreaming of writing mine since I was a little girl. I'm already upset about all the people I won't be able to fit, but I don't think my publisher would be happy with a fifty-page thank-you list.

Let's start with family:

Deepest gratitude to most of my ancestors. I am so grateful for the privileges and rights you sacrificed for me to enjoy. I will always do my best to honor that and work towards even better for the next generation. I hope I make you proud.

Definitely *not* to or for the ancestor I discovered while researching my family genealogy who willed his two favorite slaves to his son when he died, though I hope his ghost is horrified that I am related to him by blood and by every word in this book.

Again, always, to my mother Laurie Meade. Many of my peers didn't see themselves in the books they read until they were all grown up, but you wrote me as the star of my own picture books yourself. I've always had a home in storytelling thanks to you. You are the reason for this.

To my siblings, but mostly my youngest brother. My seven-years-delayed twin, my Leebee Esquire, my first idea sounding board who thinks he deserves royalties for listening to me rant about plot and then saying "Okay, but what if...space?" And his perfectly sane legal assistant girlfriend Hailey Chambliss, I don't know how she puts up with either of us.

I don't know where to begin with acknowledging my friends, because I truly do not know what I have ever done to deserve such overwhelming support. This has not been an easy road for me, but so many of you have stayed and refueled me along the way and I'm so grateful to travel it with you:

First off, a monumental debt of gratitude for anyone and everyone who has ever contributed to help keep my family housed.

My history with poverty and financial insecurity has been a roller coaster that still has not stopped, but you've never let me ride alone. Especially to Laekan Zea Kemp for organizing a community auction that is the sole reason we were able to stay housed the winter/spring of 2022. I don't know if I'll ever be able to fully thank the writing community for repeatedly believing in me like this, but I will do everything I can to pay it forward.

To Shelley Krause and Mary Jinglewski, for supporting me in ways that allow me to empower myself and trusting in my judgement to do so. As well as my former therapist Abigail Riedinger, for helping me find my voice and confidence in my writing again after I thought both were lost to me forever. I promised you I'd put you in these pages if I ever made it here and you always believed I would.

To Amber Chindris and Charlotte Woo, my original readers! We've been friends for over a decade now! You were the first people to support me as a writer, back when I was just a silly middle schooler writing fanfiction. You never doubted I'd go all the way.

To Kailey Steward and Mary-Allyn McCoy, the world's best booksellers and original Shadow Sister hype squad. Thanks for loving this book more than I do and talking me down from the ledge every single time.

To Megan Lally and Alena Bruzas, my first 2023 debut author friends. I'm so blessed to launch with you.

To Heather Ezell, my first in-person writer friend. I'm never gonna forget when we sobbed so hard at Barnes & Noble about you moving away that the other customers thought you were breaking up with me. I am so blessed you took the initiative to offer me a ride that fateful first day and I cannot wait to hug you in person again.

To Rachel Strolle, Tess Sharpe, Hannah Whitten, Gabrielle

Prendergast, Rosiee Thor, Gabriela Martins, Sara Samarasinghe, Sheena-kay Graham, and so many others I'm going to agonize over forgetting and strive to include in the next book. If people could just stop being nice to me so I have less people to adore and thank, that would make this a lot easier.

I know that the majority of this next group of people are contractually obligated to be kind to me because we signed contracts, but I still feel they've gone above and beyond:

To all of my #TeamElana agent siblings, but especially Anna Bright and Shannon Price. The best part of this has been growing in our careers together. I can't wait to put my book next to yours on my bookshelf. Our agent has the best taste, not only in writers but people.

To Elana Roth Parker, you were a dream agent before I even knew the term. I don't know how to put into words what it means to me to have you stick by me and believe in me and trust in my ability and potential. You are the best decision I've ever made in my publishing career.

To Annette Pollert-Morgan, my incredible editor. I've never had someone love my words as much as you do. Every edit letter is a gift, because you always build and problem solve from a core of passion for the story. Everything you do is centered around improving and growing both the story and my skill. I won the lottery when you chose me.

To Dominique Raccah and Todd Stocke for saying yes to *The Shadow Sister* and giving me a home at Sourcebooks. Also to Jenny Lopez, Kay Birkner, Liz Dresner, Kelly Lawler, Chelsey Moler Ford, April Wills, Karen Masnica, Madison Nankervis, Rebecca Atkinson, Beth Oleniczak, Caitlin Lawler, Emily Luedloff, Margaret Coffee, and so many more! I love being a Sourcebooks author, and I am consistently in awe of how many people work so hard to help the books we love come to be.

To Shaylin Wallace for your breathtaking art for the cover. And to Nicole Deal, for not running in fear from my ridiculously detailed art commission email and for working so collaboratively with me for the most beautiful print of Sutton and Casey.

Now we have reached the point of these acknowledgments where those who know me will be thinking "How did Lily go this long without mentioning Taylor Swift?" Wait no further, friends—it is time for the Swiftie Section:

To Taylor herself, for your pandemic gift that paid our rent during the worst months of the pandemic and helped me avoid quitting school in the final months of my editing certificate program. Your help allowed my at-risk mother to stay home and start our mask-sewing business with me instead of exposing herself to the virus. You saved her. You saved us. I'll never be able to repay you for that.

To the Black Swifties Group Chat and all its chaotic ride-or-die members: Ajhée, Lisa, Cass, Day, Nick, Luis, Heleena, Tati, Chanel, Shan, Exquisite, Malik, Thiia, Debby, Darling, Aria, Stasia, Hiwet, Karl, but especially to Brit for introducing me to you all and being the sister blood couldn't give me. Taylor brought us together, but it's the love and support that has made our friendship last.

And finally, to those who have read this far.

Friend or family, swiftie or stranger, you mean the world to me. I hope you liked *The Shadow Sister*. I can't wait to see you in the next chapter, wherever that takes us.

ABOUT THE AUTHOR

 Lily Meade's work has been published in *Bustle* and *Teen Vogue*. This is her debut novel, which was a finalist for the Eleanor Taylor Bland Award for emerging writers by Sisters in Crime. She lives in Washington. Follow @LilyMeade on social media and learn more at lilymeade.com

FIREreads

🔥 #getbooklit

Your hub for the hottest young adult books!

Visit us online and sign up for our
newsletter at FIREreads.com

 @sourcebooksfire

 sourcebooksfire

 firereads.tumblr.com